Duel on the Snake

By

Peter J Foot

Duel on the Snake

Copyright©2023 Peter J Foot

all rights reserved

No part of this book may be reproduced in form by photocopying or any electronic or mechanical means, including storage or retrieval systems, without the permission in writing from the copyright owner, and the publisher of the book.

All characters are fictional and any similarity to any actual person is purely coincidental.

The right of Peter J Foot to be identified as the author of this work has been asserted by him in accordance with the Copyright, Designs, and Patents Act 1988 any subsequent amendments thereto.

The author acknowledges the work of Richard Riley In producing the cover work for this book.

ISBN 978-1-8046-7240-2

By this Author

Oath of Allegiance
Strange Alliance
Jungle Haven
The Drums of War
Crown Assassin
The Warriors
The Savage Years
The Satan Seed
Southern Adventure
Exodus Five
The Shadow Man
The Final Solution
The Last Sunrise
The Key to Armageddon
The Tiger's Hoard
The House of Secrets
The Sands of Time
The Years to Remember
Seeking the Sun God
Call for Duty
The Guardians
The Lost City
Alpha One Zero
Secrets of the Desert City
A Conflict of Interest
One Step Too Far
In Defence of the Realm
A Journey into the Past
The Darwin Raiders
A Crisis in the Gulf
The Praetorians
The Legacy of Mount Sinai
A Country Betrayed

Chapter One

The Civil War had now been over for three months and the previously divided Americans who had fought each other to a standstill over the last four and a half years were now being allowed to return to their homes. The wounds many of them had sustained would eventually heal but, for a large number of the families that the conflict had divided the healing process would take years and in some cases never.

Jack Masters had been a sergeant in the Southern Army and to speed his journey home to his wife and young son he had spent some of his release pay on his faithful army horse Rex.

He arrived home to the small town of Hope just before dark. The town lay on elevated ground above a bend in the Snake River, well named as it followed a winding path down to the South. He was greeted at the door of his house by his widowed father Abe and Jack's delighted wife Jane. Their son Simon was already asleep in bed, but his father was allowed a peep at how is son had grown since he last had seen him.

Though her husband had not been expected home for a few days Jane had already ensured there was plenty of food ready for them all. While Jack's father slowly stabled the horse and made sure it had water and hay, Jane gave her husband a taste of the affection he had been missing. When he returned from his stabling duty, Abe Masters gave his son a hug and went up to his bed. Jack and his wife went up to their room shortly after, but it was sometime before they actually went to sleep, there was much to talk about.

It was barely daylight when an excited five year old boy came racing into the room and clambered all over his father insisting that his father walked him to school later. He wanted all the other children to see his daddy was home from the war and had been a sergeant. His mother was the teacher at the school and taught two classes one for the young children and one for the older ones, which was difficult but she made it work.

During the day Jack met up with Will Thomas, the sheriff of Hope, who wanted Jack to resume being a deputy on Friday and Saturday nights when the men from the two nearby ranches came into town.

As for the rest of the week Jack helped his father run their general store, which was a good business and supplied not only the ranches but the town with a variety of food and goods.

These came up once a month from Fort Worth, some forty miles to the southwest and had an army escort due to the bank bing included in their visit. Ethan Watts was the local Blacksmith and a giant of a man and also the local lay preacher who took a prayer meeting with hymns in the community hall every Sunday morning at eleven. Ma Harris ran the Boarding House and bar and on Friday and Saturday nights she had four girls up from Fort Worth to provide comfort at a price for the ranch hands.

Sheriff Will Thomas had an arrangement with the owners of the two ranches, one to the north which was the Circle 'O' and one to the south which was the Tall 'T'. One paid his men on Friday and the other on a Saturday, so they never came into Hope together. When the men arrived in they handed their guns in on entering and collected them on leaving.

The first Friday evening back saw Jack in his role of deputy sheriff waiting to the north of Hope for the ranch hands of the Circle 'O' to ride into town. When they arrived they greeted Jack with a torrent of friendly banter such as "Those Northern boys must be bloody awful shots Jack to miss your fat arse."

They dutifully handed in their guns with a grin and caused no trouble for anyone. At midnight, somewhat the worse for wear, but still in good humour, they collected their guns and rode back to their ranch.

On Saturday night it was the turn of the Tall 'T' to come into Hope and they gave a cheer at the sight of Jack Masters before saying that they all thought he was dead. They also caused no trouble and collected their guns around midnight leaving Ma Harris and her girls to count their profits and Jack to go home and comfort Jane in her bed.

On Sunday morning most of Hope's population gathered at the community hall to attend Ethan Watt's prayer meeting. Ethan was a powerful speaker and quote fluently from the bible and after prayers they sang several hymns with Ethan's booming voice leading the way. The prayer meetings never lasted longer than an hour because the men folk, including Ethan Watts knew their wives had the Sunday dinner in the oven.

Jack and his father had been discussing increasing the number of chickens they had in the large garden at the rear of their house. They only had six and proposed to increase that to fifty, so they could sell the eggs in the store. There was plenty of spare seasoned wood as an old lean to shed on their land had fallen down while Jack was away during the war. Ten miles to the north an old farmer was selling-up and he had some chickens for sale and Ma Harris had agreed to lend them her pony and trap to collect them.

On Monday Jack set to and started to build a new chicken house and by Wednesday had completed it and also fenced in the outside run. On the Saturday Jack and his wife Jane and their young son Simon borrowed Ma Harris's pony and trap and took the ninety minute journey to collect the chickens. The fifty young birds were all at the point of lay and ideal for the task the Masters family had planned for them, and the price was fair as well. By two o'clock they were back in Hope and after placing the young birds in their new home they had a late lunch.

Afterwards Simon and his father cleaned up the back of the trap and then they returned it to Ma Harris who said they could pay her with some eggs when the birds came into lay.

Texas had its fair share of law breaking in the aftermath of the Civil War, but Hope remained peaceful with the railroad to the west and east taking over from the stagecoach in the transportation of valuable cargo. From time to time Will Thomas received wanted posters of men wanted for all kinds of crime. They were artists impressions of the suspects, some well-drawn others so unclear as to fit almost anyone.

But one attracted Jack Masters' attention immediately because he had met this man briefly in the southern army in the early part of the war. Jack because of his ability to control men had just been made sergeant and they were resting up for a few days after suffering some heavy losses in battle. Some dozen men now joined them to make up for their losses including this man (now a wanted criminal) and his brother. His name was Todd Raven and his brother's name was Ike. Their stay in the unit was less than two weeks.

During that time Todd Raven, who was a brute of a man, got into drunken fights and when he saw his first taste of action he and his brother deserted. They were last spotted heading for the Mexican Border on stolen horses and were thought to have spent the rest of the war in Mexico. The Raven Gang as they were now known were wanted for a number of offences including one robbery of a bank, but as yet were not wanted for murder.

It was now two months since Jack had returned from the war and he had settled back in and it was almost like old times. The store was doing good business and the two ranches were good customers and had recently started to raise horses as well as cattle. A doctor now visited Hope once every two weeks from Fort Worth as part of a health programme for the children, but he dealt with other matters as well. Ma Harris had an extension built to her bar to deal with the summer trade and there was talk of a bank opening next year.

Will Thomas and Jack Masters did not view the prospect of a bank in Hope as a permanent fixture with any great enthusiasm. Banks held money and money attracted the wrong type especially in small towns, but anyway at the moment it was only a plan for the future. Jane liked the idea of a bank in Hope saying it would be somewhere safe to put their savings and not hide it in the teapot under the bed as most people did.

Some six hundred miles away in New Orleans the four man Raven gang were running out of money as enjoying yourself in this city could be an expensive business. In addition to Todd and Ike Raven the two others had joined during the civil war. Jake Shay was good with the knife and Silas Gibb, who was the oldest member of the gang at fifty, was good with horses. They had decided to take the train to Memphis with their horses in the cattle truck at the rear. Do a couple of jobs in the casinos there then ride clear and head north this time to St Louis.

Two days later they were on their way and after a twelve hour train journey they arrived in Memphis. Todd and Ike had been here before and knew of just the place to stay on the southern edge of the city. They stabled the horses nearby then spent a couple of nights deciding which of the casinos they would rob. Ike who had a way with the women latched on to one of the girls at the Silver Slipper club and in no time at all found out all about the money arrangements.

In Memphis all the casinos had an arrangement that at one in the morning all takings would be taken to the Central Law Office for safe keeping until the next day. There a posse of six armed deputies would ensure its security overnight. But each Casino was responsible for taking its own cash to the Law Office and that is where Todd and his Gang would hijack the Silver Slipper's takings. The Silver Slipper was where the most money was wagered, so Todd reckoned they would have the best takings each night and he was right.

The girl had told Ike that three men took the money to the Law office always by the same route they were always armed, but not always sober. Todd and the gang planned to ambush them halfway along their route with Jake Shay walking out into their path stark naked as a distraction. The other three would then strike. It worked out better than expected with two of the cash guardians falling off their horses in the confusion. One man was knocked out and the others two tied up and gagged and in twenty minutes the

Todd gang had galloped a mile or so clear of the city and then slowed down to a trot.

At dawn they found a stream and watered their horses then found a quiet spot in the hills and rested up till just after mid-day. They then rode off north at a trot until the light began to fade before they stopped for the night and had some food. At dawn the next day they had something to eat then checked the money they had taken. It amounted to about ten thousand dollars, so they continued their journey north up to St Louis with thoughts of how to spend their ill-gotten gains.

They took their time and never overtired their horses, conscious how valuable these animals were to their safety. Once there Silas Gibb who had once lived there found them a safe place to stay and they settled in. Ike sent off some money promised to the bar girl who had given him a good time and the information, but made sure Todd did not know about it.

After they had been in St Louis for a few days Todd Raven remembered that just a few miles away on the high ground overlooking the Mississippi River lived an old friend of their late father. He was a former Mississippi River boat captain named Paul Wallace. He was a bit of a rogue who did a fair bit of trading in illicit goods but never got caught. They decided to pay him a visit.

The old man was glad to see them as he was now quite lonely having recently lost his wife. They were invited to stay as long as they liked. The house was quite large and had stables and a paddock for the horses. He was fascinated by the tales they had to tell and was interested in their plans for the future. When Todd admitted that at the moment they did not have any, Wallace made a suggestion that excited their interest.

Chapter Two

The old captain told them about the Boston Mountains, three hundred miles to the Southwest of St Louis, where a gold claim could be registered for five dollars. Todd Raven looked round at his gang and then back at the old captain before saying, "But my friend we don't know anything about prospecting, but I'm sure it's bloody hard work."

The old captain laughed then shook his head.

"I am not suggesting you do any serious mining just pretend to after registering a claim and then at the right time rob the deposit office of all the miners' finds."

He then explained that once a month a military escort from Fort Smith visited the site and collected all the gold that had been mined before taking to the main bank in Oklahoma City where it was deposited in the miners' accounts.

They all sat down and had a good think about this suggestion it was something they had never attempted before. For one thing what they would be stealing would be gold dust or particles of gold and questioned how they would get rid of it.

"Leave that to me." said the crafty old captain. "The price we will get will not be the top one, but you won't be disappointed."

Over the next couple of days, they gave the matter more thought then decided to give it a try. The captain gave them some basic instruction in prospecting and found them the appropriate equipment and then they set off on a trip which would take at least ten days as they would not overtire the horses. It was an interesting journey over some fine country and Silas kept an eye on the condition of the horses. They arrived at the mining area at mid-day on the eleventh day of their journey with their horses looking in fine condition.

Todd went up to the assay office and said he and his brothers wished to register a claim and he was offered four sites and taken to them and chose the one which was secluded. He then went back to the office and noticed the large safe where the gold deposits were kept with the registered claims. The safe had a key lock and a combination lock, but clearly the combination lock was faulty because twice the official opened the safe using the key after giving the combination just one try.

Todd also noticed that at the rear of the office was also the official's home and several bottles of whiskey could be seen on the shelves, so he was a drinker. With this valuable knowledge Todd returned to his gang members. They set up camp and after a meal and some coffee he told them what he had found out. Two days after they had arrived at the site the army escort arrived to take this month's accumulation of gold to the Oklahoma City bank.

Over the next twenty days they worked patiently and had some success in their own claim and deposited the flakes and granules in the office like the other miners. Then came the night when they would put their plan into action with Silas taking care of the horses nearby while the other three carried out the audacious theft.

It was almost midnight when Todd moved up to the door of the office and glanced through the window just in time to see the official taking a final glass of whiskey before staggering to his bed. Todd tapped on the door and with much mumbling the unwary half-drunk official opened the door.

A six gun was thrust in his face, and he staggered back and fell to the floor and in seconds. Todd, Ike and Jake were inside and had him bound, gagged and freed of the safe key he had around his waist. The safe was promptly opened and the bags of gold, with the miners' names attached, were removed and transferred to four sets of saddle bags.

The official was pushed under his bed and the place was left in darkness and the door locked. Silas had the horses ready at the door and they fastened the saddle bags in place and quietly left the site. Once clear they trotted the horses for most of the rest of the night in the moonlight then as dawn broke they found a place to rest up for five hours. Silas then checked the horses. They were fine, so they had something to eat before heading off again for St Louis.

At no time during the next ten days did they ever have any indication that they were being pursued and they arrived late one evening at the captain's house confident they had made a clean get away. Captain Paul Wallace was glad to see them and listened to their story with some disbelief until the four sets of saddle bags were produced and their contents were revealed.

Wallace turned to Todd Raven and said, "Tomorrow you and I must visit someone who can dispose of this at a good price but don't forget it won't be the bank's price this gold is not legal so we will get what we can."

They had supper then went to bed.

The next morning around ten o'clock captain Wallace and Todd Raven went into St Louis to see the man Wallace had referred to. On Paul Wallace's suggestion Todd Raven carried one set of saddle bags and made sure he was wearing his six guns. The office they went to was clearly connected with shipping on the Mississippi River and the man there was obviously an old friend of captain Wallace. Introductions were made and no time was wasted in getting down to business.

One of the pouches from the saddle bags was opened and the contents placed on the man's desk. He opened several of the small canvas bags and had a good look at the contents. He indicated that the other side of the saddle bag should be opened, and it was then he sat back and nodded his head.

"Quality looks good. I would need that confirmed, but even so I would give you half the market daily gold price for this lot, what say you?"

Todd Raven looked at Paul Wallace then back at the trader.

"We have three more sets of saddle bags with a similar amount in them are you interested?"

The trader sat down open mouthed then said rather quickly, "Indeed I am. However, I need to bring in someone else as a banker, but totally trustworthy."

They agreed to meet again at the same time the next morning, so they collected the gold up and replaced it in the saddle bags and returned to the captain's home. The captain's housekeeper gave them all something to eat then they sat on the porch looking out on the river with a glass of some local hooch and discussed what price they may be offered.

Paul Wallace thought that forty thousand dollars was the highest they could expect even though the market price for gold of that quantity was around one hundred thousand. The people they were selling it to may sit on it for some time then sell it through a legitimate source at the market price.

The gang thought forty thousand was fine even though Paul Wallace would be expecting a present from that and later after a good meal and a few more drinks they went to bed content with life.

The next morning after breakfast Todd Raven, with his guns on clear display, and captain Paul Wallace with the four sets of saddle bags arrived at the shipping office. The man they had met yesterday was there and he had with him an older man who was rather stout. The contents of all four saddle bags were soon on display for the two men to check with the fat man taking a great interest. After about fifteen minutes the fat man turned to his partner and nodded his head and the man they had talked to yesterday turned to Todd Raven and said, "thirty-five thousand dollars for the lot."

Todd Raven gave a dismissal snort then said, "forty-five thousand or we walk out of here".

The two businessmen exchanged glances then the younger said, "The most we can go to is forty thousand."

"Agreed." said Todd Raven and the parties shook hands as the money went one way and the gold the other.

They had a party at the captain's house that night and they all got quite merry, but not completely drunk. They gave the captain two thousand dollars for his help, and he was happy with that. They stayed in St Louis for another four weeks then decided to head out to the west and try their luck in Kansas City which was new ground to them.

They had plenty of money for a while so no banks were in peril, but Ike needed some female company and that usually spelled trouble. Todd put a lot of time in practising his fast draw and was considered lightning fast by the other gang members. As for accuracy he could hit what he aimed at up to fifteen yards with a handgun and with a rifle up to a couple of hundred so he was a useful shot.

Once they had settled in a small boarding house on the northern edge of the city Ike decided to start looking for some female company. A bar girl was ok for a quick tumble in her back room bed, but he was looking for something a little different. Two young women caught his eye one was the junior school teacher and the other was the daughter of the Preacher who conducted the services at the small church in this part of the city. He was about to approach the preacher's daughter when a man rode past him on a handsome horse and greeted the young girl who was clearly delighted to see him. Ike also noticed that the youngish man about his own age wore the badge of a deputy sheriff, so he immediately lost all interest in the preacher's daughter.

So he concentrated on the young teacher realising that the offer of a drink at the nearest bar was not the way to her heart. He would have to be more subtle, and nature came to his aid because as he went to the school she was just leaving and a sudden gust of wind blew the bundle of papers she was holding from her clutches.

Ike ran forward and quickly gathered the papers up and then returned them to the rather embarrassed young woman.

"Thank you Sir that was most kind and I am most grateful." she said her cheeks now quite flushed.

Ike now feeling quite bold said. "May I walk you to your home my dear in case there is another mishap?"

And this was how Ike Raven first met Rosemary Mason who was the first woman to have any influence on his life, though at the time he was after just another tumble.

She allowed him to walk her to where she lived with her widowed mother in a small dwelling like so many others in this part of Kansas City. Her elderly mother was at the gate leaning on her stick and viewed Ike with suspicion, so he just raised his hat in farewell and moved on. But he had achieved two things he knew where she worked and where she lived, and he would build on that for now.

Todd had persuaded the gang to put their money in one of the banks and they had then purchased a small property with a couple of acres of pasture just outside the city limits to the north and Jake and Silas began to do the place up. Within a week the roof was now sound, and the doors and windows were as they should be. They began to give the place a lick of paint both inside and out with even Todd lending a hand. Ike even persuaded the schoolteacher to take a look but as yet had only been permitted to kiss her hand.

One problem they had not foreseen was having the ownership recorded jointly in the names of Todd and Ike Raven. Although their names did not appear on the wanted list of known criminals, but they did appear on the list of confederate deserters from the civil war in the State Capitol. An agreement had been reached in the now United States government that all deserters from the northern and southern armies should serve twelve months hard labour in a military prison.

Chapter Three

As a result, to Todd Raven's complete shock, he was surprised one morning to find outside their freshly renovated home eight armed American Troopers with a wagon and a warrant for the arrest of Todd and Ike Raven. A sergeant informed them of the circumstances and Todd was allowed to give Jake and Silas instructions on the running of the place in their absence. They were then handcuffed and placed in leg shackles in the wagon and then began the journey to Fort Smith and the military stockade.

Silas Gibb passed the news onto the young teacher of Ike's arrest and the reason stressing that Ike had only deserted because he was such a peaceful guy and could not harm anyone. The young teacher swallowed this hook line and sinker and said she would write to Ike at Fort Smith so that he knew she was his friend. She wrote every week and Ike was allowed one page out a fortnight. Life in the Stockade was brutal any insolence was rewarded by the butt end of a rifle and any escapee' received a bullet.

The inmates were housed ten to a cell with a canvas strip to lie on at night with one blanket in summer and two in the winter for comfort. The toilet was a hole in the corner of the cell one foot square with a wooden cover. One wash was allowed each day after labour which was the same each day. They were escorted into a large compound with perimeter guards and told to dig trenches in the bone hard soil then later in the afternoon you filled the trenches back in again. Breakfast was a bowl of thin porridge lunch was a hunk of dry bread and dinner was always a thick stew concoction.

Fights were frequent among the prisoners and the guards normally did not interfere and just watched unless they suspected it had been arranged to distract their attention from something else. The days and weeks went slowly by and without the strong presence of his brother Ike would have succumbed to the bullying of the other prisoners.

Of their two friends left at their small property only Silas could write, and he did once a month just to say all was well with the horses. A young doctor had been paying Rosemary Mason some attention as he had visited the school to check on the health of the young pupils. Her mother saw him as a very suitable companion for her daughter and suggested she forget all about the cowardly deserter now in jail that she had taken pity on. So it was with some regret that Rosemary wrote to Ike and told him in her next letter that she had been seeing the young doctor and with regret her friendship with Ike must end.

Ike did not take the news well and vowed that on his return to Kansas City he would seek the young doctor out and shoot him down. He would then throw the young teacher over the pummel of his horse and ride out of the city. In his twisted mind he thought that this would impress the young teacher of his love for her, and she would give herself to him without the need for the formality of marriage.

Todd listened to his young brother's angry plan with some amusement and told him with a serious expression on his face that it would work. The remaining nine months of their sentence dragged slowly by and at last came the day of their release and to meet them outside was Silas and a horse for each of them and an insistence that the ride home would be leisurely. Even Ike agreed to this because he had some planning to do but halfway home Silas told him the bad news.

Rosemary and the doctor were married, and the fair Rosemary was six months with child and in no condition to be thrown over the pummel of a saddle. Todd did not help matters by bursting into helpless laughter, so they set up camp for the night and downed between them a bottle of whiskey. By the time they reached Kansas City their plans had changed they would overnight at their property then head out West all thoughts of revenge had now been forgotten.

They found the property in a fine condition and the stables and pastures well-kept. Jake had a meal ready and they sat down and enjoyed it then talked of their plans for the coming days. It was at this point that Silas suggested that he stayed behind and looked after the property and raised some horses making good use of the fine pasture they had. It made sense and after some discussion it was agreed, and it gave them a base to return to if things got too hot in the West.

Before they headed west the next morning Todd and Ike needed to speak to their bank manager about access to their money in other branches and they were given a letter of introduction stamped to make it official. It was as they were leaving the bank they walked into Rosemary and her husband the doctor and Todd stood back with a smile waiting for Ike to explode. But it was Rosemary who took the initiative and with a smile she offered her hand to Ike and said, "How nice to see you back home and looking so well Ike please let me introduce you to Phillip my husband."

Her husband stepped forward with a smile and an outstretched hand and said, "How nice to meet you Ike, Rosemary has told me a lot about you."

Ike surprised himself by his response by saying, "You are a lucky man Phillip and I wish you both health and happiness and a wonderful first child, but we are off west and must go, so stay safe."

And with a wave he and Todd walked away. Twenty yards down the street Todd said, "Well little brother that was pretty impressive stuff it sounded as though you meant it."

Ike grimaced then said, "I was about to blow his balls off when he smiled and offered his hand, and I realised what a decent chap Rosemary had chosen and that was what mattered".

Todd just shook his head in bewilderment, and they joined up with Jake Shay and mounted their horses and began their journey to the west. They took their time and averaged about thirty miles a day and eventually arrived in Dodge City where Ike found the bar girls much to his liking. Todd was soon in great demand by the gaming joint owners to keep order by his size and his speed on the draw.

Meanwhile back in the town of Hope some young families had moved in and some new wooden small dwellings had been added to the southern side of the town. They now had a town doctor and Jane had four more pupils to her school and the town now had a skilled carpenter as well. The two ranches had grown, and they still came in on a Friday and Saturday night with slightly bigger numbers involved and Ma Harris had increased the number of girls accordingly, so business was good.

Most Saturdays in the morning Jack took Simon fishing in the Snake River for a couple of hours they made an early start and were usually home by ten o'clock with a couple of fish for Jane to cook later in the day. The following week the new doctor visited the school and checked the health of the children which was now something the Government wanted each State to do on a regular basis.

He happened to mention that his brother had got married to a teacher in Kansas City and they were expecting their first child in a few months. He then casually mentioned that the teacher had previously had a relationship with a young man who had been sent to prison for desertion during the Civil War. It was during the man's imprisonment that his brother and the teacher met and recently they both had met the man again after he had been released and his name was Ike Raven.

Jane was quite taken aback and told the doctor that she thought her husband had known this man and his brother as they were all in the Confederate Army at the time. Of course, she told Jack about the conversation when she came home that day and he gave a smile thinking well some justice was served at least. That night being Saturday Jack was on duty checking the guns in and the ranch hands were all in good humour looking forward to a few beers and a frolic with the bar girls. Just after midnight he handed them their shooting irons back making sure each six guns chamber was empty just in case of accidents.

Once back home he stabled his horse and gave it hay and water then went into the house and secured it for the night. He went quietly to the bedroom so as not wake his sleeping wife and after slipping off his clothes he slid into the warm bed. Seconds later a warm arm slid around his neck and a very warm and totally naked body was pressed up against his and a voice whispered, "Sleep or?"

Sunday morning breakfast was a little late and his father Abe had already made the coffee when Jane and Jack came rushing in from their bedroom. The eggs and bacon were soon cooking on the range and Jack was urging Simon to get out of bed. At eleven o'clock was of course the prayer meeting at the Communal Hall with Ethan Watts giving it his all. Very few residents of Hope missed this weekly event for one thing it was uplifting and good for their spirits and another was it made Sunday feel like a proper Sunday. The blacksmith apart from keeping an eye on their horses also missed very little else that went on in Hope.

Jack's father Abe had lost his wife some years ago and in recent months had become quite friendly with the widow Allen. A couple of evenings a week they spent some time together in their gardens as they were both keen on the plants and flowers. Ethan Watts chose to mention in his weekly sermon the sanctity of marriage and the importance of a relationship having God's blessing. But then seeing some eyes turning towards Abe Masters and the widow Allen he quickly added, "But a benevolent God smiles on a couple brought together by a partner's bereavement."

Afterwards, when they went home, the meat had already been put in the oven and was nearly ready, so it was only the vegetables to cook so dinner was never late. The men had a glass of beer with their dinner and the ladies sometimes a glass of wine and the children some water. Will Thomas the sheriff was hoping to go on for a couple more years, but he was having some trouble riding now so he was leaving any mounted work to Jack and another younger man called Buck Shaw who Jack had known in the army.

Buck proved his worth when two saddle tramps came into Hope and tried to get drinks on credit at Ma Harris's bar. When she refused to serve them before seeing their money, one of them drew his gun. At this she immediately fired her shot gun into the roof of the bar. Buck Shaw was nearby and ran to the scene and disarmed both men as they staggered outside. Then Will Thomas and Jack arrived.

They took the two men to the only cell they had at the back of Will Thomas's office. Fortunately, the next day the escort from Fort Worth would arrive and they would take the two men back there and charge them with disturbing the peace. They would be fined or be given seven days in the lock up and that would hopefully be the end of it. Ma Harris had given a written statement and that was all that was required as evidence.

Towards the end of the year Abe Masters told Jack and Jane that he and Edie Allen were going to get married, and he would move into her place just a few hundred yards away. Ethan Watts arranged for a Vicar to come over and conduct the ceremony from a town fifteen miles away. In the late October sunshine, it took place in the gardens of the communal hall with all their friends in attendance. Edie Allen was still a handsome woman and Jack, and Jane were delighted to see the couple so happy and so obviously well matched. Ma Harris provided a bar and several people there provided some music and the dancing went on until nearly midnight then stopped for the next day was the Sabbath.

Chapter Four

Ike had never killed a man before though he was a reasonable shot and he had practised drawing his gun and was quite quick but slow in comparison to his brother Todd. Not surprisingly it had all been over a woman and he would have happily walked away from the challenge but the lady in question was there to witness the whole encounter. The spurned lover had stuck his finger in Ike's chest and stuck his face inches from that of Ike's. He then issued a series of threats his foul breath almost making Ike heave. Ike pushed him away and said in a voice he barely recognised as his own, "Let's settle this outside."

He had not realised he was challenging the man to a gun fight; all he really wanted was to an escape from the man's foul breath and settle it with fists. The bar emptied in a flash the spectators standing well clear on each sidewalk. The girl concerned leaned out of a window with her friends around her watching with interest as two men would fight over just her.

Ike's instinct now was to try and talk his way out of this and he was about to say something when the man now standing about four yards in front of him said, "Go for your gun punk."

As the man's hand darted towards his gun, Ike's survival instinct kicked in and without realising it his hand followed the hours of practise in front of a mirror and he effortlessly drew his gun and fired two rounds at the target to his front.

His first shot struck his assailant squarely in the chest and the second just a couple of inches below that. His assailant managed just one shot, but it was fired a split second after he was hit in the chest, and it struck the ground a few feet in front of Ike Raven. Ike let his gun hand drop to his side as his tormentor crumbled to the ground. Feeling now quite dazed Ike was grabbed by the girl who proudly led her hero back into the bar and then to her room upstairs.

Ike was seen a short time later by a local deputy sheriff who explained that witnesses had all stated that the man killed had drawn first so in the eyes of the law no crime had taken place. But he did give Ike some advice the man Ike had killed had reputation as a 'fast gun' and now Ike would inherit that reputation.

The deputy added, "All the young gun slingers anxious to prove how quick they are will be looking for you my friend so be warned. The safest thing would be never to wear a gun."

When Ike saw Todd that evening his brother had already heard about the shooting and was furious that Ike had got involved in a gun fight and all over a bar girl. Ike explained about the deputy sheriff's advice about not wearing a gun and Todd grabbed his younger brother by the throat and said, "No Raven walks away from a challenge, so you stay kitted up and remember you can always rely on me."

In any case in a place like Dodge City the only people who did not carry guns were parsons, doctors and teachers, even females often had small handguns in their shopping bags. It was almost a week before Ike found himself confronted again and this time it was by young Willie Hicks who was almost eighteen and was not quite right in the head.

Where Willie had got the gun from nobody knew but it was later thought that some of the local young lads had dared him to do this and had given him the gun. Todd was all for Ike shooting the silly little sod in the legs and teaching him a lesson but Ike without knowing it earned the respect and admiration of a banker's daughter who observed the drama unfold. Willie Hicks strutted up and down in front of the Dragon bar shouting that Ike Raven was a coward and he should come out and meet a real fast gun.

Ike, ignoring Todd's advice, had already decided what he would do, as he knew young Willie from the times he had looked after his horse for him at the local stable. A crowd had already gathered some laughing at the sight of this halfwit who was about to be shot dead. Ike emerged from the bar and stepped down into the dirt street just fifteen feet from the prancing Willie Hicks. Helen James the banker's daughter put her hand to her mouth dreading what might now happen.

Ike decided he should take the initiative before things got totally out of hand, so he unbuckled his gun belt and threw that and his guns to the ground.

"I can't take you on Willie because I know you can out draw me."

Then unarmed Ike turned to walk away, while Willie did a little dance of delight waiving his gun about. However, in his enthusiasm Willie managed to shoot himself in the foot. He collapsed with a cry of pain with the crowd now in fits of laughter, but two people went to his assistance, the banker's daughter and Ike Raven. Ike carried Willie over to the only doctor who he knew would be sober at this time of day to attend to the minor gunshot wound, which was a mere graze. Later Ike took Willie back to the stables where he had a place to live at the rear. Helen James had told Ike earlier that she had admired what he had done as it had taken great moral courage to back down from a gun fight he could have easily won in front of that large crowd.

When Helen arrived home she told her father all that had occurred and how she had admired the way this man Ike Raven had behaved. Her father was very concerned he knew his daughter was of an age when every day events can have a romantic slant which could be dangerous in one so impressionable. He told her that he had heard of these Raven brothers with the elder one called Todd being a very violent gun fighting thug. He went on.

"From what you say my dear his brother Ike seems to be an improvement but please keep away from them they are not suitable for someone like you."

Helen loved her father and since her mother had died they had grown even closer together and she respected his wishes. Todd gave some thought to encouraging his brother to get closer to the banker's daughter with a view that in time it might get them easy access to the bank but then other events changed things.

Todd Raven normally never gambled but he had been tipped off how this particular card sharp worked and how to interrupt the sequence with a large bet and clean out the house. He assured Ike the information was rock solid and then put almost all the money into the stake that they had left. But Todd had been conned and his informant was in league with the card sharp and that night the biggest gamble of Todd's life was to come crashing down.

All seemed to be going well at the start and Ike had their horses outside ready for a fast getaway when they won the big prize. Then as the game reached the large bet stakes Todd's confidence grew. He recognised the clue he had been waiting for and put all his money on his next hand dealt but when it came his world fell apart it was a disaster, and he knew he had been conned. He calmly shot the card sharp and then the informer dead and as everyone dived for cover he grabbed as much money from the table as he could and made for the door.

Ike had the horses ready and Todd stuffing the money into his pockets mounted his horse and together they galloped at speed to the north out of Dodge City. Then after a few miles slowed to a trot and turned west thinking that perhaps they would try their luck in Denver. The two men Todd had shot and killed were hardly the two most popular characters in Dodge City but even so the lack of volunteers to form a posse until the next morning did surprise the city marshal.

They then set off northeast, confident that was the direction the pair was heading but by this time Todd and Ike were resting up thirty miles away to the northwest having breakfast. Before they got on the move again Todd checked how much money he had retrieved, and he was surprised to find he had all his stake money plus five hundred dollars, so he felt quite satisfied. Back in Dodge City over breakfast the banker showed the headlines of the morning paper to his daughter which read, *Raven brothers kill two and flee City.*

As a result, wanted posters were issued and for the first time Todd Raven's name appeared on one in which he was wanted for murder and his brother Ike as his accomplice. One eventually reached Hope and was placed on the wall of sheriff Will Thomas's office and was seen by Jack Masters.

It took Todd and Ike twelve days to reach Denver making sure they never overtired their horses. Once there they had the local blacksmith check their horses over and had them re-shod then they checked into a boarding house on the edge of the growing city.

Photography was of course now a growing industry, but law enforcement was still catching up and as yet convicted prisoners were not routinely photographed so no photograph appeared on the wanted posters of the Raven brothers, just a poorly drawn artists impression which could fit almost anyone man of that age.

Employment was not hard to find in the gambling clubs of Denver for men of the calibre of the Ravens and both were soon at home in the Red Hat club and enjoying the free drink and Ike the girls while attending to their protective duties. The owner soon realised that he had hired a ruthless fast gun and his club became trouble free almost overnight and the brothers had an increase in wages. Ike had his pick of the eight bar girls but sensibly spread himself around to keep the girls happy.

The weeks went quickly by then suddenly a sudden fever struck the city and spread quite dramatically initially through the older population. There were quite a few deaths then it seemed to mutate and spread into the younger population and Ike became quite ill. A doctor advised Todd his brother stood a better chance of survival in the higher mountain air so Todd and one of Ike's girlfriends took him twenty miles to a remote cabin in the hills.

Todd only stayed overnight then drove the buck board back to Denver but had left Ike and the girl with supplies for a week. The week saw Ike make a good recovery and when Todd returned and stayed for the night the next morning they all were ready to return to Denver. Thankfully the illness was on the wane and a trapper was blamed for bringing the disease down from an Indian reservation where the disease was rife.

The brothers spent another three months in Denver then Todd began to get itchy feet and wanted to move on. He mentioned it to the boss of the Red Hat and he offered him more money to stay but Todd had made up his mind. The Red Hat boss asked him where he was aiming to go and Todd just said vaguely, "Oh, somewhere south."

The boss said, "My brother runs a club like this one in Amarillo and he could use someone like you and you brother if you are interested?"

So, a few days later Todd and Ike headed south for Amarillo with a letter of introduction to the owner of the Firelight Club. It's about three hundred miles from Denver to Amarillo and they took their time and never overtired their horses, so it was just before mid-day on the twelve day of their journey that they arrived in their new place of work. As usual the first thing they always did was to find somewhere near the edge of the large town to stable their horses and live. This they did quickly and booked into Widow Clancy's establishment with stables run by her son Joseph. She saw them settled in and gave them directions to the Firelight club.

The club was a ten minute walk from the Clancy Rooms and was almost identical to the Red Hat club in Denver. When they asked to see the owner, a large man stood up and barred their way but noticed that Todd had a confident swagger about him and when the letter was produced seemed only too pleased to escort them in. The owner greeted them pleasantly enough then took the letter and scanned its contents then offered them both his hand. He then turned and indicated the large man at his side by saying, "This is Jake, he is my house manager, and you will get on fine".

Chapter Five

Strangely enough despite his initial reservations Todd Raven and Jake did get on well together. Jake never carried a gun but was very useful with his fists and the two in combination proved a formidable obstacle to any troublemakers at the Firelight club. Ike's role was to make sure the girls were not short changed by the punters who paid for their service as a dance partner or for more intimate entertainment. The club was a thriving business and one of the more successful ones in Amarillo which did cause some local friction, but Jake and Todd quickly dealt with that and received a bonus. After they had been there for a couple of months the Raven brothers really felt they had made a wise choice in coming to Amarillo. The money was good, and Ike was enjoying as much female company as he could handle and for free. Then an unexpected problem arose the owner became quite ill and his brother who they had worked for in Denver at the Red Hat club came down to install a temporary manager.

The new manager or manageress turned out to be the brother's sister from the east who had a business degree and demanded to look through the books on her arrival. The sick brother was taken to Denver by his elder brother so as to be given the chance to recover in the clean mountain air. The sister after two hours studying the books sent for Jake and Todd and though inviting them to sit down viewed both of them with ill-disguised contempt. Then she said, in rather withering tones, "My brother appears to have been running nothing more than a gambling house and a brothel".

She poured herself a glass of water then went on.

"However, from a business point of view it appears to be most profitable whatever it moral shortcomings might be. I have undertaken to carry on and run the business until my brother is well enough to return and take charge and I am counting on you two monsters to help me achieve this. Are you prepared to work alongside a weak woman like me?"

Todd Raven glanced at Jake who nodded, and Todd said, "I don't see no weak woman in this room lady but in answer to your question you can count on us and we will make sure your stay here is trouble free."

The brother's sister stayed a month, and the stay was not without its moments of humour with Ike complaining to his brother that his weekly pay slip had five dollars deducted for in-house entertainment. When Todd checked with the manageress she said, "Your brother does not have free use of the girls he must pay when he slakes his lust like everyone else."

Then she added, "I have given him some discount, but he should show more self-control."

At last, the now well again brother returned, and the sister said her goodbyes giving the somewhat embarrassed Todd and Jake a hug and kiss for their help. It was a while before the visit of the sister was forgotten but things quickly returned to normal, and Ike stopped paying for his pleasures.

Three hundred miles away to the east in the Town of Hope Jane had found out that she was pregnant, so they were both hoping for a girl this time. They had expanded the store building so they could take in more stock as now they had more custom. They now had a full time bank and Will Thomas left all the riding duties to Jack and Buck and just looked after the sheriff's office and walked around town keeping the peace. Because all of Hope's buildings were constructed of wood Ethan Watts the blacksmith had constructed a hand driven water pump in case of fire and had trained a group of young volunteers in its use. From time to time Will Thomas got updates on people still on the wanted list and much to his and Jack's surprise they found that Todd Raven was no longer wanted for murder as both the men he had killed had discharged their weapons, so it was considered a fair gun fight. Jack had his suspicions that money had changed hands and he was right for the owner of the gambling club was a friend of the owner of the Firelight club who owed Todd Raven a favour.

The two ranches to the north and south of Hope were doing good business in cattle and horses and there was talk of a railroad branch line being constructed across to Hope from Fort Worth to collect the cattle for market. Another teacher was now in post in Hope he was married and had two small children not quite of school age. He had been used to teaching older children so with the numbers of pupils they now had they now split them all into two separate classes. With Jane teaching the five to nine year olds and the other teacher Adam Summers teaching the rest. Adam Summers wife was also a qualified teacher so when Jane was off having her baby she would cover the vacancy until and if Jane wished to return. Both Jane and Jack got on well with the Summers family and after a short time became really good friends. In conversation Jack found out that Adam had been Medical Assistant in the Southern Army during the Civil War and one of his brothers had been killed fighting for the south and the other had died of wounds while fighting for the north. It was typical how that war had split the families apart with some the division never healing.

Simon now was almost ten years old and quite fascinated by the fact that in his mother's bulging stomach was an addition to their family. He knew from the conversations that he had overheard from older boys that his father had placed a seed there and in his naivety assumed it had been purchased from their store. Simon was hoping for a brother but then on some reflection thought he may grow bigger than me and decided that a sister would be a safer option.

Early one morning Simon was woken by a great deal of noise and some anguished cries of pain from his parent's bedroom and then saw his father race across to the doctor's house. For the next hour he hid under his two pillows to shut out any noise but then he heard his bedroom door open and he surfaced to hear his father say, "Come and say Hello to your little sister Sue Ellen".

Fortunately, there were no complications with the birth or the after affects and Sue Ellen was a healthy bonny baby with Jane making a rapid return to normality. Rachel Summers was covering Jane's classes until her return with Jane thinking whether she wanted to go back or not. Abe Masters and his wife were delighted to be Grandparents again and a date for the christening of the child was being discussed. It was soon decided, and Ethan Watts arranged for a Vicar to come and conduct the simple ceremony. After Sue Ellen was three months old Jane did go back into teaching for a short time with Abe and his wife looking after the baby. But her heart was no longer in it and she decided to become a full time mother again. The store was doing good business so there were no financial problems and the schoolteachers pay was only one dollar a day.

The owners of both the cattle ranches had complained to sheriff Will Thomas that they were losing small numbers of cattle to rustlers each week always on the nights that their ranch hands came into Hope. So Will took over seeing in the ranch hands on those evenings and Jack Masters and Buck Shaw went out and kept an eye on the grazing herd from a position of vantage. It was not long before it was clear something was disturbing the cattle and then they could see three mounted men cutting out four of the beasts and moving them north.

Jack and Buck followed at a distance and found a mile or so further on a horse drawn cart and the four cattle were being urged into the back of the cart. Jack and Buck let the loading be completed then they moved in each firing a warning shot in the air. The three rustlers did not hesitate as ranchers often punished rustlers with hanging without the bother of a trial and galloped off at speed to the north.

Jack and Buck watched them go then led the horse drawn cart and its load of prime cattle back to the ranch owner who had now gained a fine sturdy wagon and four fine horses and had not lost a single animal. That was the end of the rustling in the Hope area and the sheriff, and his two deputies enjoyed prime beef joints each Sunday for a year.

Ma Harris built another extension to her premises as her business was booming as the ranchers had taken on more hands. There was very little crime in Hope with the occasional theft from the store by a light fingered youth being punished by a couple of whacks from Ethan Watts on the offender's backside in public. The Communal Hall was in need of some attention and a group of volunteers was formed to see the work completed.

Jane Fuller and Rachel Summers volunteered to make some curtains for the five windows and some minor carpentry work was required but the main task was the repainting.

Over the next two weeks a transformation took place and on completion Ethan Watts held a prayer meeting of celebration to thank those involved for the splendid work they had done. As he watched the huge blacksmith come Preacher perform Adam Summers thought what a great Shakespearean actor he would have made. With that great thunderous voice and delivery Summer's was lost in admiration as Ethan called for God's Blessing on everyone by name who had helped in the Communal Hall project.

Afterwards they all enjoyed some coffee and cakes that the ladies had provided though the men would have preferred something stronger but it was a religious occasion. Afterwards Ethan Watts called for order and said, "My friends I think that from now on this building will be known as the Peoples Community Hall, it may seem to be a belt and braces title but to me it reflects the work you have all given to this project."

A loud cheer went up clearly this met with everybody's approval.

Jack Masters had acquired a buckboard and two young sturdy horses specially bred for this task. He now was able to deliver the supplies to the ranches to the north and south which gave him extra business. It also meant that if his stores stock was running low he did not have to wait for the monthly wagons to arrive from Fort Worth. Jack found that if he left early in the morning from Hope he could do the resupply in one day by giving his horses a three hour rest while reloading the supplies in Fort Worth. He was always home before eight in the evening and the stores unloaded and the horses fed and watered before ten.

Life in Hope continued on its quiet peaceful way until one hot summer's day in the late afternoon a young man rode into town and decided to stop at Ma Harris's for a free drink. Ma Harris did not like the look of this man but never turned away the chance to make a few cents, so she poured him a beer then put her hand out for the money. The young man drained the glass in one then slammed it down on the bar and said, "Fill it up again."

"Money first." said Ma Harris. "You ain't paid for the first one yet".

The young man grinned.

"Where I come from the first beer is always on the house, so fill it up you old bag or I'll do some damage."

In reply, Ma Harris produced her shot gun and thrust it the young man's stomach.

"No, you mouthy young punk, pay up or I will do some damage."

The young man threw some money on the bar and walked out. Once outside he drew one of his guns and fired three shots into the coloured glass sign over the door smashing it completely. Sheriff Will Thomas who had just come out of his office across the street called out to the young man.

"Put your gun down son and walk slowly over to me. I am the sheriff of this town, and we won't have any wild shooting."

The young man calmly reloaded his weapon then turned and faced sheriff Will Thomas.

"Just get out of my way old man and you won't get hurt and I'll ride out of your stinking town."

By now several people had gathered and Ma Harris was desperately looking for a spare shot gun cartridge. sheriff Will Thomas had positioned himself between the young stranger and his horse determined to face this threat down.

"It's your final warning son drop your guns and raise your hands over your head and walk slowly towards me."

The young stranger just grinned then drew his right handgun in one slick polished movement and shot Will Thomas twice before Will's hand could reach his gun.

Chapter Six

The young stranger then walked slowly to his horse and gazed with contempt at the onlookers who had scurried away then he mounted his horse and rode slowly north out of town. Will Thomas was still alive, one bullet had struck his sheriffs badge and deflected into his upper arm the other round had hit his shoulder, but he lost a lot of blood. Jack Masters had been at the back of the store when he heard the shooting, and his first thought was to see that Will Thomas had the services of the doctor. Then he and Buck Shaw collected their weapons and set off after the young stranger but after two hours there was no trace to the north and he had not been near the ranch there.

Frustrated they returned to Hope to find that Will Thomas had now improved and was expected to make a full recovery. A report of the shooting was sent to the marshal in Fort Worth and over the next few days Will Thomas made a steady recovery. But as Will made a return to full health he made it clear that his days as sheriff of Hope were over.

Jack Masters was the popular and logical choice to replace him and with Abe's wife Sarah looking after Sue Ellen it meant Jane could now work full time in the store with Abe. The young stranger who had shot Will Thomas had been involved in another shooting to the north. He had now been identified as Jed Miller who had been the sole survivor of a small gang of bank robbers who had been killed while attempting to rob a bank in Mexico City.

The shooting in the north had been after a bar brawl and no one had been hurt as Miller and his friend fired shots in the air as they raced out of the town. Will Thomas had now recovered and had been given a job as door man at the bank, so he still carried a gun but was hoping not to have to use it.

Some distance away in Amarillo the lives of the Raven brothers had taken on a comfortable air, they both had good jobs which they enjoyed and were well suited for and the money was good. Todd was the more ambitious of the two and dreamed of having not just one club bearing his name but a chain of several. Ike was quite happy with less responsibility and some willing female at his beck and call. The owner of the Firelight club had never been fully fit since his last illness and his brother did not want to buy him out, so he offered the sale of the club to Todd and Jake who jumped at the chance and within a week the sale went through. Despite the difference between the two men, they got on really well, but Ike always thought that his brother would find a reason to kill Jake and take over the club. They made slight changes to the club and extended the back premises which were now a full time brothel and the money rolled in.

They decided to change the name of the club slightly to give it a more welcoming appeal, so it was now called the Fireside Club. Within a month of Todd and Jake taking over the ownership of the club the profits had increased by one third and everyone employed there received a bonus unheard of in those austere times. Some of the other club owners in Amarillo were not too happy with this competition which had reduced their earning by almost a half.

For once they forgot their individual differences and put the money together to hire four hard men to go and wreck the Fireside club one evening at the height of its business. Fortunately, one of Ike's former girl friends who was still working at one of those establishments got to hear of the plan and passed the word onto her former beau. When the four hired hard man arrived at the club prepared to create mayhem they were met at the door by the towering figures of Jake and Todd with six club wielding security staff behind them.

Ten minutes later without a blow being struck the four men were riding out of Amarillo with the deed unaccomplished but the money for it in their pockets as they always were paid in advance. Todd and Jake took their revenge in a business way by reducing their prostitute's fees by half for a week causing two of those competitors to close down. The former girlfriend was offered a better job and a cash bonus for the information she had provided.

For almost a year life could not have been better for Todd and Ike Raven and their good friend and partner Jake and then suddenly out of the blue tragedy struck. One morning just after eleven they were drinking coffee after realising that last night's takings were the best ever when Jake slowly got to his feet complaining of a pain in his chest. As Todd rose to ask his friend if he needed a doctor the mighty Jake suddenly crashed to the floor on his back. Ike, without being told, ran to get Doc Summers.

As Todd Raven bent over his friend for almost the first time in his life concerned for someone other than himself Doc Summers arrived. He quickly carried out an examination then shook his head and turning to the stricken Todd Raven he said.

"I am afraid he has gone."

From that moment on Todd Raven lost all interest in the Fireside club and sold it to the first eager buyer. Then he and Ike stayed in Amarillo just long enough to give Jake a good send off and have a fine memorial stone placed over his grave. They had a sizeable bank account between them, and Jake had left everything to Todd as his only friend. They decided to head for El Paso about three hundred and fifty miles southwest and new territory to them and try their luck so they transferred their money to a bank there and were given a letter of introduction.

They took their time over the journey and never put their horses over more than thirty miles a day. The country was pretty wild and rugged and some of the nights were cold in the hills, and they needed a fire most nights. They came across some odd characters who Ike would have kept clear of but with Todd at his side he feared no one. El Paso sits on the bank of the Rio Grande and was a place that people tended to pass through than stay and make their home. It was pretty rough and ready and that suited Todd in his present mood and all Ike wanted was a bath and the services of a woman.

They found some reasonable accommodation for themselves and their horses with Ike complaining that the horses had the better deal. The four bed hotel was run by a

Chinese couple who clearly thought everyone liked rice, but the place was clean and that made it stand out from the opposition.

The second night they were there Ike got into an argument over a bar girl and guns were drawn but before shots were exchanged the local sheriff stepped between them and confiscated their weapons. He then coolly said, "You can pick these up tomorrow when your good sense has returned."

Todd who had watched this taking place confident his brother was the quicker and better shot was very impressed and asked who the sheriff was. The man next to him put down his beer and said, "Oh he's new around here only been here about six months but has got quite a reputation. His name is Wyatt Earp."

About a week later Todd heard that the local sheriff had been summoned to Dallas and was to be given the title of marshal and a roving commission in the State. A new man came in as sheriff and did a decent job of keeping the peace by fining any gun play with five dollar payments.

Todd Raven took his letter of introduction down to the manager of the bank of Texas and after reading it the manager was most affable. Todd was assured that his money was secure in the bank of Texas and the two men drank a whiskey together. It was as Todd was leaving the manager's office with the manager at his side that three armed men burst into the bank firing their guns in the air. As everyone dived for cover Todd Raven shot all three, two with his right handgun and one with his left. The manager staggered to his feet an enormous expression of relief on his face and grasped Todd by the arms.

"My dear sir, you are a hero you saved the bank and the people's money, and what shooting they all got what they deserved."

Two of the three were still alive but only just and one died as the doctor was examining him but the other had only a shoulder wound but was bleeding badly.

The sheriff arrived and the wounded man was patched up then moved to a bed in the cells and the undertaker removed the other bodies. The sheriff had a word with Todd Raven saying, "It was a good job you were here Mr Raven and good enough with a gun to prevent this robbery I congratulate you."

But when the sheriff went back to his office he looked through all his wanted posters wondering how someone that good with a gun was not a peace officer. Todd and Ike were to spend another six months in El Paso before deciding to move on and gave the matter some thought before deciding on a move to Laredo almost four hundred miles to the south. Laredo is on the Rio Grande and close to the border and a hot spot of smuggling between the two countries but on their two weeks ride south Todd and Ike were not aware of that at the time.

The journey south was not without incident two saddle bums with almost a full bottle of whiskey inside them tried to rob them as they made camp on their second night. Todd shot them both but left the rough burying to Ike after breakfast the next morning. It was not a wasted journey as they now had two more half decent horses that were in better condition than their previous owners.

They eventually arrived in Laredo to find a Fiesta in full swing but quickly found some decent stables and a rooming house nearby. Todd met someone who he had worked with some years ago and who he felt he could trust and the two were soon in deep conversation. Ike had his eyes on a couple of Mexican bar girls whose short dresses were attracting a great deal of attention. The goods being smuggled were of a mixed variety but mainly brandy and whisky, the goods went north, and the money went south. The reason for all this business was simple Mexican labour was cheaper than that in the American States.

It took Todd and his new partner Wally Tyne a week to muscle in on the business spending two afternoons at the funerals of their opposition. Within a month Todd Raven was top dog in this dangerous business and some of the smaller outfits just became his carriers. Even Ike was surprised how ruthless his brother had become he had always been hard but since Jake's death he had changed.

He had a routine now for almost everything every Saturday night after two drinks he had a woman. Sunday morning he trimmed his beard and had a bath then did the accounts and checked the week's profits. After a meal he would go for an hour's ride then come back and have a drink with Ike.

During the week it was business occupying his full attention with him now being almost as close to Wally as he was to Jake. They always got good notice when any rare attempt by the authorities to stop the smuggling was to take place and the informants were always well rewarded, so the business flourished.

Chapter Seven

Back in Hope sadly Jack's father had died leaving Edie once again a widow however she was now very closely involved with the family looking after Sue Ellen while Jane was working in the store. Even Simon now was able to help his mother in restocking the lower shelves and feeding the chickens was a task he enjoyed.

The population had grown by about twenty over the last year as a man who had arrived to try and grow grapes to produce wine had brought his Italian family with him. Jack was trying to work out just who they were for the town's records, and it turned out to be Mother and Father, son and his wife and four children, two uncles and their wives six children and two cousins. This large family were no trouble and had money to build some stout timber houses on the large piece of land they had purchased.

The children were an asset to the school as they were well behaved and spoke good English and two of the girls were talented artists and helped the other children less gifted. Most of the citizens of Hope who were initially wary of the newcomers were very impressed with how hard this new family had worked. And in a fairly short time they had turned their rough couple of acres of ground into a well cultivated area almost ready for the vines to be planted.

Jack Master's duties as sheriff were not hard work and he found time to help Jane with restocking with Buck Shaw covering for him. He had always been a naturally good shot and from time to time rode off into the hills to do some shooting practise. He was also a very quick draw which came of practise and natural ability plus a regular waxing of his holsters to ease a rapid extraction. Jack had killed men during the war purely on the basis that if he had not killed them they would have killed him. If the occasion occurred during law enforcement he would apply the same principle it seemed the right and obvious attitude to take.

Jack had never discussed this with Will Thomas or with Buck Shaw, but he knew every man had his own way of dealing with this as it was a personal thing. Gunfighters of course were different to them it was almost like the luck in a turn of the cards, the difference being instead of holding the Ace of Hearts you were the faster draw. One night a worried mother called at Jack's house saying her son had gone fishing down on the Snake after school saying he would be only a couple of hours. Jack asked where the boy normally went, and he knew the spot well, so he contacted Buck Shaw, and they collected their horses and a couple of lamps and set off. It was a dark but clear night, and they rode down both banks near the spot for a mile each way but there was no sign of the lad. So, they rode back to Hope and spoke to the mother who had two other children, but her husband was away working in Fort Worth.

It was Buck Shaw who suggested the boy may have run away to see his father in Fort Worth and as he said this the older child a girl burst into tears and said to her mother, "He told me not to tell you but that's where he's gone to tell dad to come home."

Jack Masters said, "Well we can't do anything now, but at first light I'll take the buck board and drive down the Fort Worth. We'll track him down and pick the young rascal up. One night out at this time of year won't hurt him."

The mother was relieved, even though her son would be out all night, and Jack and Buck went to their homes. Jack told Jane he would be off early in the morning to catch a runaway on the Fort Worth track. At five o'clock Jack got up had a quick breakfast and made some coffee then put some in a flask and went out and got the buck board ready. It was now almost light, and he started the horses off at a trot down the track to Fort Worth he had gone less than six miles when he spotted a young figure walking slowly ahead of him and Jack slowed his two horses to a walk so as not to alarm the lad.

The boy did not realise who it was at first until Jack said, "Going somewhere son?"

"Oh, it's you sheriff. I'm going to Fort Worth to see my dad." said the boy.

"You can't go without your mother's permission, and she has not given it so you can return freely with me, or I can arrest you. What's it to be?"

"I'll come back with you please sheriff." said the lad, tears now just beginning to trickle from his eyes. Jack turned the buck board round and helped the lad aboard then gave him some coffee from the flask and a couple of biscuits Jane had baked yesterday. Jack took the boy straight to his mother who was already up and anxiously waiting for news, and she rushed forward and on seeing her son and wrapped her arms around him. She expressed her thanks to Jack Masters then hurried her son indoors to give him breakfast and later a good talking to.

Jack took the buck board back to the stables and fed and watered the horses then went into the house where Jane was busy cooking breakfast and gave her all the news. Later that morning one of the ranch hands came into Hope from the Circle 'O' with news that one of his colleagues had been shot dead trying to fend off a group of rustlers during the night who had taken a dozen cattle.

Jack and Buck rode out to the Circle 'O' and with a posse of four ranch hands all armed went after the rustlers who could not move at any great speed with their small prize. It was late in the afternoon when they caught up with the rustlers watering their stolen cattle at a small stream. Seeing there were four rustlers, Jack sent Buck and two of the posse round to cut off their route of escape. Once they were in position he and his two men moved down and challenged them.

Jack and his two colleagues sat astride their horses, hands near their guns and just five yards apart. After Jack had made the challenge one of the four rustlers stepped forward.

"You've got a big mouth sheriff considering you only got three guns and we got the drop on you with four."

He allowed himself a laugh then said. "Just drop your guns and get off your horses and start to walk back to town we could do with some spare mounts."

Jack allowed himself a smile then said. "The drop is on you Mister I have men behind you, so you drop your guns, or you risk taking a bullet. Which way is it to be?"

The man did not hesitate and went for his gun, but Jack with practised ease drew and fired in one the bullet striking the man's thigh almost before his gun had cleared its holster. Seeing this happen his fellow rustlers threw their guns to the ground and Jack indicated they should now give aid to their wounded colleague.

Two of the ranch hands would escort the cattle back to the Circle 'O' and the other two hands would help Jack and Buck take the four rustlers back into Hope. They got there just before the light failed and the wounded man was seen by the doctor who removed the bullet none too gently. Will Thomas was only too happy to stand guard in the cells overnight and they would be moved to Fort Worth in the morning because a murder had been committed.

At six the next morning the four rustlers were taken in the buck board to Fort Worth all hand cuffed and fastened together by a gang chain with the wounded one protesting at every bump in the track. Jack Masters was driving and had two volunteer guards one being the mighty Ethan Watts all armed. Halfway there, Jack paused for twenty minutes to rest the horses and Ethan Watts took the opportunity to ask the four rustlers who had shot the ranch hand.

The wounded one, clearly the leader said. "Keep your mouths shut boys they can't hang us all."

Ethan Watts laughed then said, "Oh that is where you are wrong my friend. There is now such a thing as collective responsibility if a group of men are involved in a killing. If the guilty one does not step forward the court then all are found guilty by association, and they all hang."

There were a few seconds silence then the youngest of the four rustlers shouted at the wounded one. "I'll not swing for what you did Dixie."

Ethan Watts clapped his hands together and said, "Good we now know who did the killing."

On arriving in Fort Worth, they handed over the prisoners to the marshal with the information that the wounded prisoner was the man who had killed the ranch hand and they explained how they had found out.

On the way back to Hope Jack Masters said to Ethan Watts, "I have never heard of a verdict of collective responsibility and guilt by association."

"That's odd Jack." said Ethan, "Neither have I."

It was about a month later when the four rustlers went on trial in Fort Worth and they were all found guilty the same day. The one Jack had wounded was sentenced to hang and the other three were sent to prison for five years. The sentence of hanging took place a week later the owner of the Circle 'O' and two of his ranch hands were there to witness the event. Ranch owners always thought that there was nothing like a hanging to curb for a while at least the practise of rustling and for several months that was true. Jack had heard that some serious rustling had taken place much further north where the gangs had access to big city buyers down here that was not the case the markets were further away.

The two busy nights for Jack and Buck were still Friday and Saturday when the ranch hands came into Hope to spend their money at the vastly enlarged and improved premises of Ma Harris. Then of course on Sunday all that sinning could receive absolution of sorts under the far from tender words of guidance from Ethan Watts. Strangely enough the Italian family that had recently arrived though of course Catholic always attended taking a full part and singing happily along with the hymns praising the same God. They had good reason to be content as the young vines had taken well to the soil and were growing at about the same pace as they would in Italy.

One morning two men rode into Hope and booked into Ma Harris's establishment and asked to see the sheriff. Jack went to see them, and they said they were from the railroad company and were considering a spur line for the transport of cattle to the main line at Fort Worth. It would not come into Hope but would have its terminus the other side of the ridge.

Jack suggested that they should discuss these plans with the Hope Residents Committee and their chairman Ethan Watts, and they agreed to do so. Jack Masters went straight to see Ethan Watts who immediately rushed off to see the bank manager and the doctor and asked Jane Masters to act as their secretary. Then they all went to see the railroad men with Jack now minding the store. The meeting went on for some hours with the railroad men surprised at the detail the committee demanded.

Lunch was taken with just one glass of wine at Ethan's insistence. To keep our heads clear he had said. At four in the afternoon, it was adjourned until the next morning so that the railroad men could consider overnight what had been discussed. The advantages to Hope would be a weekly train service to Fort Worth arriving at Hope at 0800hrs on Friday and returning at 1600hrs. The disadvantage would be several times a year several hundred cattle being driven through Hope and over the ridge to the railroad terminus.

The committee called a meeting of the town's residents that evening to discuss the proposals so far made. The meeting went well with the majority being in favour of the railroad spur as it would give them the opportunity to see friends in Fort Worth. The next morning the committee met up with the railroad men and went over just a few minor points. By lunch time it was all decided, and Hope would have its spur Line and work would begin straight away. It was anticipated to take about six months to lay the track over the thirty mile stretch from Fort Worth to Hope and perhaps a couple of weeks to complete the terminus there. The two railroad men then returned to Fort Worth and the people of Hope felt they were now really on the map of America.

Chapter Eight

On Monday the work started with the skilled work crews all setting off to perform their different tasks. Already a couple of hundred yards had been prepared for track laying and ahead of them a gang cleared the route of larger obstacles blocking their way using explosives where necessary. Ahead of even them the route markers using maps and compasses, so the route was accurate and precise using the skills they had learned over the years. The two ranch owners at the Circle 'O' and the Tall 'T' were delighted with the news of the building of the spur line. Driving their cattle to market several hundred miles cost them money as the condition of the cattle suffered during the long trek. Getting them to market in a prime condition would be worth thousands of dollars so they looked forward to increasing their herds.

It was about ten days later when Jack Masters made a restocking trip into Fort Worth that he saw evidence of the progress of the Hope spur. Work was in progress fairly close to the existing track and Jack could see the ground being cleared at some pace and then as he neared Fort Worth he actually saw some laid railroad track. He carried on into Fort Worth and completed his purchases and then on his return journey which was quite late in the day the men were still working. He noticed that several additional sections of rail were now in place, and he now had no doubt that the work would be completed on schedule.

After he had placed the goods he had purchased in the store he went round to see Ethan Watts and told him what he had seen, and Ethan said he would tell everyone of the progress at the Sunday service. Jane was preparing the evening meal when Jack went home so he told her and Simon what he had seen while they were enjoying their meal. Though Sue Ellen was not very interested finding the rice pudding more to her liking.

When the Circle 'O' ranch hands came in on Friday night they had a couple of young new men with them who were most reluctant to hand in their guns. Jack Masters was quite patient with them and said, "Look its simple enough if you keep your guns I won't allow you into town."

The other ranch hands spoke to the young men and reluctantly they handed over their weapons. Later around midnight when the men left Hope the two young men were both so drunk they were flung over the saddles of their horses and their fellow ranch hands took charge of their weapons. The next day Jack mentioned the two new fellows to Buck Shaw and suggested they may in the future cause trouble. But the pair did not last another week at the ranch as they were caught asleep at night while guarding the herd and the foreman promptly sacked them. They were last seen heading north with a week's pay in their pockets.

Work on the railroad spur was progressing well and the grape vines appeared to be flourishing and apart from an outbreak of chicken pox at the school the small township of Hope was having a good year. Then almost overnight the Circle "O" ranch to the north had twenty cattle suddenly become sick and before the day was out they had died. The twenty had wandered slightly ahead of the main herd but had still been in sight of the ranch hands.

In those days there was no official veterinary organisation dealing with life stock and very often an ordinary doctor would be asked for an opinion. The Hope doctor was asked by the Circle 'O' owner if he would give his opinion of the animal's death and he went out and examined the dead cattle. He could see no evidence of disease and the suddenness of their death made him suspect another cause. He made sure all the other cattle were kept well away from the area where the dead cattle had been grazing and took some samples of the grass there.

By the evening the doctor was satisfied something in the grass had poisoned the cattle, but he did not have the facilities to establish what exactly it was. The ranch owner asked him, "Could someone have spread something on the grass with the intention of causing this?"

"Well, it is possible but who would wish to do this?" enquired the doctor. "

"Well, my foreman sacked two young men a couple of days ago and they rode off north." said the ranch owner.

So, Jack Masters was informed, and he and Buck decided they would take a day's ride up to the north to see if the young men were still around causing mischief. They set off early and after thirty minutes reached the spot where the cattle had died then an hour later found traces of a recent overnight camp. They proceeded with caution keeping well apart knowing how the two young men liked guns. They rested the horses for thirty minutes at mid-day then twenty minutes later saw some wood smoke ahead and dismounted.

They secured their horses and went forward cautiously on foot and were able to take the two young men completely by surprise as they sat drinking some coffee as their horses grazed nearby. Buck already had his gun trained on the two men, so they made no move to draw their weapons and Jack quickly disarmed them. Buck had a look through the saddle bags on the two horses and came back with a canvas bag half full of grey powder.

"What's this then?" he asked looking at the two men.

One looked at the other then one said, "Oh, its stuff we used when we worked for the railroad people; it stops the undergrowth choking up the points."

"Oh, so that is what you used to kill the cattle in revenge for being sacked by the Circle 'O' the other day." said Jack Masters. "You are both under arrest."

The two men remained silent as Buck handcuffed them both then the camp was cleared, and the men placed on their horses and the ride back to Hope began with the horses tied loosely together.

Three hours later they went through the Circle 'O' and paused briefly to rest and water the horses and without Jack and Buck there the two men would have been lynched. Thirty minutes later they were under lock and key in Hopes small Lock Up and would be taken to Fort Worth in the morning for eventual trial.

The wilful killing of life stock as an act of revenge would be harshly dealt with if they were found guilty and there would be not much doubt about that. Jack Masters took the buck board and the two prisoners into Fort Worth the next morning Will Thomas came as his escort but both prisoners were hand cuffed and in a leg chains, so were unlikely to cause trouble. They handed over the prisoners to the marshal just after lunch with the evidence and statements. Then after a coffee and a bite to eat and a chance to give the horses a rest for an hour they started off back to Hope.

They noticed how well the railroad spur was progressing and Will Thomas thought it would be finished ahead of the six months schedule. They arrived back in Hope just before it became dark, and Jack thanked Will for his help then took the horses to the stable and gave them a rub down then some fresh water and hay. Sue Ellen was already in bed, but Simon was doing his homework and Jane had put Jack's dinner in the oven. Jack quickly had a wash then sat down to enjoy his meal and when he finished he told Jane and Simon about the progress of the railroad.

The colder weather came, and the vines survived this as they had been selected from hardy stock. It was a milder winter than of late and it did not seem to last as long though further north they had a hard time of it. The spur line was completed two weeks earlier than anticipated and the last piece which was the terminus constructed just above the Snake river took only two weeks to complete.

The railroad company had decided that it would run a service twice a week to Hope instead of once so on Monday and Friday the citizens of Hope could go into Fort Worth at 0800hrs and return to Hope at 1600hrs. What the generous railroad company did not tell the citizens of Hope was the change to twice a week had been because they then qualified for a government grant towards the spur building costs under the improvement to the community scheme.

Ma Harris took immediate advantage of the new service as a quick way of bringing her girls in from Fort Worth for the weekend activities. Jack could also bring his fresh stock in much quicker this way and though it would give the citizens of Hope the chance to shop in Fort Worth their taxes made their goods dearer than Jack's and Jane's store in Hope.

Just a month after the line opened the first herd of cattle were due to be collected by a special train of ten cattle trucks which could carry five hundred animals. Jack and Ethan Watts were still not happy about five hundred cattle being urged through the narrow streets of Hope and over the ridge to the railroad spur and decided to look for an alternative route. The first herd would be from the Circle 'O' which was to the north, so they went to the northern side of Hope to find a way round or over the ridge. Less than half a mile out of Hope they found what could be the answer and with a little work may well solve the problem for the Circle 'O'. Jack and Ethan rode slowly down this rough track alongside the Snake the area was wide enough to accommodate the animals and the water was only three feet deep if they fell in.

It just required some of the larger trees to be felled and volunteers from Hope could do this as it would keep the cattle of Hopes streets. At the terminus the cattle would be right opposite the loading ramps and could be watered at the Snake before being loaded. Ethan Watts was a great organiser and the next day had four men working to clear the route while Jack Masters went to see the owner of the Circle 'O' to tell him of the plan. The rancher came down to Hope with Jack to have a look at the route suggested anxious not to have his animals damaged on the way to market. But Ethan and his volunteers had done a fine job and the rancher was impressed and said, "Once five hundred beasts have been this way once it will be a fine road."

A few days later the cattle train was due at 0700hrs, and the cattle moved down at 0630hrs with hardly any problems with the citizens of Hope hardly aware it was happening.

The fireman on the train seeing five hundred cattle moving around across the river decided to give them a toot on the whistle as a welcome without the driver's permission and almost caused a stampede. Fortunately, the ranch hands quickly controlled their animals, and the driver gave the fireman the rough end of his tongue. Then the loading went quite well with a few lessons learnt for the future. Afterwards Jack and Ethan had a look at the new trail the cattle had used, and it now had the look of a well-used route.

Over the next few weeks, they worked with the help of the ranch hands from the Tall 'T' to clear a similar route from the south along the Snake for the Tall 'T' to use and this was completed well before it was needed. The good people of Hope were delighted that a railroad spur that had been built primarily to move cattle at the behest of the Cattleman's Association was of great benefit to them without any great inconvenience to their way of life. On Sunday Ethan Watts led a prayer of thanks as regards the new railroad spur and he was well supported.

Chapter Nine

After almost a year in Laredo making good money Todd Raven felt the urge to move again Ike was not that keen and Wally Tyne would stay and run the business on their joint behalf. Todd fancied Houston and persuaded Ike to go with him and if that did not work out they would try Baton Rouge. What counted in their favour was they had money and were not starting in business from the bottom.

After a few days in Houston which sits on the banks of a shallow water bay they noticed a couple of clubs next to one another that had seen better days. One was a low grade drinking and gambling den and the other a cheap brothel used mostly by the fishermen who often paid in kind not adding to the aroma of the place. Todd bought both places for a very reasonable price and turned one into a fish restaurant and the other into a respectable gambling club. Within two months both businesses were thriving and the only one complaining was Ike who had to look elsewhere for a girl for the night.

Of course, Todd Raven was hardly the most popular man in Houston and his arrival had put several noses out of joint and these particular people employed others to exact retribution that they were unable to achieve. This was nothing new to Todd Raven and he employed scouts to warn him of approaching trouble which he usually handled himself.

On this particular evening the local sheriff had brought his family to the restaurant for a fish supper and Todd had made sure that they were given a nice table over to the side of the room. The place was busy and about three quarters full when three men strode in and called out, "Where is the gutless Raven hiding. Have we got to wreck the place." Todd Raven had been sat talking to a customer, but he now stood up and said, "Let's discuss this outside boys, like real men."

This was not how the three men wanted it but now they had been challenged in front of a large group of people and they made their way outside still confident of disposing of Todd Raven. Once outside the three faced Todd Raven who gazed at them with utter contempt before saying, "Well it's your play boys."

One of the three made the first movement towards his gun followed instantly by the other two but they were not just fast enough, and Todd Raven's two guns were fired as their fingers tightened on their triggers. The three gunmen spun round and crashed to the ground, two had died instantly the other twitched twice before joining his fellows in whatever life follows this one. There had been an audience of about a dozen people who could not resist the opportunity of seeing a real gun fight including the sheriff who had felt it his duty to attend.

Almost the first person who rushed to the scene was the local undertaker who quickly measured up the deceased then enquired, "Who would pay for the funeral?"

Todd Raven who was now talking to the sheriff turned and said, "I will, but no flowers."

So with a contented smile on his face the undertaker and his assistant placed the three bodies on their cart and took them off. Meanwhile the sheriff had moved back to his family after assuring Todd that he would be having a word with the parties behind tonight's fiasco, and it would not be repeated. Todd Raven made a personal visit to the various clubs over the following days and in each one was received with courtesy. One closed the week after and Todd bought the other two and turned the one that had closed into a decent class brothel and let Ike run it. He now controlled nearly all the entertainment industry in Houston but then a strong willed woman came into his life.

She was married to a lawyer who oversaw most of the legal business in Houston and they had been married for four years but it had been a marriage destined to complete the image of respectability and had nothing to do with love. They had always had separate bedrooms and the lawyer's sexual tastes was restricted to fair haired young men, but he was very discreet. Ella Fellows was a fine looking woman and she had thought her husband's initial reluctance to be intimate was down to a deep shyness but then he explained that her role as his wife was purely for show. Money was no problem, and her dresses made her the envy of most of the ladies of Houston.

She met Todd Raven purely by chance and they had a coffee together and an hour later she allowed this great thug of a man to make love to her in his room. Once was not enough for either of them and an hour later they repeated the act again but in a less frantic manner.

From then on they met once a week and it was not long before the husband was made aware of his wife's affaire. He decided to confront her after dinner one evening and as they were enjoying a brandy with their coffee he casually said, "I would have thought you would have chosen someone a little more civilised to bed down with than that thug Raven my dear."

His wife laughed, "That thug Todd Raven satisfies my needs in the same way as your fair haired bum boys satisfy yours, so let's leave it at that shall we."

The last thing Ralph Fellows wanted was a scandal. He could live with his wife being unfaithful but any suggestion of him and young men would see him blacklisted in all the Southern States. Todd learnt a lot from Ella not only in a basic hygiene sense but in how to use a knife and fork properly and breaking wind in a crowded room on a social occasion is not what a gentleman does.

Twelve months just sped by the business was good and the money rolled then a sequence of events led to tragedy. Ralph Fellows had recently become infatuated with a young fair haired lad who had recently joined the staff and had been spending a lot of time with him. This had upset the one who up to that time had been his regular favourite who then plotted his revenge. He did this by writing to the local newspaper saying that Ralph Fellows sleeps with two young fair haired men, and they engage in sexual acts together.

The letter was not published, but a lot of the staff knew of its existence and the editor told Ralph Fellows about it. Fellows thought that his wife had sent it and confronted her at her bedroom door. The argument continued out onto the landing where after her repeated denials he struck his wife violently across the face. She staggered back and her heel caught in her dressing gown, and she fell backwards down the stairs.

Her head crashed down with sickening force on the marble staircase and Ralph Fellows shouted to Leo the butler who had witnessed the whole scene to fetch the doctor. Despite the doctor's best efforts Ella Fellows died two hours later of what was thought to be a fractured skull. The sheriff was informed and took statements from Ralph Fellows and from Leo the butler but after reading through them both it was clear the blow contributed to her death. Todd Raven on hearing the news was shattered and was about to go and kill Ralph Fellows when Ike said, "Let the courts do the work for you."

Ralph Fellows was charged with Domestic Violence contributing to his wife's death and released on bail, two days later he took his own life.

Houston was never quite the same for Todd Raven after that and six months later he sold off all his business interests in Houston at a very nice profit. They made their way to Baton Rouge on the Mississippi River and spent a month there deciding whether or not to start up another business empire there. Ike was keen but there was not enough going on for Todd to get his teeth into and with New Orleans just a hundred miles away the lure of that hot spot was too strong. You needed money to enjoy yourself in New Orleans and Todd and Ike Raven certainly had that. But Todd was after setting up in the gambling and brothel business and you not only needed money but muscle to succeed in that and Todd and his brother had both in abundance.

They spent a few evenings wandering around the various gambling clubs eyeing up a couple they fancied to start their New Orleans empire. Todd quickly spotted a switch being made in a card game with most of the other players too drunk to notice. The House dealer was overconfident and was doing it too often so Todd played a hand in the next game and when the switch took place Todd challenged him. The whole saloon went deathly quiet and the other players in the game who had seen their money disappear with monotonous regularity looked on with interest. The dealer did not like the steely look in Todd Raven's eyes or the way his hands hovered near his guns.

"I may have misplaced a card my friend it was by accident of course and I apologise, and I gladly refund your stake."

"Not good enough." said Todd. "You made the same mistake four times in the last four games, so you have cheated all these good people out of their stake money."

The club's owner had now arrived with two muscular assistants and demanded to know what was going on.

"It's simple enough." said Todd Raven. "Your dealer has been cheating the customers."

The former players all joined in a chorus of "He took our money by cheating."

The owner turned to the dealer and said, "Get out of here you are fired."

He then instructed his assistants.

"See that these good people get their money back."

Then turning to Todd Raven, he said, "Would you care to join me for a drink of a glass of fine brandy Sir?"

As they made their way upstairs to the office Todd saw the Dealer go into another room close by, which prompted Todd to ask, "A relative?"

"Yes." said the owner, "He's my brother."

Todd laughed. "Well, he needs to polish up his act because any real big-time gambler would spot his routine within a couple of moves."

"I don't know your name Sir." Enquired the owner.

Todd smiled then said, "Oh, its Raven. Todd Raven."

The owner's hand shook slightly as he poured out two rather generous glasses of fine vintage brandy then he said. "I have heard of you and that you have several clubs further west Sir."

Todd told the owner whose name was Bart Hobson that he was on the lookout for a couple of run down establishments that he could put money into to turn them around, but they had to be in the right location. Todd explained the two establishments would be totally different one would be a decent restaurant with gambling encouraged. The other near the docks would cater for the sexual needs of the sea faring trade and the two places would be miles apart. Over the next few days Bart Hobson showed Todd Raven around the best and worst of New Orleans and a week later Todd found the properties he wanted.

Purely by chance he had gained the lifelong gratitude of Bart Hobson when arriving one morning to be taken by Hobson to see a range of potential properties he walked in on a dramatic scene. A tall wild eyed man had Hobson by the throat and a knife poised to strike down into his chest ranting on about being cheated out his life savings. Todd drew his right handgun and fired twice, one shot hitting the man's raised knife hand the second hitting his arm.

A doctor and the sheriff were summoned in that order and later after Bart Hobson had discussed the matter with Todd Raven no charges were made and the gambled money was returned. It was after this incident that they came across just the type of run down establishments they were after, and Todd got them both for a knock down price.

Chapter Ten

Todd decided that in naming both establishments he would remember his friend Jake so the up market eatery and gambling casino would be called J&T's. The brothel would be less sophisticated in its title and be known as Jake's Cat House. It took two months for both places to be redecorated and re-equipped and Todd brought in selected experienced personnel from their other establishments to make sure on opening they got off to the best start. Todd made sure his staff at the gambling tables did not play the same games that were played at Bart Hobson's he wanted to attract the more sophisticated and high roller player.

Some nights they made a loss but that was very rarely, but the games were straight, and it attracted the right people. The cat house always made money and the girls there were looked after and were seen regularly by the local doctor. Ike ran that side of the business, and he was always on the lookout for fresh talent.

Todd always recruited some local muscle which he insisted on selecting himself he paid them well and he made sure they did not go overboard with their duties. All were good with their fists and some with their guns but none of them fancied taking on Todd Raven who had a reputation not many could equal. Six months into the business and Todd made some minor changes to the gambling side but business was very good, and the bank manager was always pleased to see him.

Todd was wary about what he did with his money and all the persuasion about investing in companies did not appeal to him. He always saw good land as a sound investment and preferred that to property. He could read and write but his education was very basic but with his brutal personality and skill with his guns that was all that was needed to be a success in those early times in the west.

They had been in New Orleans almost a year when Ike became ill began to cough a lot and lost a lot of weight. Todd could afford the best medical opinion in New Orleans and did so and was advised his brother had a severe chest infection that would benefit from some clear mountain air. Todd immediately offered his establishments to Bart Hobson at a reasonable price and a deal was quickly done. They would go to Denver and then to a place called Colorado Springs which had a reputation for treating the sick. Most of the journey was covered by train and frequent overnight stops as Ike's condition was causing his brother some concern. Eight days later saw them settled in the Colorado Spring's health resort with Todd Raven's money ensuring Ike had the very best attention.

There was a strict no smoking rule in the rooms and Todd had to go out into the garden to have a smoke but even this was frowned on by the staff. Todd found the regime there a complete and utter bore but his brother did appear to be making progress and that was what mattered. After three weeks Todd made an excuse and went into Denver for a couple of days had more than a few drinks found himself a woman for the night and the next morning decided to return to re-join his sick brother.

The hired horse drawn buggy dropped him at the entrance to the health resort and he walked over to where Ike's room lay but a doctor called out to him.

"Mr Raven we have been trying to contact you since last night. Your brother took a turn for the worst yesterday evening and passed away just after midnight."

Todd felt the rage boil up inside him and wanted to take out the hurt on someone close bye, but then a strange calmness came over him and he just said, "Can I see my brother?"

"Of course." said the doctor and led the way to where Ike's body lie covered by a white sheet, the strong scent of flowers filling the room. The white sheet was pulled back and Todd Raven was left alone with his brother for a few minutes which gave him time to say his goodbye. A few minutes later Todd Raven had enough control to make arrangements for the burial the following day in the beautiful nearby cemetery. He also ordered a gravestone to be placed at the appropriate time with Ike's details clearly inscribed.

That evening out of respect to his brother he did not get drunk and gave some thought to what he would do next for the first time without his brother for company. The next day there was a small gathering for the funeral as the staff always attended these sad events. Later Todd settled the account and took a hired buggy into Denver where he was to spend a couple of days then he decided to go down to Laredo and see how Wally Tyne was doing. He went by train, and it took him almost a week with some overnight stops but on arrival he was greeted like an old friend. Wally was genuinely shocked by the news of Ike's death. The effect on Todd Raven was strange in that this very brutal man had lost in a fairly short space of time the three people that he really had only cared about, first Jake then Ella and now Ike.

He spent three weeks with Wally most of the time he was drunk and looking for trouble and in the end Wally persuaded him to move on. As soon as Todd was sober Wally gave him his guns back and Todd embraced his friend before he moved off heading for Arizona still a rich man and not yet wanted for murder. Todd took almost five weeks to make it to Phoenix using Ike's horse as well as his own during the journey it almost made it feel his brother was still with him.

On arrival he found a decent blacksmith and stable for the horses and once they were taken care of he found a rough bar nearby and walked in. Two large men were arguing at the bar and Todd pushed his way between them and ordered a beer. A deadly hush fell over the usually noisy establishment as the Carr brothers resented strangers and pushing in like that was asking for a kicking.

Sam Carr tapped Todd Raven on the shoulder and said, "If you buy me and my brother a bottle of whiskey and apologise we might let you just walk out of here in one piece mister."

Todd took a mouthful of the beer then turned his head and spit the contents into Sam's face and then swung the glass round into the face of the other brother. He followed this up with a short barrage of punches to the head and bodies of both men leaving them stretched out and moaning on the floor. Todd then drew one gun and laid it on the bar before saying, "Anybody else?"

The barman poured Todd another beer and said, "This one is on the house mister, but be careful those brothers have got friends."

Todd watched as the two brothers were carried out of the bar and gradually the place began to return to normal, but all eyes were still on Todd Raven. Todd had two more beers then as he was about to leave a deputy came in and asked him if he would call at the sheriff's office.

Todd agreed and went there straight away and had an interesting chat with the sheriff who advised him on one of the better places to book a room for the night. Todd was warned by the sheriff that the Carr boys were part of a gang of six violent thugs who were good with guns as well as their fists and that they would be out for revenge.

Todd found the place the sheriff recommended and booked in for seven nights. The next day after breakfast he went round Phoenix looking for a place to buy and found one then bought it for a decent price but it needed money spending on it but he had plenty of that. He went to see the sheriff and told him about his business deal and as he left the sheriff's office he was confronted by Sam Carr across the street.

"You are good with your fists stranger, but how good are you with a gun?" shouted Carr in a loud voice that attracted a number of people.

"Too good for you young Carr." answered Todd Raven. "But let me by you a drink and we will make a fresh start".

But Carr was after blood, and he laughed. "You are a gutless coward stranger and I'm going to fill your belly full of lead so stand by to draw."

He then walked towards Todd Raven then less than fifteen paces away his hand darted towards his gun, but he was always a split second slower than Todd. Sam Carr's bullet struck the ground five feet in front of Todd Raven, but Todd's had already smashed its way into Carr's chest. The sheriff and his deputy had witnessed the whole scene, but Ben Carr was the only one of the gang who moved over to the body of his brother. The very last few words his brother spoke surprised him. They were painfully croaked out. "So fast."

The sheriff and his deputy escorted Todd Raven away from the scene to ensure there was no more shooting. Then a short time later sitting down in the sheriff's office drinking a strong whiskey laced coffee the sheriff gave his opinion.

"Ben Carr is not going to forget this, but strangely enough they won't all jump you one night and kill you as he would see that as dishonouring his brother's memory. As none of them can beat you on the draw they will bring in a hired gun so until then you can sleep easy."

Todd laughed and thanked the sheriff for his advice and left he really did not care whether he lived or died and if they hired a hit man then so be it. Over the following two weeks he engaged the services of carpenters and painters and contacted Wally Tyne for some of his spare staff for the gambling tables. The place was to be called 'Jakes Den', for Gambling and Fine Foods and he intended to have it running in a month's time.

Two days before it was due to open the deputy came to see him and advised him that a stranger had arrived in Phoenix and was staying with the Carr gang, so he was to be on his guard. The next morning Todd went down to 'Jakes Den' to make sure that the final arrangements were in place for the opening tomorrow evening. He spent two hours there and as he left he noticed a tall thin man watching him from across the street, so he walked into a bar he often used and where now he was well known.

He ordered a beer and had taken a couple of sips when a hush descended on the busy saloon. Todd Raven knew without looking that the tall thin man had entered the saloon and they had some business to settle. Without looking at the stranger Todd said to the barman, "Give our new friend a beer it's a warm day."

The barman poured out the drink and took it to the man at the end of the bar.

"Thanks for the beer when I have drunk this we have some business to settle outside, if that's agreeable?"

"It's agreeable." said Todd and sipped away at his beer until the glass was empty then he followed the thin man out into the street. They faced each other some twelve paces apart with a sizeable number of people including the Carr gang watching on. Todd Raven called out to the stranger, "It's your call stranger, you can still walk away with no harm done, but I'll not slap leather first."

"Die then." shouted the stranger and drew and fired, but somehow Todd had fired first and the stranger's bullet struck the ground between Todd's feet. What Todd Raven had done was he had spent several hours turning his right hand holster into a swivel holster, so you did not have actually draw the gun to fire it, just tilt and pull the trigger. The stranger was not dead, but his gun shoulder was badly smashed by the heavy .45 round. It was three weeks before the stranger was fit enough to leave Phoenix and Todd Raven paid his doctor's bills and was a regular visitor and the two became friends.

The Carr gang had paid him in advance and never once came to see him and they never bothered Todd Raven again after that, which was a bonus. The Stranger and Todd never discussed who would have won a real shoot out, but it did not matter really and they parted as friends. The 'Jake's Den' was a great success and Todd spent another year in Phoenix but then felt the urge to move on.

Chapter Eleven

Back in the town of Hope the sidewalk had been smartened up and now almost four hundred people lived in or close by the cheerful community. The two ranches to the north and south had expanded and brought business to Hope especially on Friday and Saturday nights. Jack Masters only rarely had anybody to lock up in the three cells at the sheriff's Headquarters and that might be just for a few hours on a Friday or Saturday night.

Jane now had two young women helping at the store they were both from the Italian family and had a good business sense and were completely honest. The weather was very hot, and the children had been given the afternoons off from school with some work to do at home in the evening to make up for the lost school time. But of course, children being children they all had a lust for adventure and two of the boys wandered off into the hills.

Two of the parents came to see Jack at about seven in the evening when the boys failed to return to their homes as arranged. Jack and Buck knowing there were still at least two hours of daylight left set off in the direction the lads had taken with some extra water bottles and an oil lamp. Both men knew that in these hills there were several small caves but no water, but the only real danger was a fall and a snake bite. Further up in the mountains there may be a mountain lion, but they were rare these days as most had been hunted almost to extinction.

Every now and then they stopped and called out the boy's names. At midnight Jack told Buck to ride back to Hope but he would stay here for the night just in case. Buck assured him that if the boys had returned he would come back out and collect him and then he left. Jack poured some water into his sweaty Stetson and gave his horse a drink then sat down and listened to any sound which might be the boys.

When Buck arrived back in Hope the boys had still not returned, and he told the worried parents that Jack Masters was staying out in the hills all night with a lamp on and Buck and any volunteers would go out again in the morning. It was almost one o'clock in the morning when Jack thought he heard someone call out so he immediately shouted, "I'm over here" and waved the lamp over his head. He heard someone crying and stumbling towards him and moved forward himself. It was one of the missing boys clearly in a state of collapse and he fell forward into Jack's arms. Jack eased him to the ground and gave him a drink of water which the boy tried to gulp down, but Jack made him drink it slowly. After a minute or so Jack asked him where his friend was, and the boy said he has hurt his leg and he's about a couple of hundred yards over there.

Jack placed the boy on the horse then following the boy's directions he led the horse and boy towards where his friend lay. Ten minutes later Jack found the lad and quickly gave him some water then attended to his injured leg. It looked like a clean break and Jack put a shaved tree branch as a temporary splint then tightly bound it.

It was almost one thirty in the morning, and he needed to get the boy to a doctor so he helped him onto his horse then helped the other lad up behind him to make sure he did not fall off. Then Jack led his horse off down the mountain on a two and a half hour hike with his two rescued lads.

Just after four o'clock in the morning he was knocking on the doctor's door, and he was quickly ushered in without a word of complaint. An hour later Jack was sharing a coffee with the boy's parents and his horse was getting a lot of attention too. Jack took his horse back to the stable and saw it had water and hay then went home had some breakfast then went to bed and slept till one in the afternoon.

He had to tell Jane the complete story then went to see how the injured lad was getting on making sure Buck was with him as he deserved some of the credit. They found the lad with the broken leg in good spirits with five of his school friends listening to his very vivid and highly dramatic story of his rescue from the den of the mountain lion. One of the school friends turned to Jack Masters and said, "Did you have to shoot the lion to get Mike away sheriff?"

Jack smiled and said, "No, when I got there the lion had fled so we were lucky, but I would have liked to have seen it because they are a rare sight now."

With the sheriff and Buck there, Mike's friends quickly departed, and Jack Masters said to young Mike, "What's all this nonsense about being in the mountain lions den?"

"Well, its sounds better than the true story of just falling of a rock while playing about and the girls were very impressed."

Jack Masters put his hand on the young boy's shoulder and looked him in the eyes then said, "Are you going to go through life telling lies to try and convince people that you are someone that you are not young Mike?"

The boy gave this advice some thought then said, "I know what you mean sheriff and I'll make it right when I see my friends next. They will hear the real story and not the one about a fantasy lion."

Jack and Buck had a word with the parents then went back to the real work of trying to find out who had tried to break into the premises of Ma Harris during the night. There were marks on the outside rear door where someone had tried to force it open. All the outside doors of her premises were of the double variety made by the local carpenter. She also employed a static night guard who though old was armed and would have tackled an intruder. The would be intruder had to be a stranger to the town because all the locals knew of Ma's security arrangements and would not risk being shot by old Luke her night guard.

Jack and Buck went around Hope asking people if they had noticed any new faces in town, but no one had seen any strangers. Jack saddled his horse and rode a mile out of Hope and had a look around the foothills for any signs of a camp or a recent fire. After a couple of hours, he was about to start back when he could smell smoke, but he could not see any.

The slight breeze must have brought the scent of smoke to his nostrils, so he headed into the direction of the wind. A couple of hundred yards further on he noticed two horses tied up under a copse of trees and a wisp of smoke coming from a fire there. Jack dismounted and led his horse forward into the small camp where two men lay stretched out asleep.

"Had a busy night boys?" enquired Jack. Both men rolled over and reached for their guns, but Jack already had them covered.

"I'm the sheriff of Hope." said Jack Masters. "Tell me what you two men are doing out here and where you were last night?"

"We are just looking for work sheriff. We called in that small town late last night, but everything was shut even the lodging house door was jammed."

"Well," said Jack, "The owner of that lodging house says you tried to break in so you will have to come back with me and explain that you were not."

"And if we don't want to do to that?" enquired the larger of the two men his hand reaching for his gun.

"I'll have to shoot you both in the legs and then go and get the buggy to take you into Hope so what's it to be?"

An hour later the two men were trying to convince Ma Harris they were only after a room for the night. Surprisingly they did have the money to pay for it in their pockets and after some discussion she offered them a week's work painting several of the rooms with food and accommodation as part of the pay.

Just as a precaution Jack and Buck checked their pile of wanted posters but to their surprise the two men did not appear to be wanted for anything. To Jack and Buck's total amazement Ma Harris asked the two men to stay on another week and paint some more rooms which they did to her complete satisfaction then they were hired by the owner of the Circle 'O'. The first grape harvest was slightly better than expected and a few months later the wine that it produced was given surprisingly good reviews for a young wine.

The young lad whose leg had been broken made good progress and was soon able to walk with the help of crutches but after a couple of weeks these were no longer necessary. The train journeys into Fort Worth were popular and provided the teachers with the opportunity to broaden the children's view of the area.

A spell of very hot weather caused some fires up in the hills but they were no threat to the town of Hope because a thunderstorm saturated the area and the fires fizzled out. The men from the Circle 'O' caused some trouble at Ma Harris's after drinking too much and Jack and Buck had to lock them up for the night. Jack took Ma Harris to task over this because she could see they were drunk but still sold them liquor just to grab some extra money. So no fines were issued just a warning about future conduct.

On the Circle 'O' as on the Tall 'T' ranches about half a dozen families lived on the ranch slightly apart from the main accommodation for the ranch hands. It had not been unknown in the past for some of the wives to become infatuated with some of the younger ranch hands but usually it was quietly dealt with. Sadly, on this occasion the husband was not so forgiving and when he caught his wife and the young ranch hand on the spare bed together he shot the young man dead.

A message was sent into Hope for Jack Masters to investigate what had happened and the wife unwilling to see her husband and father of her two children hung for murder told a false story.

She stated that the young ranch hand had attacked her in the bedroom and was trying to rape her when her husband heard her cries of distress. The husband of course confirmed her story and said he had to shoot the man as the young man was armed and tried to pull his gun. Two of the young man's friends said the wife and their friend had been having an affair for over a month and it was common knowledge amongst the other wives. Jack felt this was far from being a straightforward matter and that he and Buck needed to speak to more of the people in both camps.

The owner of the Circle 'O' wanted the matter quickly dealt with and the death of one young ranch hand did not bother him too much. However, his wife did not share the same opinion and was well aware of what had been going on and insisted that justice should prevail.

So, Jack Masters got a note stating that the wife was lying to protect her husband and to protect her reputation and it was quite clear where the note had come from even though it was unsigned. The marshal had come up from Fort Worth as technically the ranch fell out of the jurisdiction of the Town sheriff of Hope. Together they interviewed the wife and husband and then the friends of the young man who had been shot.

All were interviewed separately then the wife was seen again and this time her story began to unravel, and the truth began to emerge. What had was taking place was with her consent but when her husband burst in she was so terrified of what he might do to her she made out she was being attacked. She then said as her husband drew his gun the young man reached for his and that was when he was shot dead. Jack Masters and the marshal looked at one another they now had the true story now it was up to the court and jury in Fort Worth to deliver a verdict.

The husband and wife were taken to Fort Worth in custody to await trial which should take place in about two weeks. Both Jack Masters and Buck Shaw would be required to give evidence and the case was not expected to last very long.

When the case did come before the court there was no doubt the jury had some sympathy for the husband when he claimed that he was protecting the honour of his wife. This sympathy did not extend to the wife who the jury felt was the cause of all this trouble and deceiving her husband into committing this fatal act.

The judge agreed and sentenced her to eight years imprisonment and the husband to just one year to cheers from the court. The children were to be looked after by the grandparents until the husband's release and his old job on the ranch was to kept open for him until then.

Chapter Twelve

Todd Raven had a decent bank balance and a good horse and decided to head east with no particular destination in mind. He stopped off in Albuquerque for a couple of months chiefly to rest his horse and enjoy a couple of women. The Rio Grande always fascinated him with its frequent changes of colour causes by storms further upstream. He made and lost some money in the gambling clubs, but no card sharp ever tried to cheat him as his reputation was well known.

During his stay he was involved in a couple of brawls, but no gun play and when it became time to leave he had enjoyed himself and had not added to the graves in the cemetery. He decided next to head for Denver, but he would break his journey in Puebio, which is on the Arkansas River and do some fishing. The only one satisfied with Puebio was his horse who had been placed in a good stable Todd found the place an absolute dump and the fishing hopeless so after a week he rode on to Denver.

He kept away from the part of the city where he was known and kept a low profile in a quiet hotel. It was here that he read in the newspaper one day of the trial at Fort Worth of the man and woman from the Circle 'O' Ranch and saw the name of sheriff Jack Masters as one of the witnesses. He remembered their brief meeting during the Civil War and smiled as he read the full story of the trial and the verdict.

After two months in Denver, he needed to move on so he decided to head east and try to start a business in Omaha on the Missouri River. It took him nearly a month to get there as he never over-extended the distance travelled daily. He found a decent hotel and stables nearby for the horse, Omaha was a busy place where cattle were traded but what was of great interest to Todd Raven there was plenty of money about.

After a week he found the place he was looking for it was run down and full of gutter trash begging for free drinks. He bought it cheap sacked everyone except two young bar staff and then ripped the place apart brought in some decent decorators and carpenters and in a month had the place refurnished. Wally Tyne sent him two decent card men to run honest tables and he recruited six young dancers himself.

They allowed the restaurant side to build up itself as demand increased and within six months Todd Raven was making a nice profit but paying his loyal staff well. One advantage Todd had and that was of his reputation. There were four other club owners who would quite happily contribute to a gang of heavies smashing Todd's place up but the sheriff had warned them of what Raven was capable of. As a result, they left him alone to ply the more upmarket trade while they took their money at the lower social end.

A card player joined Todd Raven's team from Denver on recommendation his name was Lou Wightman, and he was a real asset. He had a routine where before a game. He would offer to tell the players what their prospects were for the evening. To some he would say "Your wife will be pleased with you tonight." and others "Go home while you can still afford the fare."

The punters loved it and strangely he was right more often than he was wrong, but he played a straight game. Todd was quite happy because the Wightman table very rarely showed a loss at the end of the evening. Todd Raven watched him in action one particular evening, and he had four quite big money gamblers on his table, and he had warned three that they would lose tonight. The reaction of the three was they insisted that the games were played with cards that they provided, and Lou said as long as the packs are brand new and the seals are unbroken that's fine.

The games took place and the three lost heavily and their fourth friend won several pots there were no complaints and they left at midnight with handshakes all round. The next day later in the morning Todd had a word with Lou Wightman and asked him how he decided on who would win that evening if the games were straight. "Oh, the games are straight Mr Raven. I guarantee that. I just get that sense of who will be lucky and who won't." He then added,

"If I study someone long enough I very often sense what will happen to them later in life, but I keep that normally to myself."

They enjoyed a coffee together and then Lou Wightman left. Todd Raven would have liked to have asked this man to study him and give him some forecast of his future but did not know how to even suggest this. However, Lou Wightman found this large brute of a man with a fearsome reputation with his fists and guns fascinating and was already watching his every move.

Over the next twelve months the business flourished two of the other four clubs went out of business and Todd bought them both for a song. He tidied them both up and turned one into a brothel and the other into a bar and eatery and soon both were doing good business. Todd was on good terms with the sheriff and his two deputies, and he made sure the security team he employed stayed well within the law.

Todd began to feel he wanted to move on again life was becoming a little too comfortable and he needed another challenge. Kansas City was a couple of hundred miles south so he decided that would be his next stop.

He liked and trusted Lou Wightman and placed him in charge of all the Omaha business and drew up papers to that effect in the solicitor's office. Strangely enough Lou Wightman was not surprised by the promotion and was already compiling an outline of Todd future life. He was keeping all this to himself at the moment but at some time he would show Todd Raven what he felt the future held for him.

When Todd started his journey to Kansas City he planned to take at least a week and initially would stay at the property he owned jointly with Silas Gibb on the outskirts of the City. At about the halfway stage in his journey Todd encountered a young rider down on his luck and he shared some of his food with him.

During the night the young man decided to relieve Todd of his valuables and was given a good beating as a lesson. As soon as it was daylight Todd stuck him on his horse and gave him twenty dollars and said, "If I see you again I'll kill yah."

The young man rode hastily off north, and Todd continues at a more leisurely pace south feeling the day had started well. It was just after mid-day after a week of travel that Todd Raven arrived at the property he owned jointly with Silas Gibb.

The place was an absolute picture the wooden property was freshly painted white with curtains at the windows and there was a woman hanging some washing on a clothesline. The adjoining pastures were neatly fenced and about ten young horses were grazing there opposite to their stables.

Todd dismounted and walked over to the gate and the woman had finished hanging out the washing and she smiled and came over.

"Can I help you?" she said, some colour coming to her cheeks.

"I hope so." said Todd Raven. "I am a friend of Silas Gibb and I jointly own this property."

"Oh, you are Mr Raven. Please do come in, Silas will be back in a few minutes. Please let me give you some refreshment."

Within the next few minutes Todd's horse was being cared for and Todd was being offered a choice of cooling drinks. He was on his second cooling drink when Silas arrived and the two embraced as old friends do. Then Silas formerly introduced Rachel who he had married last year who had been an army widow. Rachel asked Todd which of the two spare bedrooms he wished to sleep in. As he hesitated she quickly said, "This is your home too Todd so which bedroom shall I make up?"

So, it was decided, and this was to be the most stable period in Todd's life and he and Rachel became really good friends.

Todd had been back at Kansas City for almost a month before Rachel saw the side of him that Silas had told her had become almost legendary. They hired out their horses to visitors to the city providing they were decent people who would treat them well. On this occasion two young well-built businessmen who had plenty of money turned up and demanded two horses for the day. Rachel was not keen on renting them out because of the way the two men were behaving, and Silas had gone into the City on business.

Todd was in his bedroom reading a newspaper when he heard raised voices and clearly heard a man's voice say, "We will take these two horses, you stupid woman, and pay when we return. Now get out of the damn way or you will get hurt."

Todd stormed out of the house as the two men were about to unfasten the gate to the compound.

"Are you alright Rachel?" he asked.

"Yes." she replied. "But I don't want these men to ride those horses."

Todd walked over to the gate and confronted the two men.

"Let those horses go free and get off this property now. Is that clear?" said Todd.

The two young men looked at one another and laughed then one said, "What have we here, the farm lame brain? Go away before you get hurt old chap."

Todd stood his ground not wanting to make a scene in front of Rachel, but the two men were now itching for a fight as both had been considered fine boxers at their colleges. They dismounted from the horses and both advanced on Todd giving him one final warning to stay clear from the gate.

They stood now close to Todd Raven and the two men exchanged a final glance and then launched their attack. Todd ducked under a couple of rather wild swings and countered with a crisp body blow to each man in the lower chest. This surprised them but they came again and this time they were met with some hefty blows to their heads and faces which deposited them on their backsides.

Silas Gibb had now returned and at Rachel's urging suggested to the two men that that should be it. A bucket of cold water was provided for the men to freshen up and Rachel handed them a towel to dry themselves. Then Todd suggested that they leave adding, "And don't bother to come back."

As they left one of the men shouted, "We will be back with the sheriff and charge you with assault."

An hour later the two men returned with the sheriff, who knew Todd Raven and to the surprise of the two men he shook his hand, greeting him like an old friend. The circumstances of the incident were then explained with Rachel telling most of the story which the two men did not deny.

"So, you were asked to leave, and you failed to do so?" said the sheriff, addressing the two complainants. Then he asked, "Who swung the first punch?"

"Well, we did. This man needed a lesson in manners." said one of the two men.

"Well," said the sheriff. "You chose the wrong man here young gents he could out box six of you at a time and outshoot you too. You are lucky you are still walking. So, I suggest you stay clear of Mr Raven."

The sheriff stayed for a drink then went back into the city and had a word with the fathers of the young men to make sure they kept out of trouble. But at least they did not bother them at the farm again though Todd did see them in Kansas City Centre on one occasion. At Todd's suggestion they bought some ponies and Rachel taught young children to ride which added to the farm's income.

Chapter Thirteen

Rachel had a sister whose husband who had been badly wounded in the Civil War and now they had been turned out of their rented house and needed a place to live. Todd said he would find them a small place locally, so Rachel told them to catch the train to Kansas City. Todd bought them a cottage about a mile from their place so Rachel could take the buggy and visit them as often as she liked. He was in the local bank in Kansas City making the final arrangements with the manager as to the purchase when three armed men burst in demanding money. Everyone fell to the floor except one of the cashiers and Todd Raven, even the manager hid behind his desk.

"Put the guns down boys, before someone gets hurt." said Todd as two of the gang started to take money from the tills. The leader waved his gun round toward Todd Raven and said, "Down on your knees, big mouth."

"Never." said Todd as he drew and fired in one fluid movement sending the gunman crashing to the floor.

The other two went to draw their guns but Todd's cold voice saying "Your choice boys" made them think twice and they meekly raised their hands one still full of dollar bills. Within minutes the sheriff and his two deputies were there and after twenty minutes things were almost back to normal. With the bank manager insisting that Mr Todd Raven's business was given top priority at all times from this moment on.

A couple of months later the sheriff called and had a quiet word with Todd and told him he had heard that a friend of the man Todd had shot in the attempted bank raid was in the city planning revenge. Not wanting Rachel and Silas to be put at risk Todd decided to move into Kansas City for a few days until this matter was settled so he booked into a City Centre Hotel.

On his second night there he had just finished a very pleasant evening meal and decided to go into the crowded bar for a drink and some company. He was enjoying a beer with two men at the bar when a sudden hush fell on the previously noisy room. In the mirror above the bar Todd could see what had caused the room to grow silent stood in the doorway of the bar were two men. One carrying a Winchester rifle in the crook of his arm the other stood his hands poised at his waist his eyes darting around the crowded bar. Todd knew they were looking for him and he was ready for them but not in here, so he stepped forward with his hands slightly raised.

"I think your business is with me but not in here some good people might get hurt, so let's move out into the street and do it right."

The man nodded and waved his accomplice back into the street and Todd Raven quite confident the fight would be a fair one followed on.

As the protagonists made their way outside so did their audience who quickly lined the sidewalk each side of the street. As the two faced one another Todd indicated the other man friend with the rifle enquiring, "Is he part of this?"

"No." said Todd's adversary. Then turning to his accomplice, he said, "You play no part in this Sam. Is that understood?"

The other man nodded and placed the rifle between his feet.

"Your call." said Todd and stood braced for the first movement, which was lightning fast. It seemed both men fired at the same time, but Todd must have just had an edge as his bullet found its target whereas the bullet of his opponent clipped Todd's right ear. His adversary slumped to the ground and Todd's concern now was the rifle bearing friend, but he had rushed to aid his dying companion. A doctor came over but could do nothing and the man passed away within a few minutes with the sheriff and one of his deputies keeping the onlookers back.

The man's friend came over to Todd Raven and noticed the trickle of blood running from the nicked ear lobe and said, "Well at least he drew blood."

Todd smiled. "Yes Sam he was bloody quick. I'll take care of the funeral. Give me his name and age and I'll have a small stone put in place, so he won't be forgotten."

Sam scrawled the details out and handed them to Todd then shook his hand and rode off out of Kansas City. Two days later Todd and the sheriff plus a couple of onlookers saw Luke Starr buried and a week after that a small headstone was placed there stating his name and that he was twenty five years old. Todd moved back in with Silas and Rachel and took an active part in running the now thriving business but as the weeks went by he began to get that feeling that he needed to move on and gave some thought as where it should be.

He decided to move back west to Wichita in the Arkansas Valley he had never been there, but he heard that it was a busy place full of men anxious to sell cattle and timber. Both Silas and Rachel were genuinely sorry to see him leave he had brought some excitement into their lives and had helped with the resettlement of her sister and her sick husband.

Todd took a leisurely four day ride over to Wichita found a decent stable for his horse and a nearby boarding house which was run by a Chinese couple and was spotlessly clean. The next day he went over to a branch of his bank and asked to see the manager and presented a letter from the manager of the Kansas City branch.

On reading the letter the atmosphere changed dramatically and coffee was summoned and twenty minutes later on leaving Todd was assured the bank was delighted to welcome him to Wichita. Todd Raven spent the next week looking around for some business to invest in though he did not want to go back into bars and restaurants.

He became very friendly with the Chinese couple whose boarding house he was staying at and was most impressed with how hard they worked. The husband told Todd that his brother ran a laundry three streets away and employed twenty people but the hot water boiler was old and needed replacing, but his brother could not afford the cost so it looked like the business would fail. Todd explained to the man that he would be glad to invest in the firm as a sleeping partner and would meet the cost of a new boiler if his brother was agreeable.

So the next morning after breakfast they went road to the laundry and as they approached the office they heard raised voices. An American voice said, "Listen to me you Chinese monkey, this week's hotel laundry bill you will do for half the normal fee because you are desperate for the money to keep this place going, is that understood!"

At this point Todd and the owner's brother entered the office and Todd Raven looked the American making the threat in the eye and said, "No Sir that is not understood."

Then he followed this up by saying, "I am this man's potential partner and any failure to pay the bills will lead to the goods being sold to recover the costs involved."

The man now had calmed down and went to leave saying, "I will pay as normal for the service this week but in future I may go elsewhere."

As he left the boarding house owner turned to Todd and said, "There is no elsewhere."

For the next hour Todd and the two brothers talked business and Todd was shown around the laundry and noted what needed replacing. They then shook hands and Todd was a partner and the brother was told to immediately arrange for the work to begin to replace the boiler and anything else that was needed. Todd went to see the bank manager and told him that any bills concerning the Chinese Laundry repairs should be debited to his account as he was now a partner.

The manager asked him if he was interested in any other good business that needed a helping hand and Todd with a rather suspicious look on his face said a cautious "Yes." The manager smiled at this cautious approach from this strange brute of a man then told him of a family whose baking business had been doing so well but had been hit by a neighbour's fire. This had almost put them out of business and because they had no insurance they could not afford to rebuild what they had lost.

They were still trying to run a business, but it was now from a family kitchen and almost hopeless. Todd was immediately interested and asked where these people lived, and the manager offered to take him there in his buggy. The family turned out to be originally from Holland and had been in America for twenty years the discussion lasted two hours and during that time Todd Raven agreed to finance the rebuilding of the original premises to a higher standard and cover the cost of renting some temporary suitable accommodation so that the business could continue.

Work was to start straight away, and the bakery lost very little business as their customers stayed loyal. Over the next four weeks Todd Raven spent most of his time watching the resurrection of his two investments and it gave him a surprising amount of pleasure. Of course, there were a few people in Wichita who had heard of Todd Raven's exploits elsewhere and thought this generosity was a cover for some criminal act. This did not include the sheriff who was a friend of the bank manager, but he had an ambitious deputy who saw Todd Raven as a dangerous man up to no good. Also, this deputy fancied himself as being fast with his gun and practised for hours in front of a mirror.

The men working in the logging camps tended to let their hair down at the weekend and came into Wichita to enjoy some drinking and the bar girls. There were always minor disturbances but on this particular Saturday night a shop was broken into, and the owner beaten up and robbed. The man was not discovered until the next morning when his daughter called to see him he was alive but quite badly hurt.

Of course, all the revellers had returned to the logging camps, so no one had any idea who was responsible, but the young ambitious deputy was determined to blame Todd Raven. The sheriff asked the deputy why should a man like Raven who had plenty of money smash his way into a shop to and beat up the owner steal some.

"Because," said the deputy, "he is a violent thug, and we should arrest him."

The sheriff knowing that the deputy was not going to let the matter drop decided he would have a word with Todd Raven to clear the matter up so he went to see him. He explained to Todd about the break in and the assault on the shop's owner and then about his deputy's suspicions.

"What time did this occur?" asked Todd.

The sheriff looked at his notes and said, "The shop keeper said he was attacked at about ten o'clock."

"Well," replied Todd, "from about nine o'clock till midnight I was the guest of the Dutch family of bakers and I am sure they will confirm that."

The Dutch family did confirm this, and the sheriff told his deputy that he should start looking for someone else most likely in the logging camp. But to the sheriff's amazement his deputy said, "Of course those Dutch people will give him an alibi they owe him money, so they have no choice."

The sheriff told his deputy to sit down then said, "You are a good lad Steve, but you have got this wrong about Raven and its dangerous. Have I got to take your gun away?"

The deputy agreed to go up to the logging camp and see what he could find out but after he left the sheriff's office he went straight to see the mayor of Wichita who was his uncle. The mayor had always felt responsible for Steve because his father the mayor's brother had been killed in the Civil War and the mayor had been having an affair with Steve's mother ever since. His own wife was a cold woman and relished the fact that she now no longer was required to submit to her husband's lustful demands.

He explained to his uncle his suspicions about Todd Raven and that the sheriff could be part of a conspiracy to hush things up. The mayor knew that his nephew was rather impetuous and coveted the sheriff job, but was also aware of the great love the mother had for her son and had no wish to jeopardise that relationship. So, he told the nephew he would make some discreet inquiries and hopefully sort the matter out.

The mayor went to see his good friend the bank manager who had handled Todd Raven's business since he came to Wichita and was a member of the same Masonic Lodge. After some discussion the bank manager said, "Leave this with me old friend I'll get this sorted out."

Two days later a man was brought into the sheriff's office by two burly loggers, and he confessed to breaking into the shop and hitting the old man and he returned some of the money stolen.

Chapter Fourteen

The solving of the attack on the shopkeeper came as a relief to the sheriff, the bank manager, and the mayor and to some extent to Todd Raven the only person not delighted was the deputy sheriff. The work to upgrade the laundry was at last completed and to budget but the bakery took a little longer than planned and cost a little more than anticipated. This was not a problem as far as Todd Raven was concerned money came into his account from his other business interests which were all being managed by his friends who were shareholders so benefitting from success.

The turning point in the relationship between the deputy and Todd Raven came about purely by chance. One evening quite late Todd had decided to have a meal at a place that served decent food and had a reputation for straight gambling tables. He had been at the table for about an hour and had won a few hands when three men walked in and went to the bar. One took a hurried drink and went back outside leaving the other two eyeing the money on the card tables.

It was then that the eager young deputy sheriff appeared and ordered the two men to unbuckle their gun belts and allow them to fall to the floor. One drew his gun, but the young deputy out drew him and fired and the wounded man slumped to the floor of the bar. The other man unbuckled his gun belt and allowed it to slide to the floor and the deputy moved towards his prisoners. It was then Todd Raven called out a warning saying, "There is another man with them sheriff watch your back."

The deputy glanced over to where Todd Raven stood and said, "Keep out of this Raven I'm in charge here."

It was then that the other man entered through the swing doors gun in hand, and it was raised to fire into the back of the deputy. Todd Raven drew and fired twice his bullets striking the gunman in the chest and he crashed back onto the floor. The deputy swung round realising what had happened and who had saved his life and for the moment he felt lost for words.

Todd Raven checked the body of the man he had shot and then asked the deputy if he needed any more help with his prisoners. The deputy had just slipped the cuffs on the unwounded prisoner and the doctor was checking the wounded man. To Todd Raven's surprise the deputy held out his hand and as they shook hands nothing was said, and it did not need to be.

From that day on in the few months further that Todd Raven was to stay in Wichita they always had a smile and a wave when they met which was quite often. At last came the day when Todd decided that it was time to move on this time he would move east and keep going until he felt the urge to stop. It would be by horse and train and as no destination was clearly decided upon there was no time frame.

After two months on the road, he found himself in Birmingham Alabama an expanding mining community with several hard men jostling for power.

Todd Raven amused himself with a couple of bar girls for a few weeks but then started to look for a business opportunity. He converted some rundown stables on the outskirts of the town into a brothel which pleased the organised female religious group who opposed the several in Birmingham itself. He then bought a failing bar and restaurant spent some money on it and sorted out the staff retaining those who he thought had promise.

After a month it was making money and the staff shared in the profits when they reached a certain level. The sheriff came to see him and told him that there were several businessmen who resented his presence in Birmingham but his reputation meant at the moment they would do nothing about it. Todd thanked the sheriff for his warning this was nothing new to him someone was always out to add Todd Raven's name to a notch on his gun butt.

Six months after he arrived in Birmingham Todd Raven went to see his bank manager who always was pleased to see him. The matter that concerned the bank was that according to their records Mr Raven had never made a will.

As soon as the two men were settled and drinking their coffee the manager raised the subject of the will.

"You must make a decision on where you want your money to go on your death Mr Raven, have you no relatives?"

"Nobody at all." said Todd Raven. "The best thing that I can suggest is that if and when I die all my properties and monies be realised and then divided among all the people that I employ."

"Well, that is most generous." said the bank manager. "Are you absolutely sure?"

"Yes." said Todd. "I assume if I die without a will the State will confiscate the lot."

The manger nodded his head, then said, "In that case I will get our legal department to draw up a document to confirm your intentions."

The two men then had a brandy and Todd went on his way.

In another part of Birmingham three men sat discussing the success of Raven's two business ventures. One owned a couple of brothels badly hit by the new competition and the others owned saloons less affected by the new restaurant, but they resented any competition.

"We could hire a hitman." suggested one man, with the other two looking rather uneasy at the prospect. After another ten minutes it was decided that Will Thorne would find out the cost of such a venture and report back. Mr Thorne in his enquiries over the next few days found that there were quite a few gun fighters for hire in the adjoining states. But when the name of the target concerned was mentioned the number dropped and those that remained interested mentioned a price that the trio were not willing to meet. So, they decided to live with the competition and try to compete and in doing so improve their business.

Two did manage to improve, the brothel improved the quality of the girls working there and one of the saloons improved the quality of the food served but the other saloon went out of business. Todd Raven noticed this but was not greatly bothered his business was doing fine and he was looking for more opportunities to expand.

A couple of times he had been called into the bank to discuss his will as the bank's lawyers had made suggestions about the precise wording of the document. Eventually the manager assured him the matter was now resolved and the greedy hands of the State would not profit from his demise only his loyal work force. Todd signed three copies and the matter was now decided with one copy going to Washington Records, one in the bank vault and the other in Todd's safe custody. Six more months went by, and Todd was getting that feeling that he wanted to move on again, but where?

Then a decision was made for him as he received a letter from Rachel to say Silas was quite ill and could he come back to Kansas City as they needed him there. Todd instructed his bank manager to sell all his business interests at the best price and move his account back to Kansas City. Then he collected his horse and mostly by train but occasionally by horse he reached Kansas City in four days.

Kansas City had been struck by a bout of flu and Silas had had a severe bout of this which had led to pneumonia which almost killed him. Todd Raven took control of the business enabling Rachel to devout all her time to care for her husband. It was a month before Silas was well enough to sit up in a chair and another two weeks before he was back on his feet. Todd had relished the opportunity to help his old friend and decided to stay on for another month or two.

The time passed quite quickly and towards the end of the second month Todd Raven was beginning to speculate where to try his luck next was it to be east or west. Then as very often happens in these cases fate tends to take a hand and suddenly news broke that gold had been found in free land just north of Fort Morgan.

Todd knew that Fort Morgan was not far from Denver and that the government were selling licences to parcels of land in this gold field to prospective miners. So, he said his goodbyes to Rachel and Silas and started off to Fort Morgan which would be mostly by horse. It took him six days to make the journey as he never overtired his faithful steed and on arrival he was surprised that the number of licences issued was small.

He soon found out why when he applied at the office for a licence himself as a five hundred dollar deposit was required to ensure the holder of the licence was a fit and proper person. The idea was of course to keep the riff-raff away from this gold field and therefore keep it law abiding. If the licence holder chose to leave at any time the deposit was refunded. Todd paid his deposit and was issued with a licence and the plot number the whole area was being patrolled by the military as an additional security factor. Todd's plot included a cave area which was large enough to shelter him and his horse, so the canvas shelter he had purchased was surplus to his needs. The plots to his left and right were vacant, and the road was his southern boundary only the plot to his north was being worked by two men.

A small stream ran through most of the plots providing the important water supply to each plots static pond for washing the ore. Todd made himself some coffee then went down to the onsite store and stocked up including some hay for his horse. When Todd had been issued with his licence he had been told that all gold found had to be sold through the government agent at the price set by the Washington Treasury. This was to prevent hoarding and selling at times when the price of gold was rising it also stopped theft. Todd was not an expert miner, but he had mined before and he knew roughly what to look for.

Over the next few weeks, he heard that some of the miners had made some good finds worth several thousand dollars. Todd's finds had been more modest but enough to cover his expenses and give him some satisfaction.

One of the plots to his right was now being worked by two youngish men who gave him the occasional wave he always responded but did not want to get friendly with anyone in this community. Most of the finds were in powder or tiny grain form but now and again a slightly larger fragment might turn up but anything larger than pea size was rare indeed. Todd had been hacking at a particularly hard piece of rock which had some signs of holding the precious ore.

He was about to take a break from his labours when his chisel broke off two fragments of the rock. He picked them up to examine them more closely and discarded one almost straight away as being just plain rock. But the second piece though slightly smaller had a certain look and feel and he began to feel a sudden surge of excitement but he needed to examine it more carefully. He took out his magnifying glass and scanned the small rock and his heart leapt it was a pure gold nugget.

Chapter Fifteen

The wave of the influenza virus had affected the small town of Hope but mainly the more elderly residents. The exception had been at the Circle 'O' ranch where over half the cowhands had been laid low. The owner had asked for help from the owner of the Tall 'T' to the south, but he was anxious not to have his men infected so he kept them away. So, sheriff Jack Masters was asked if he could get six men to keep watch on the large herd there at night.

Jack managed to get four men and they did the job for a week with just one rainy night making it unpleasant. The family store was doing well, and Simon was progressing well at school and Sue Ellen would start junior school in the mornings next year. One morning a military posse arrived in Hope having ridden from Fort Worth overnight looking for three army deserters who had broken out of the army stockade in Fort Worth.

They rested up in Hope for three hours then asked sheriff Jack Masters if he would act as a guide through the hills to the north to any likely hiding places.

Jack left Buck Shaw in charge and left with the posse telling Jane he would be away no more than a couple of days. With Jack the posse now consisted of six men so they could move quite quickly over the undulating ground. As they moved into the rockier higher areas Jack noticed the tracks of shod horses and they moved more cautiously as the Lieutenant in charge of the posse had said the men had stolen some weapons from the armoury as well as the horses.

The light started to fail and it was decided to make camp for the night and post two guards. They lit a small fire and had some food and then enjoyed a hot coffee. They put the fire out and bedded down two on watch for one hour at a time until dawn. The night passed without incident, and they quickly brewed up some coffee and had some biscuit then prepared to begin the search again.

They had been on the move for about twenty minutes when they came across clear signs of a night camp. The embers of a fire were still warm, and the trio could not be that far ahead, so they moved on with added caution. Jack who was leading the way noticed that his horse was becoming a little twitchy a sure sign other horses were nearby.

He stopped and dismounted and told the lieutenant and as a result one man stayed with the horses and the remainder moved forward on foot. Thirty yards further on and they heard voices and they crept nearer then clearly they heard one voice complaining that as his horse was lame he should ride double. Clearly his fellow escapees did not fancy being slowed down like this and told him to catch them up when he could later on. It was then that the Lieutenant ordered the posse to move in and only shoot if necessary.

The posse rushed forward shouting "Drop your guns" and to Jack Master's surprise the three men did just that. Later he put their reaction down to them being soldiers and used to obeying orders knowing that an ordinary armed robber would have gone for his gun. The three men were handcuffed, and they began the journey back to Hope with third deserter handcuffed to the reins of his lame horse and walking it home.

It was almost eight in the evening when they arrived in Hope and Jack locked the deserters in the jail for the night. Ma Harris accommodated the posse and Ethan Watts took care of the horses and treating the lame one with one of his special remedies. On arriving home Jack had to explain to Jane all about the pursuit and capture of the three men as he ate his evening meal. Later as they lay in bed she insisted he replayed the story but somehow it was never finished.

The next day being Friday the posse and the prisoners plus their horses were able to travel back to Fort Worth by train which enabled the lame horse more recovery time. The result of their escape would mean an extra two years on their sentence and lead to an enquiry into how they managed to escape anyway.

Sadly, after a brief illness, Ma Harris died and her younger sister from Fort Worth had been named as her sole beneficiary in her will. She was not like her sister at all and viewed the prospect of running a saloon come boarding house and a weekend brothel with absolute horror. As a result, she sold it to two brothers from Dallas who installed a manager to run it on the same lines as Ma Harris had done.

Jack Masters made some enquiries about the activities of the two brothers in Dallas and they ran a string of gambling clubs and brothels all with a dubious reputation. Hope needed somewhere like Ma Harris's for the ranch hands to let off steam at weekends and it did bring income into the town because without the ranches to the north and south Hope would struggle to exist.

Jack called a meeting of the Hope town committee an unofficial body that kept an eye on the welfare of Hope. It consisted of Jack Masters, Ethan Watts, the doctor and the bank manager and two others who were not available. They discussed the demise of Ma Harris and the transfer of her business and the reputation of the buyers from Dallas. It was decided that they should allow the business to continue and see how it was now run before taking any further action.

For the first two weeks the 'Doll's House' as it was now called was run as it was in Ma Harris's day and the committee began to relax. Then the next Friday night all hell broke loose as the prices for the drink and the women had suddenly doubled. Also two armed men were on the entrance and two thugs inside ready to chuck out any objectors and the boys from the Circle 'O' went in to face that.

Desperate for a drink and a woman some of the men parted with their hard earned money but others went back to where Jack was posted collecting their guns. They explained the situation to him and fearing a mass shoot out he took all their guns and locked them in the jail. Then he went over to the 'Doll's House' closely followed by the unarmed ranch hands. As he approached the entrance the two armed men stepped forward and one said, "That's as far as you go sheriff this is private property."

Jack kept walking and one of the men pulled a gun and Jack shot him twice in the legs the other one backed away his hands away from his guns. The two thugs now appeared then backed away when they saw the drawn gun in Jack's hand and the expression on his face. The manager rushed forward his hands up to his mouth with concern and Jack wasted no time in laying down the rules.

As from now all prices for drink and the services of the women must return to what they were under the regime of Ma Harris if not this place will be closed down. The manager accepted what Jack had instructed and refunded the excess charged earlier to the ranch hands. Jack pointed to the wounded man.

"Get him to the doctors and dispense with your armed guards and thugs a good business does not need them." Jack hung around for another thirty minutes but all was now calm but he wondered how the two brothers in Dallas would take this as they had a reputation for getting their own way. The next day he explained to Ethan Watts what had happened and Ethan felt sure that the two brothers would react in some way and of course they did. The brothers took legal advice as to whether the sheriff's action was legal and they were advised that it was. So they decided to sell the business and make out of it what they could.

Jack Masters and Ethan Watts suggested to the owners of the two ranches that they offer to buy the property without disclosing who they were. As a result they bought it at a good price with the town of Hope undertaking to keep it in good condition and profiting from the supplies sold. The name of the establishment was changed again but this time to simply 'Ma's House'.

The bank manager recently had a new safe fitted not only with a key lock but as an additional security measure a combination lock as well. The problem was the manager whose task was to remember the numbers in the combination lock kept forgetting what they were. He discussed this problem with Jack and Buck and a solution was decided upon whereas he wrote the numbers down and they were kept in a locked cell which was never used. So if he needed to refresh his memory he would pay a visit to the sheriff cells.

Of course, this was against all banking rules and if widely known could get the manager into a lot of trouble. However things went well for months until one day when thirty minutes after the bank closed its doors and the safe was closed and locked for the day the bank inspector paid a surprise visit. He spent thirty minutes going through the books had a coffee then said to the manager, "Open up the safe old chap I need to see that the money held balances with the books."

The chief cashier used his key to partially unlock the safe leaving the manager to apply the correct numbers to the combination but his mind went blank. The cashier knew what the problem was and wondered how the manager would get out of this. The manager half stumbled to his feet then fell over in a faint causing the bank inspector to instruct the cashier to fetch the doctor. The cashier did as he was instructed but he also saw Jack Masters and explained what had happened and Jack quickly wrote the numbers on a small piece of paper then made his way to the bank.

The doctor and Jack Masters helped the bank manager into a chair under the concerned eye of the bank inspector. After a brief examination the doctor gave the manager a small glass of brandy and Jack pressed the piece of paper into his hand and it was acknowledged with a grateful nod.

"I feel much better now." said the manager and as a result Jack and the doctor left. A couple of minutes later the manager stood up and walked slowly over to the safe and dialled in the correct numbers of the combination lock. It took the Inspector almost an hour to count the contents of the safe then he was satisfied. As he left he shook the manager's hand and said, "I am most impressed with the way you put the bank before yourself and head office will hear of this, goodbye and good luck".

Later that day Jack Masters found a bottle of brandy on his desk with a note saying simply 'With Grateful Thanks'. The strange thing was but from that day on the bank manager found that the safe combination numbers were easy for him to remember even though they had to change them on the first of every month. His doctor put it down to shock and Jack Masters thought he was probably right.

A few months later he was offered promotion to a larger bank in Dallas but he declined the offer citing not wishing to disrupt his family arrangements at this particular time but he was given a raise in salary instead. 'Ma's House' was now very popular with the ranch hands on Friday and Saturday nights partly because the prices were now back to what they were. Also as the ranch owners were the proprietors every now and then the drinks and the girls were heavily discounted to reward loyal attendance.

That idea came from Buck Shaw and even Jack Masters was surprised when the Ranch Owners agreed to it but it worked well and was not abused. The whole town of Hope benefitted from a contented workforce on the doorsteps because it meant they spent their money without causing trouble which was to everyone's benefit.

A new classroom was added to the school so that the senior pupils could do some private study under minimum supervision and it was obvious that in a very short time another teacher would be required on a full time or part time basis. A retired colonel and his wife came to live in Hope and they had a pleasant two bed one floor property built on the north side of town. They had a daughter who taught maths and geography so she quickly joined the school staff. She was rather attractive and in her late twenties and it was thought that she was married, but where her husband was remained a mystery.

Chapter Sixteen

Not wishing to make any fuss about his find, Todd Raven duly presented it to the officials in the assay office for weighing and valuation. Eyebrows were raised and the officials consulted their books then said, "This will have to go to Denver for an expert valuation, but we think it will value out at least fifty thousand dollars."

Todd thanked them and told them he wanted to hand in his licence and have his five hundred dollars refunded. That accomplished he explained he was now off to Denver and his bank manager would take care of the money from the sale of the nugget. He collected his faithful horse and started off they covered about half of the fifty miles then rested up for the night in a sheltered hollow not far from a quiet stream. He removed the saddle from his horse and allowed it to browse in the succulent grass near the stream then realised he had almost made up his mind on his next destination California.

He lit a small fire and boiled some water for coffee then having made a strong brew he ate some trail biscuits which he always found filling. He had two mugs of coffee and then as the light began to fail he put his small fire out. He like many men who spend a great deal of their life outdoors can usually smell rain but tonight the air was dry.

He settled down for the night lying on just a rough canvas sheet and covered by a horse blanket his head resting on his saddle. His horse grazed contentedly nearby and Todd Raven knew that the animal would give any warning of approaching danger. Todd Raven woke to feel the pleasant warmth of his horses back against his with the first signs of dawn in the morning sky. As Todd and his horse struggled to their feet from their resting positions they both broke wind as if in salute to the new day.

Todd lit a fire to boil water for coffee and also to fry himself some bacon as a special treat to break up the monotony of hard tack. An hour later he put out the small fire and made ready to travel the twenty five miles to Denver. It was about two in the afternoon when he completed his leisurely journey. He found a boarding house and stables on the edge of the city that at first glance seemed OK. He found out later it was run by the widow of a parson who had left his wife just enough money to set up a small business and she was making the most of it. The food was plain but good and the rooms were spotless and the stables had the same conditions. Todd Raven had taken the one remaining room and met his fellow guests at dinner that evening.

Two were elderly women in Denver for a week or so for the funeral and will reading of a close relative. The other three were men, one was a salesman and the other two were connected with the rail company.

His fellow diners were quite intrigued when Todd Raven though neatly dressed came down to dinner wearing his guns. The meal was eaten with just the odd word of comment but the two women were eager to learn more of their gun carrying fellow guest, but it had to wait until coffee was served in the lounge and the atmosphere became more relaxed. Then with a cup of coffee poised at her lips she asked, "Tell me sir, have ever had any occasion to use those guns you so proudly carry."

Todd put his coffee cup down and turning to the elderly woman he said, "Sadly in my business I frequently have, but it not something that is a suitable subject for an occasion such as this."

"Well said Sir." exclaimed one of the railroad executives, then added, "Just what is your business?"

"It's in the past tense now." said Todd. "It was the very dark side of the gambling clubs in the southern cities."

After a week in Denver with several meetings with his bank manager Todd was beginning to think again about California. He wondered about going back to Phoenix Arizona and seeing how 'Jakes Den' was doing it certainly held memories, not all of them pleasant. He did not need the money, but he needed the excitement and he realised that he enjoyed causing trouble. He gave some thought to forming a small gang but to do what? He did not fancy robbing banks because it would be like robbing himself.

One morning he woke up and decided there and then he would start the journey to Phoenix that day, so just before mid-day he saddled up and started out with no particular time frame in mind. He took his time travelling just about twenty five miles a day for a week then giving his horse a couple of days rest. He took a fairly direct route first to Albuquerque where he took a week's break from his travels and where his horse was re shod.

Then at the same gentle pace onto Phoenix where he found a suitable boarding house with a decent stables nearby. Todd Raven gave himself a day to recover before he went into Phoenix and checked on how 'Jakes Den' was performing. As he entered he was immediately recognised by some of the staff he had appointed and warmly welcomed. The manager came out of the office delighted to see him and anxious to show him how well the business had done.

"Any problems at all?" enquired Todd who knowing what Phoenix was like there had to be something of concern.

"Well," said the manager, "last week two men called and offered special insurance against vandalism, but I told them that we carried all the usual insurance we needed."

Todd nodded then said, "But they said they would be back?"

"Yes." said the manager. "This evening."

"In that case," said Todd. "I will be here to meet them."

That evening Todd had a very pleasant meal at 'Jake's Den' then went into the back office to see if the two insurance men showed up. Todd and the manager were enjoying a glass of beer when they heard a commotion from the kitchen and some women screaming so they rushed back to investigate.

Apparently a man had rushed in the back door and smashed two trays of drinking glasses that were in trays on a kitchen shelf, he then had run off into the darkness. The kitchen staff quickly tidied up and Todd and the manager returned to his office. It was about thirty minutes later when one of the waiters brought the two insurance men to the office. They seemed surprised to see Todd Raven sitting there with the manager and the manager just said he was a friend.

"Have you thought anymore about our offer because these acts of vandalism are happening all over the place and our weekly policy insures your protection." announced one of the insurance men.

Todd Raven then spoke and asked how much this insurance would cost a week. The insurance man smiled and said, "To you my friend we have a special offer for just two hundred dollars it will give you complete protection what do you say?"

Todd Raven got to his feet and drew both guns.

"My name is Todd Raven and I own this place and if you and your tin pot gang come anywhere near I'll blow the guts out of every one of you, is that clear?"

The insurance men got to their feet trembling with fear one saying, "We did not know you owned this place Mr Raven here's twenty dollars to cover the glasses."

Then they actually ran out of 'Jakes Den' with Todd and the manager enjoying a celebratory brandy in their wake. Nothing more was heard of that particular nasty little outfit and no doubt they moved on somewhere else and tried out their scheme there. A rather mature but attractive female guest had taken residence at the boarding house and was in Phoenix in connection with the reading of the will of her late husband. They had been living apart for several years due to his frequent infidelity but he had assured her that she would be well taken care of on his demise.

The will reading was to take place in the offices of her husband's solicitors in four days time and during that time she and Todd Raven became quite friendly. She was clearly nervous about the whole business though she did have a copy of the original will. When she told Todd Raven she had a copy of the will he assured her that in that case she had nothing to worry about but if she wanted him to he would escort her to the reading.

On the day arranged they made their way to the solicitor's offices and were surprised at the number of people in the room set aside for the reading. At last the solicitor appeared and announced that he was here today to read the Last Will and Testament of William Grainger. Then the solicitor went on to say, "Mr Grainger makes several Five Hundred Dollar gifts to four named ladies whose names I shall not read out to save them from any embarrassment."

He leaves the bulk of his estate to his business partner in the hope that their success will continue and at the end he makes mention of his estranged wife Lucy Grainger with the comment she gave me very little, so I leave her nothing.

Lucy Grainger sitting next to Todd Raven gave a little sob then burst into tears, but Todd Raven had the feeling that something was not right.

So he stood up and asked, "Who is the business partner who benefits from the bulk of the estate?"

The solicitor looked up in surprise then asked, "Who are you Sir?"

Todd Raven smiled, "I am Mrs Grainger's Legal Representative," and slapping the holsters of his six guns he said, "And I want answers."

By now most of the people had left the room and the solicitor looked warily around then said, "I think we should go to my office to discuss this Mr Raven so if you will both follow me."

Lucy Grainger had now composed herself and eagerly followed the solicitor and Todd into the office where they all found chairs to sit in. The solicitor looked far from happy and waited for Todd to make the first move, so he did.

"You are the business partner who benefits from the bulk of the estate are you not?" challenged Todd Raven.

"Yes, but it is not illegal to benefit." said the solicitor.

"Yes it is." said Todd. "You witnessed the will and witnesses are not allowed to benefit from a will."

The solicitor put his head in his hands and gave a little moan of distress. At this point Lucy Grainger handed Todd the copy of the original will and he quickly scanned it. Todd then suggested to the solicitor that there was a way out of the mess that he had created and fifteen minutes later it was all arranged for another will reading for tomorrow at the same time. This time there were not as many people present as before and the Solicitor read out the true last wishes of Lucy Grainger's husband with the bulk of his estate coming to his wife. With the matter completed they then went back to the solicitor's office where over drinks they discussed the disposal of the business.

Todd Raven knew that Lucy Grainger wanted money to ensure she could enjoy a comfortable life and he knew the solicitor and his friends wanted to keep hold of the business chain which was earning good money. After an hour he had talked the solicitor into buying out the widows holdings at a fair price leaving everyone feeling they had a good deal. Now comfortably off Lucy Grainger moved into the best hotel in Phoenix and insisted Todd Raven came with her. They spent the next two months together with Todd providing the rough love making this woman had longed for but to now she had never experienced. But then Todd moved on further west but where?

Chapter Seventeen

Colonel Rogers and his wife had settled well into the town of Hope and their daughter was enjoying her role as teacher at the local school. Their daughter was known as Mrs Fairchild so obviously there was a husband somewhere but where? Buck Shaw was quite taken by the attractive Janet Fairchild and when she expressed a wish to learn to ride he was quick to offer his services. Jack and Jane Masters had a great affection for Buck and the last thing they wanted was for this pleasant man to be hurt. However from the start it was Janet Fairchild who did most of the running with Buck very happy to tag along in her wake.

At his wife's suggestion Jack did ask Buck if he knew anything about Janet's husband. But all Buck would say was that Janet had said her husband had been part of Custer's Command but had not been in the battle when Custer and his men were all killed. Jack began to think that there was a dark secret behind all this and something that colonel Rogers and his wife would want no part of and he was not far wrong.

About a week later Buck had taken two horses to the house of colonel Rogers by arrangement to give Janet an hour's riding instruction before it became too dark. As he arrived he heard the colonel angrily cry out, "I won't have a picture of that snivelling coward in my house take it out and burn it."

Buck sensibly held back for a few minutes before formally arriving at the house and said nothing to Janet as they went for a slow ride for about half an hour. It was about a month later when Janet told Buck the true story that as Custer's command approached the Little Big Horn her husband, who was a lieutenant, was instructed to go back to major Reno and tell him to provide immediate support. Her husband failed to do this saying he became confused and got lost and that his horse went lame. He faced a court martial and was dishonourably discharged from the army in disgrace. Her father had forbidden her ever to have contact with him again and she was not sure even where he now was as his family had disowned him as well.

The colonel and his wife begun to take a liking to Buck Shaw it had not been like that at first but they began to realise he was a decent man who clearly thought the world of their daughter. One thing that still upset the colonel and his wife and that was his daughters still using her married name of Fairchild. Life went on in Hope with everyone getting one pretty well with one another until a stranger came into town asking a lot of questions about the school teacher and her husband.

Buck Shaw got to hear of this and immediately sought out this person who had booked into Ma's House for a few nights. Buck found the man in his room looking through some letters he had in a case and Buck wasted little time in wanting to know what this man was after. Within a few minutes Buck knew who this man was and his heart sank he was in the same room as Janet's disgraced husband.

"If you go anywhere near the colonel's home he will shoot you dead." said Buck. "And his wife or Janet will not be able to stop him such is the loathing he has for you."

Richard Fairchild looked at Buck Shaw and said, "I have a feeling Mr Shaw that you have more than just a passing interest in my wife?"

"I won't deny that I am very fond of her but as to her feelings that I cannot say" commented Buck, then he added, "But what are you really here for?"

"A distant relative has offered me work in England where I can make a fresh start he has sent me money for the fare and I want to know if Janet will come with me as I can afford her fare." replied Richard Fairchild.

Buck gave the matter a few minutes thought then said, "I'll take your offer to Janet as I am taking her for a riding lesson tonight but keep away from the colonel's house and I'll get back to you later tonight".

Later that evening they had only been riding slowly away from her father's house for a few minutes when Janet said, "There is something wrong Buck what is it?"

They dismounted under a small copse of trees and in just a few minutes Buck explained all to a shocked and surprised Janet Fairchild. Buck was surprised how composed Janet had remained and she just said, "Take me to him Buck but stay close by."

Within a few minutes they were at Ma's House and at the door of Fairchild's room which was opened at the first tap. He went to embrace Janet but she pulled back and just offered her hand and insisted Buck witness what was to follow. She allowed him to make his offer then told him clearly their marriage was over and she wanted nothing more to do with him and if he had any decency remaining he should honour that. She then turned and left and said to Buck "Come on let's finish our ride"

The next morning Buck went along to Ma's House but Richard Fairchild had checked out and taken the Friday train into Fort Worth. From that day on Janet stopped using her married name of Fairchild and became Miss Rogers. This delighted her father, who never became aware of the mystery visitor. Buck Shaw became a regular guest at the colonel's house and he often took the colonel fishing in the buck board as the old boy could not walk very far.

It was about two months after Richard Fairchild had left for England that Janet had a letter from his solicitors in England it was to tell her that Richard Fairchild had died of pneumonia after catching influenza, but he had nothing in his estate to leave her. A copy of the death certificate was enclosed with the letter and of course that meant that Janet was now a free woman and free to wed again. Her father was delighted at the news and felt a shadow had been lifted from the family.

Janet told Buck a couple of days later when they were out for their usual ride together and Buck very cautiously enquired if she would consider marrying again. Janet gave Buck a sweet smile and said, "Well, it depended if the right man came along."

Buck wanted to know more and said, "And what would the right man look like then?"

Janet laughed, "Well, Buck he would be tall, ride well and be something like a deputy sheriff and be a decent man just like you Buck."

It was a couple of days later when Buck took the colonel fishing that he plucked up courage and asked the old man if he could have his daughter's hand in marriage. Colonel Rogers put his rod down and grabbed Buck by the hand.

"My wife will be delighted at the news as am I. So let's get back and tell her and drink a glass to celebrate this wonderful news."

Within a few days the whole of Hope were aware of the coming wedding and all of Buck's friends had set to in building a two-bed cabin styled home on some land Buck owned on the north side of town. The wedding took place a month later. At Buck's insistence, Janet wore white and almost the whole of Hope attended the service in the richly decorated communal hall. The vicar from Fort Worth conducted the service and Ethan Watts led the singing. The happy couple spent a week at the best Hotel in Dallas and Buck, somewhat nervously, waited until his bride had got into bed before he came into the bedroom and undressed. When he got into bed and their bodies made contact Janet said, "Oh Buck you still have your gun on."

But Buck said, "That's not my gun Janet, it's my thing."

Janet gave a delighted giggle.

For the first two days the honeymooning pair never left their room then they went out for just an hour or so then rushed back to their room. The week sped by and then it was time to return to Hope via Fort Worth where Jack Masters collected them in his buggy. The look on their faces told Jack what kind of week the two had enjoyed and he was delighted for the two of them because they were both good friends. He drove them straight to their new home as food and everything had been finished for their return and it was already eight in the evening.

Jack drove off and Buck carried Janet over the threshold of their new home and inside it was a delight. On the table well covered up lay a cold supper and a bottle of wine stood in the cooler. Janet checked their bedroom the bed was ready and the room was full of flowers.

Within a week it was as though they had always been together with a well established routine already in place. Some heavy rain made the main street in Hope a mess and everyone was trying to keep to the wooden walkways and of course horse traffic made it worse. After a few day of warmer weather things gradually got back to normal but the main street needed a lot of small stones as a surface just to make it usable all the year round. The railroad company provided the answer because they had a grade of stone for their tracks and always had a surplus of small gravel they were anxious to get rid of.

They dumped it off in Hope for free and the Hope community took care of dispersing the gravel on the main street making the surface in time more stable. After six months of marriage Janet was not surprised to find that she was pregnant much to the delight of Buck but to her mother and father too. Jack's wife Jane would return to teaching when Janet had to temporarily give up her role for a few months so everything was now arranged.

A gang of four young bank robbers had been reported as being active some fifty miles south of Hope by the marshal at Fort Worth and Jack and Buck and warned the bank manager to be on his guard. The manager had taken notice of the threat and had hired a veteran of the civil war in his sixties to sit just inside the bank door with a shot gun just in case.

So when two young men with guns drawn burst into the bank he promptly fired both barrels into their lower legs. This caused their two accomplices waiting outside to mount their horses and gallop out of Hope closely pursued by Jack and Buck. The two remaining would be robbers ran straight into four ranch hands just outside Hope and so all four were now in custody. Hope's doctor spent two hours removing bird shot from the legs of the two wounded by the veteran who received a bottle of whiskey for his prompt action.

The next day the marshal came up from Fort Worth with a small posse and a horse drawn buggy and took the prisoners into Fort Worth for trial on several charges across the State. Janet Shaw of course was very concerned that her husband had been involved in a possible shootout, but she has a talk with Jane Masters and that made her feel better. A sign had now been placed over the entrance to the bank on the advice of their solicitor it read, "If you enter this bank in an aggressive manner you are at risk of being shot."

Three weeks after the bank raid, the District judge sentenced the four men to five years hard labour after pleading guilty to four charges of bank robbery and attempted bank robbery. He told them it would have been ten years if they had not pleaded not guilty and wasted the time of the court over a trial.

Janet stayed teaching until the end of seven months then Jane took over then almost at the end of the ninth month she gave birth to a fine healthy baby boy. Janet and Buck had already decided on the Christian name for their first child and had selected one for a boy or a girl so their first child was to be called Robert. It was very suitable because it was the name of Buck's late father and was Janet's father's name.

Three weeks later Ethan Watts and the vicar organised the baptism and the christening in the communal hall and almost all of Hope were in attendance. To the colonel and his wife it was like being given an extension to their lives now as grandparents and they enjoyed every minute. With so much support so close at hand Janet was able to return to teaching after three months and Jane was able to return to the family store.

Chapter Eighteen

The goodbyes had all been said and Todd collected his horse and enough supplies to last a week and headed south towards Tucson about one hundred and fifty miles away. He had no plan but would take things as they came he knew little about Tucson apart from it being on the Santa Cruz River and it had a violent past. As usual he took a very leisurely journey allowing his horse almost to decide when they had travelled far enough for the day.

So it was noon on the seventh day of their journey when he rode into the outskirts of Tucson and soon found a place suitable for his horse and himself to stay. The stables and boarding house was run by a Mexican family and by their standards was quite clean. The woman of the house with breasts like pumpkins said she did washing for just a few cents an item, but stressed, "No funny business in this house."

The food was plain but good as was the coffee and if you wanted a bath a boy would bring water to a tub in the yard.

Later that evening after his meal Todd took a walk into Tucson with his guns clearly on show to anyone interested. It was dark when he entered 'Ladies Bar' full of half drunks and nobody fitting the description of a lady. His smart appearance immediately attracted some attention as he knew it would and two local roughnecks staggered to their feet and lurched towards him. When they were about six feet away Todd said, "That's close enough boys your smell could stun a skunk."

One went for his gun but Todd's lightning-fast draw had the onlookers gasping in surprise. Todd waved for the man to re-holster his gun saying, "If you fancy your chances I'll be available, but only try it when you're sober"

Then he walked out of the bar having made the impression he had intended to. By the next day various versions of this smart stranger's appearance in the 'Ladies Bar' were circulating Tucson.

The main attraction of the story was how fast this mystery man was with a gun, but adding to this was why having out drawn a drunk he did not bother to shoot him. Being the top man in Tucson meant running the most successful gambling clubs and brothels and your position was always under threat. The top man at that time was Aaron Levy a rather small tubby man but a brilliant business organiser his enemies noted he had two faults one he was not ruthless enough and the other was he was a Jew. Levy was proud of his Jewish faith and put that down to his lack of ruthlessness, so when he heard of this stranger in town he wanted to meet him. He needed a fast gun to ensure his own protection and thought this stranger might be interested in protection duties.

The first Todd Raven knew of Mr Levy interest was when a young man brought a letter to his lodging house inviting him to take coffee with Mr Levy at eleven o'clock at his home.

The young man said, "If you are agreeable Sir I am to take you there."

Todd agreed and was taken in a smart horse drawn buggy to a smart house on high ground overlooking the Santa Cruz River.

Aaron Levy met Todd Raven at the door and introduced him to his very attractive wife and young daughter. Then the two men went into Aaron Levy's study for a private talk with their coffee and sat down in two beautiful leather chairs. Aaron Levy asked Todd what his name was and where he was from and Todd gave a brief summary of the last five years of his business dealings. Aaron Levy was surprised and wrote down a great deal of what Todd had said and then told Todd what his problem was. It appeared he and his family were constantly under threat from several other players in Tucson's entertainment world who resented his success.

"I need someone like you near me at all times Todd not only to protect me but my lovely wife and daughter."

"Why not pay a hired gun to kill off these people who are a threat to you and your family. That's what they are doing to you." said Todd.

"That would be against my religious beliefs I could only kill in direct defence of my loved ones and their methods are far too subtle for that." said Levy.

Todd drank some of his excellent coffee then he said, "Mr Levy I don't do protection work but I have some sympathy for your situation so give me a list of all the people who have made threats against you and we will see what we can do."

He left the Levy house an hour later with a complete list and a very anxious Aaron Levy in his wake. Todd went first to the branch of his bank and asked to see the manager who was not available until Todd produced a certain letter then he was rushed in to see him. Todd received a good deal of information on the people threatening Aaron Levy and the state of their business affairs which were in a fairly dire state.

The manager of the bank was becoming quite enthusiastic and said, "If Aaron Levy drops his prices for a week and offers a bonus this could tip all of these other businesses over the edge into bankruptcy but he would need to watch his back".

The next morning Todd Raven went back to see Aaron Levy and suggested he did what the bank manager had outlined. Levy agreed to do it starting next week but was fearful a murder gang would be after him. Todd assured him that would not happen because he was going to warn the other club owners and offer to buy them out before they were ruined. He went to the larger of the two organisations first and noticed how shabby the places were. He was asked to hand over his guns and refused but then was allowed in to see the owner.

As Todd Raven faced the owner, who had a gunman stood either side of him, smiled and said. "You can see that I have adequate protection Mr Raven."

"I am afraid you do not," Replied Todd, "because by the time they shoot me you will be dead. So can we start talking business now?"

Twenty five minutes later a rather pale faced owner sat opposite Todd Raven the hired guns had been sent on their way seeking pastures new. At last the owner found the energy to speak barely managing to say, "Your offer is hardly generous Raven."

Todd Raven smiled before saying, "Well it's in cash and you are unlikely to get a better one."

There was a very short pause and the man said, "I accept."

Todd then quickly rammed home that if the other three clubs accepted Todd Raven's terms he would receive a financial bonus on completion of the business. The club owner looked nervously around. "Have I your word that they will not know of this arrangement between us because if they did they would kill me."

"Here's my hand on it." said Todd. "As one gentleman to another."

With this former owner's support the other three club owners only took a day to decide to accept Todd Raven's terms and the business was rapidly concluded. Todd's bank manager was delighted to have conducted most of the business then helped in the resale to Aaron Levy of all the vacant sites most of them to build more small dwellings for renting. Todd made a profit on the deal and in the process made some friends and a few enemies.

Tucson lacked a hospital or anything like one with most towns and even cities having the very basic medical facilities such as just a doctor or a nurse. Aaron Levy decided to build a medical care centre and employ at least a doctor and a couple of nurses. Treatment would be free to the poor and those who could afford to were asked to contribute to the cost of their treatment.

Todd Raven spent some time on the river boats, which did mixed work, most of it legal. Fishing and the movement of goods up and down the river was the legal trade but being close to Mexico and their cheaper hooch was a good earner but somewhat risky.

After almost four months in Tucson Todd Raven decided to move down into Mexico and see what Magdalena was like it was just over a hundred miles south over fairly barren country. He took extra water for the journey even though he could follow the river for a while but this was bandit country. It was on the second day of his trip south and the trail led through some low sand hills and his horse was a bit twitchy a sure sign that other horses were around.

Todd Raven dismounted and left his horse to graze while he carefully moved thirty or forty yards forward. After covering half that distance he could smell the aromatic odour of cheap Mexican tobacco. Cautiously edging his way forward he caught sight of three men in an ambush position on either side of the track. Two had rifles and the other had a hand gun all were ready to spring their trap but Todd sprung his first.

"Buenos Dios Senors." said Todd Raven suddenly standing up both his guns at the ready. The three bandits may have been caught by surprise, but they reacted immediately. Sadly for the bandits only one shot went anywhere near its target but it was close. Todd cautiously approached the three bodies. Only one required a 'coup de grace' and with that completed he went to find their camp.

Their belongings amounted to almost nothing of value, they had not been very successful bandits. Todd took their guns and horses to sell in Magdalena and covered the bodies with a few inches of sand. He was just a day's ride out from his destination when he came across a Mexican Military patrol and the young Officer in charge warned him about a small gang of bandits who were very dangerous.

"Oh, I met them." said Todd. "I have their guns and horses and I buried them about thirty miles back."

The Officer looked at Todd in disbelief but his sergeant said, "I know this man Sir, he is very fast with his guns and his fists and you can believe what he says."

Todd had an army escort into Magdalena where he sold the guns and horses and then presented the money to the Mexican armies orphan children's home. This of course made him very popular with the mayor and the local army commander as he knew it would. Todd Raven spent an enjoyable three months in Magdalena did not shoot anyone and had the services of two very attractive maids at the small hotel he had decided to stay at.

The one sad part of his stay was that his faithful horse that had accompanied him across many miles for the last eight years died suddenly in its stable one night. However his new friends in the Mexican Army presented him with a fine replacement mount and one morning he headed north not quite sure where he wanted to go. He paused briefly in Tucson then again in Phoenix before making a decision to try Salt Lake City which he finally reached in six weeks.

Each day he restricted his new horse to between twenty five and thirty miles and was pleased with his performance. He had to admit that his new horse Tex was a worthy successor to old Rex who had been so loyal.

Utah was a State with many cattle ranches all wanting to get bigger and grab one another's land. Salt Lake City was at the centre of these activities and Todd Raven had only been there a couple of days when he witnessed a taste of the violence quite common there. His hotel had stables at the rear which suited Todd and he had just come down for breakfast in the small dining room at the end of the larger bar area.

The local sheriff was having breakfast at an adjoining table and Todd decided to have the eggs and bacon similar to that the sheriff was enjoying. Two men were drinking beer at the bar when three men came in and confronted them accusing them of cutting their bosses fences and stealing land.

The sheriff gave a sigh put down his knife and fork and he went over and told them to settle their quarrels elsewhere. The men went out into the street and within seconds gunfire was heard and the sheriff rushed out to see what had happened. The two men who had been drinking beer at the bar had been shot dead and the three men who had confronted them were seen riding fast out of town.

Chapter Nineteen

The sheriff returned to his breakfast and just glanced over at Todd Raven and said, "The undertaker is going to be busy today."

When breakfast was over, they were drinking some extra coffee when the sheriff told Todd that this was a common occurrence these days but could be a prelude to a full-scale range war between the bigger ranchers. Two Ranchers in particular were putting pressure on smaller ranch owners to sell up or make their lives almost impossible by restricting their access to water.

The two ranchers were related by marriage and certainly not the best of friends but family ties would prevent any major bust up between them. This information intrigued Todd Raven because if the two major players suddenly took on one another the minor players stood a chance of survival. He surprised the sheriff by asking a lot of questions about the big players and then later on that morning introduced himself to his local bank manager.

The manager was initially a little distant until he read Todd's letter of introduction from his previous bank manager then he was very helpful. The two Ranch owners Todd was interested in had accounts with another bank but the manager knew a great deal about them and clearly did not have much time for them as most of his clients were the smaller ranchers. This pleased Todd because the more people he could get who had influence in Salt Lake City to help with his plan the greater chance of success.

The family bond between the two ranches was fairly simple the eldest son of the owner of each ranch had married the young daughters of each of the other families. It was not a business arrangement the couples had been childhood sweethearts and the arrangement genuine. The sons of both families were not happy the way their fathers were treating the other small ranchers but both their fathers were strong wilful men in their early sixties.

Over the next few days Todd Raven found out a great deal about the two ranchers and it was inevitable that his curiosity would attract their attention. As a result one evening after he had enjoyed an evening meal Todd was taking the cool air on the side walk near his hotel when a large figure approached him.

"You the out-of-town big mouth asking all the questions?" enquired the foul breathed thug.

"I am he." said Todd. "Who wants to know?"

There was no reply just a large fist aimed for his nose which Todd easily avoided and countered with a rapid right and left that left his would be assailant flat out on his back. The grounded man grunted and reached for his gun but his hand was quickly crushed under the weight of Todd's highly polished boot. A small crowd had quickly gathered including the deputy sheriff who quickly disarmed the man and took him off for a night in the cooler.

The sheriff arrived and he and Todd had a beer in the bar and Todd was informed that the man was a heavy from the 'Bar T' who did a lot of the bosses persuading.

"The word has got out you are asking a lot of questions and they won't like that Mr Raven so watch your back, they know now that you are no mug so it's likely to be a bullet."

That may have been the original plan of the two big ranch owners but they had been had been carrying out their own investigation of this nosey outsider now they knew his name. What they quickly found out about Todd Raven caused them to call off their 'War Dogs'. They decided that with his background he would be a better ally then an enemy so one of the ranchers invited him over for a tour of the ranch and Sunday lunch.

Todd Raven was not completely surprised by the invitation and accepted it but informed his now friend the sheriff. So on the Sunday morning he rode out to the 'Bar T' ranch and dismounted in front of a fine house with a fine garden leading to a massive ranch area.

The man who led his horse to the shelter of the stables was the heavy who Todd had met before and Todd politely enquired, "How is the hand?"

The man just scowled and grunted but Todd noticed he was not wearing his guns. Samuel Taylor the rancher came to meet him his hand outstretched.

"Welcome to our home Mr Raven we have much to discuss."

Todd was to spend four hours at the ranch and was treated to a fine lunch and met the family who were extremely pleasant. He also toured the ranch with Sam Taylor it was huge and heavily stocked but there were some smaller ranches to the south on fine land which he looked at with envy saying, "The bastards won't sell."

Todd just looked at him and said, "If you were them would you?"

Sam Taylor looked at Todd Raven.

"You are right. We are approaching this in the wrong way but I need to cross that land to sell my beasts or go a hundred miles north and they lose condition."

"How long would it take for your cattle to cross your neighbours land?" asked Todd.

"Two days at the most through a fenced channel which then would not disturb his cattle." said the rancher.

Todd smiled. "I take it you would pay a fee to cross that land and deal with the fenced channel?"

"Of course." Said Sam Taylor. "It would save us thousands of dollars and hours of work."

Todd thought for a moment then he asked, "Does your friend have the same trouble moving his beasts to market going for miles around ranches that will not sell?"

"Why yes," said Sam Taylor.

"Exactly the same problem that I have."

"Well," said Todd, "why don't we try and come to the same solution then!"

Todd left the ranch an hour later with Sam Taylor going to talk to his ranch owning friend to the north and Todd agreeing to talk to the small ranch owners who were being pressured to sell against their better judgement.

Todd Raven went back into Salt Lake City first and had a long chat with the sheriff about the plan. He agreed to come out with Todd to meet with the small ranch owners concerned so they knew the offer was genuine. Over the next two weeks Todd and the sheriff visited all the ranchers involved but once it became clear that this was not a clever plan to cheat them of their land they listened carefully to what was being offered. The problem was that in some parts of the west once a person had passed his cattle through it he could claim ownership of that land by 'rite of passage'. The sheriff had a legal document setting out the temporary arrangement and the payment agreed plus a promise to make good any damage incurred. Agreement was finally reached just a week before the big two ranches were due to start moving their cattle to market.

For the first time five thousand head of cattle were allowed the quicker route to market to the south and the same applied to the ranch to the north. Both ranch owners sold their animals at a higher price because they were in excellent condition because of the shorter journey. Todd Raven was told by the sheriff that the post of mayor of Salt Lake City was becoming vacant and there were several people who thought he would be a fine choice for the post. The idea filled Todd with horror and he immediately made plans to leave but needed to talk to his bank manager first.

He had a meeting with him the next day and when he was asked where he was off to now he said, "I am going to try Reno in Nevada and do some gambling."

He packed his saddle bags with trail food and a bag of oats for Tex he had his map and a compass but seldom needed either and stuck to twenty-five or thirty miles a day.

He came across several other riders in his journey but they were all saddle bums on the lookout for some easy money and they did not fancy taking on Todd Raven. He took six weeks to reach Reno and arrived in the evening he quickly found a decent stable for Tex and then booked in at a nearby boarding house. His room was small but clean and the bed was quite firm with clean bed linen.

He went down to supper there were four other guests but nobody was talking just eating so Todd followed suit. The food was quite good and you were expected to clear your plate by the lady in charge who was fat but could not be described as jolly. Blackberry pudding and custard was the sweet followed by strong coffee.

Todd then apparently broke the house rules by saying, "Thank you, I enjoyed that."

The fat lady immediately put her finger to her lips indicating complete silence at meals but as she turned away her face indicated she had enjoyed the compliment.

The fat woman said to him as he was leaving the dining room "The front door is locked at eleven o'clock but if you come in later the back door is open all night."

Todd wandered out into the street and then stood on the side walk and watched a little of the night action in this a quiet part of Reno. He then went back to the boarding house and up to his room and decided to go to bed as it was just coming up to eleven o'clock. He lay there for a while then drifted off to sleep, just waking once during the night until he heard a horse and cart outside at first light.

For some strange reason the fat lady allowed talking at breakfast and lunch, but imposed a strict silence at dinner. It mattered little to Todd Raven as the food was good and there was plenty of it and he was not greatly interested in what his fellow guests had to say.

After breakfast he made his way into the main part of Reno and quickly found a branch of his bank. He presented his letter of introduction and was shown into see the manager who greeted him somewhat warily. That changed fairly quickly when he realised just how much this client had invested in the bank and a request for a few thousand dollars for gambling purposes created no problems.

The manager was about to warn his client about the ruthless activities of these gamblers when he suddenly remembered reading about this man and he wisely kept his mouth shut. Todd spent the rest of the day deciding which club he would honour with his presence and decided it would be the "Sin City" tonight.

After he had enjoyed the evening meal in silence he finished his coffee and wandered out into the street and walked down the sidewalk for about two hundred yards into the gambling hub of Reno. The Sin City gambling club was almost in the centre of five brightly lit clubs which were quite busy although it was still quite early in the evening.

Todd Raven took a brief look into several of the other clubs before finally entering Sin City and then wandered around before finally seating himself at a table where three men were already starting to play a hand of cards. He was dealt in and within seconds spotted that the club dealer was in league with one of the players. Todd put his cards down and said in a loud voice. "Can we all have a card from the bottom of the deck like your friend here?"

Two men immediately came over to the table and confronted Todd Raven who just said to two of his two innocent fellow players. "See what the dealer has on the bottom of the deck."

One of them grabbed the deck and on the bottom was a sequence of Kings and Queens clear proof that the dealing was rigged. The two heavies led the dealer and the involved card player away and the manager brought over a bottle of brandy as a peace offering.

Todd had a couple of glasses of brandy with his new found friends then decided to try one of the other clubs which had wheel games. He spent almost three hours there and won almost four hundred dollars. It was just after midnight when he arrived back at his boarding house and went in through the back door and quietly up to his room.

After breakfast the next morning he decided to go for a ride around Reno so he saddled up Tex and spent a couple of hours looking around the perimeter of the city. He then took Tex back to the stables and gave him a good wash down and a special treat of oats. After lunch he made plans for the evening intending to go to several of the gambling clubs but to try and avoid the card games which had a bad reputation.

Chapter Twenty

The town of Hope was having a celebration over nothing in particular, but because they all felt like getting together and enjoying themselves. It was planned to start at lunch time with games for the children then go on till midnight with dancing for the grown-ups. 'Ma's House would organise the drink and the wives would get together and organise the food. The married couple from the two ranches would be invited but not the single men who could not be spared anyway. Jack and Buck did not anticipate any problems, but they had their cell block for anyone who got out of hand.

There were now quite a few twelve-year-olds in the town, but of chief concern were three girls from the Italian family who were now seventeen. They had already attracted the attention of some of the younger ranch hands when they came in on Friday and Saturday nights. The girls were innocent enough, but they did not understand how attractive they were to men who had too much to drink.

The day went off well and it was well past midnight before things began to quieten down Jack Masters and Buck did not have any trouble and after breakfast the next morning they were congratulating themselves on a well organised and orderly event when one of the Italian families reported that one of his daughters was missing. She was one of the seventeen-year-olds and had been last seen at eleven o'clock last night dancing with others in the main street.

Jack and Buck immediately questioned her friends if she had a special boyfriend and who had she been last seen with. They were told that the girl was the shyest one of them all and did not make friends easily and the last person they saw her with was Ethan Watts.

Ethan confirmed this and said, "She asked for a drink of lemonade, and I gave her some and she sat drinking it on the seat by the hall."

Buck went over to the seat and there underneath was a half empty glass of lemonade so the search for the missing girl began there. Someone told Jack Masters that some strangers were camped just outside of the north side of the town, so he rode out there to check them out. He found three men asleep in a canvas lean-to and a woman making coffee over a small fire.

Their four horses were grazing nearby and the woman in her early thirties smiled a greeting and said, "My man and his two brothers ain't wanted by the law, sheriff. We just come here looking for work."

Jack Masters explained about the missing girl and the woman said they had arrived here at about eleven last night from Fort Worth. When Jack returned to Hope Buck suggested that their wives should talk to the friends of the missing girl and Jack agreed so it was arranged straight away. The two girls were clearly much happier talking to two women who had known them during their school days. After some persuasion they eventually revealed that their friend had been seeing one of the younger ranch hands called Rico who took her for rides on his horse.

They insisted she said she would only been away an hour and could not imagine what had happened. Jack and Buck were now very worried and rode over to the Circle 'O' where they knew a young ranch called Rico worked. They saw the Ranch owner first and he gave them permission to search for young Rico who was supposed to be rounding up strays. Eventually they found him coming out of a rocky area not where you would normally find strays.

At first he denied all knowledge of the girl then he admitted that once or twice he had given her a ride on his horse. Jack Masters tried a shot in the dark by saying, "How badly hurt is she Rico?" Most of the colour drained from Rico's face and he barely whispered, "I think she may have broken her arm."

Ten minutes later they were at the small cave where Rico had set up a temporary home for his beloved now nursing an injured arm after falling from his horse.

Buck went back to Hope to collect the doctor and to give the parents the welcome new that their daughter was safe. He then returned with the doctor and the buck board to make the journey back more comfortable. Fortunately, the arm was not broken just badly bruised, but the girl's parents were deeply hurt by her behaviour and from then on their freedom was restricted until they were eighteen. Rico could have been charged with abducting a minor, but the girl's father knowing he was to be sacked from the ranch dropped the charge and Rico went back to Mexico. The four visitors camping on the boundary of Hope were offered work by the Italian wine making family. They always needed ditches digging and fences put up. They proved to be good workers and settled in to be an asset to the community.

One morning just before noon a posse rode in from Fort Worth in pursuit of three bank robbers who had last been seen heading in the direction of Hope. Jack and Buck managed to get together two small possies of four men and while the Fort Worth posse headed north they searched the rocky areas to the north and south. In Jack's posse were the two younger brothers who had arrived just a short time ago and had now found work digging ditches. The one called Luke had particularly sharp eyes and as they moved through a series of large rocky outcrops he drew Jack's attention to a small trace of fresh horse dung.

He dismounted and pressed it with his foot then said, "It's still moist sheriff they can't be that far ahead."

They moved on and not more than fifty yards further on behind a large rocky outcrop was a lame horse. As they moved towards it several shots were fired which struck the rocks behind them and they took cover and edged towards the firers.

Jack decided to try a bluff and he shouted out "You have given your position away and the other posse is moving behind you and you are one horse short so give up now."

They could hear the three robbers in angry discussion and clearly in disagreement. Then a shot was fired, but clearly not at them then the sound of horses galloping away then a volley of shots and then silence. Jack turned to his men and said, "I think they just ran into Buck's posse but let's go and see who they just shot."

Just a few yards further on they found one of the bank robbers who had been shot in the dispute he was not dead but close to it, it was probably his horse that had gone lame. They made their way down to where Buck and his posse were checking over the bodies of the other two robbers and by now their companion had died. Jack made sure that Luke got the praise he deserved for spotting the small scrap of horse dung.

All the stolen money was recovered from the saddle bags and the three horses became the property of Hope stables as the lame horse quickly recovered. Luke and his brother Seth were placed on Jack's reserve deputies list and six months after they had arrived in Hope Luke and one of the Italian girls were going out together with the full approval of the parents. Jack was pleased with the way Simon his son was developing he could ride well now and could be trusted to go fishing on his own.

Sue Ellen was also growing into a well-behaved young lady and doing very well at school with high marks in most subjects. There was some talk of the railroad company running a daily service to Hope but there was not any demand for it now and the fare would go up for a more frequent service. The real problem was the railroad company was losing money and was desperate to find ways of making some.

Fortunately, someone heard of their problem and offered them a military contract to carry ammunition, weapons and men as required and the Company jumped at the opportunity. The Circle 'O' apart from breeding cattle had for the last couple of years bred horses and had gained a fine reputation for its young colts and when ten went missing from their corral they asked Jack Masters for help. These lively young creatures were not easy to steal and would have to be secured in a long chain together, but it was thought the thieves had a twelve-hour start.

Jack Masters took three men, including Luke who had good tracking skills, and they set off from where the animals had been corralled later that morning. At first the track was easy to follow but after a couple of hours it moved into rocky country where the ground was bone hard. They carried on till darkness caused them to stop and rest up till daylight when they could begin the search again.

Luke had the early morning watch and when dawn broke Jack rose from his sleeping position to find Luke missing. He was about to rouse the other two when Luke reappeared and said, "They are about a mile over that rise and having trouble with the colts that they hobbled for the night."

Within minutes Jack and his team were on their way and went carefully over the rise and almost ran straight into the ten colts linked up together and trying to drag a thick tree trunk as an anchor. The four thieves were still sorting themselves out from their breakfast and were shocked to find this unwelcome company, but they still went for their guns. This was a mistake and two paid the ultimate price while the other two would go to trial nursing their wounds. Only Luke suffered a minor wound to the arm and Jack rode back to Hope with him and put him in front of the doctor. Then he took the buggy out to collect the bodies and the Ranch owner had his men collect the colts.

The marshal came out from Fort Worth and collected the two wounded robbers and that night Jack and his team were given a special dinner by the grateful ranch owner. This also included their wives and Luke's girl friend who was so proud of her wounded hero. Luke's brother Seth was now seeing the sister of his brother's girlfriend and it was with the full consent of the parents who thought both young men were hard working and very suitable for their daughters.

Three months later there was a double marriage of two brothers and two sisters it was a splendid affair, and it was talked about for weeks afterwards. Not long after that the older brother and his wife who Jack Masters had met that day on the outskirts of Hope decided to move into Fort Worth leaving his two younger brothers to enjoy their new lives.

Jack Masters later found out that the man had been offered a post at the military depot there because of his experience as part of major Reno's command at the Battle of the Little Big Horn. What role he had actually played was not clear, but he had an honourable discharge from the army for his services.

The trial took place in Fort Worth of the horse thieves, and it only lasted a day. The surviving two thieves pleaded guilty and then had the nerve to ask the judge to consider their punishment served by the pain of being shot. The judge nearly fell off his chair and when he managed to pull himself together he told them "I was going to give you each five years hard labour, but I now have decided to make that six for your audacious cheek, being shot was in my view rather getting off lightly, take them away."

Everyone was delighted with the judge's remarks because in the past sentences had been considered too light and offenders had been back up to their old tricks in no time at all. It was quietly whispered that the two Ranch owners were members of the same Freemasons Lodge as the judge but of course the Lodge membership is secret but who knows. Jack Masters and his men who were ready to give evidence if it had gone to trial were relieved it had ended early.

Chapter Twenty One

Todd Raven was to spend a couple of months in Reno he moved around the various clubs, but he now avoided the card games which were mostly dodgy. The various wheel games were a much fairer option and gave a better return to the steady gambler. He did not make any particular friends during his time there but then he did not make any enemies. When he finally decided to move on he did so with more money than he had arrived with which was no mean achievement. When he told the fat lady he would be leaving at the end of the week she surprised him by saying, "I shall be sorry to see you go at least you appreciate good food."

On the morning of his departure Todd even surprised himself by handing her some flowers as a token of his appreciation. Then he could not get onto Tex quick enough to start the hundred-mile journey to Sacramento.

The City of Sacramento takes its name from the famous river that it rests on the banks of and in its early days was a hub for the movement of timber and fishing. It was now a busy work centre mainly for timber with a small entertainment side. Todd was interested in the business side for a change and there were several small firms eager to become larger but did not have the funds to achieve this.

Todd made himself known to the manager of the branch of his bank who drew his attention to a small family business consisting of a widowed father and his two sons and their sawmill. It had done good business because it paid a fair price for the logs brought down by the workers from the forests. But recently their sawmill had been damaged probably by a rival firm who wanted the timber but at a cheaper price. And with that business out of action the loggers had to sell their timber to the other firm at a cheaper price.

Todd Raven was given a letter of introduction to the father of the stricken timber firm by the bank manager but on his arrival at the premises he was greeted with suspicion by all three family members. However, they listened to what he had to say, and they began to take a keener interest but the suspicion still hung in the air. Todd had just finished outlining his offer when two men from one other rival timber mills arrived with an offer to buy the troubled firm out.

The father promptly said, "No thank you, we are continuing in business with a new partner."

One of the two men stepped forward and said, "If you know what's good for you, you old fool, take our offer and be thankful or fill a grave up yonder."

At this point Todd Raven stepped forward and confronted both men and tapped his guns then said, "I have considerable experience of filling graves gentlemen and if you come threatening my friends again I will add you two on to my extensive list."

The mean look on Todd's face and his general attitude were enough to send the two rival mill owners on their way.

The father turned to his two sons with a smile on his face and said, "Boys, let's shake hands with our new partner."

Todd spent another two hours with his new friends finding out what was required in terms of new machinery or repairs. Trying to Impress upon them the importance that they should start the repairs and order the parts straight away but at the same time still buy in the timber as before. The two sons were called Jake and Ethan both sturdy lads no doubt good with their fists but neither wore a gun.

Todd decided that he should stay nearby for the time being and the old man was happy to have him as a guest for a while. The loggers were more than happy to sell their timber to the old man and his two sons again even though it was just stacking up in a huge pile now. The other two mill owners were furious their plan to force to make the loggers sell cheap had misfired and they were in danger of going out of business.

They were forced to go cap in hand to the old man and ask him to sell them some of his wood which he did at a much higher price. Two weeks later the sawmill was back in production and producing finished sawn timber the other mills could not match so within another month they went out of business. The father bought the better one of the two on Todd's advice and put the elder of the two sons Jake in charge they then improved the machinery and business improved.

Late one afternoon the sheriff of Sacramento came out to the sawmill and spoke to the old man. He told him that he had heard that the embittered mill owners had paid two men to set fire to both sawmills that the old man now owned. The father called Todd into the conversation and together he and the sheriff worked out a plan to foil the arson attempt and arrest the wrongdoers. The attempt was to be made during the late evening just before midnight.

By eight o'clock the sheriff and his group were in position at the main mill. Todd and Jake and his group were in position at the one recently bought. They all had half a dozen buckets of water with them just in case a fire started. It was just after eleven thirty when three men rode up and lit some oil-soaked rags fastened to sticks. They approached both buildings and were about to throw the lighted torches through the open windows when the defenders struck. Within a few minutes six men were in custody and the torches were put out harmlessly.

By the next morning the sheriff had Statements from the six men implicating the two former mill owners in the plot to burn down the two sawmills. The courts did their business quite quickly and within a month the former mill owners were serving five-year prison sentences and the fire raisers two years.

Todd Raven spent another twelve months in Sacramento then the urge to move on became impossible to resist. He thought about San Francisco less than a hundred miles to the southwest then decided on a quieter spot and settled for a spell at Fresno less than two hundred miles south. He took his time over the journey and the route was quite busy, so he was not short of company and he came across some decent folk.

It took him and Tex eight days to complete the journey and Fresno was awash with small farms where you could stay for a few days and either pay board or work to pay off your keep. Todd Raven lodged with a young family and did a mixture of both paying some days and working on others though he could afford pay right through. The two children were aged seven and eight, a boy and a girl who went to the local school in the morning then helped in the fields in the afternoon.

The father and mother were both about thirty years old and the mother was still very attractive. Juan the father was a well-built young man of about six feet in height and he never seemed to stop working and he quickly gained Todd Raven's respect. Most of the small farmers had joined a farmers' cooperative so they could get their produce to the markets in San Francisco at a good price.

It had worked very well for a long time but lately the wagons had been held up by masked men who demanded payment to let them pass and this was ruining their business. Todd immediately became interested and offered his services to Juan and his friends. The local sheriff was sympathetic but as it was happening beyond his boundaries of responsibility which was the town area of Fresno he could not act. Todd arranged to go with the next load of fruit to be sold in San Francisco and he would sit up next to the man driving the horses.

The arrangement with the carts for a quick delivery to the city was that halfway between Fresno and San Francisco the carts did a change of horses, so the one hundred miles was completed in one night. The fruit arrived at dawn just as the market traders wanted it and in a very fresh condition as it had travelled through the cool night air. The men on the wagon quizzed Todd on what would happen when Todd told them that this time they would not be paid.

Todd smiled then said, "Well that's up to them, they can either ride off in a sulk or slap leather."

As a concerned gasp went up Todd said, "But you need not worry. If they choose to go for their irons I will deal with it. Just trust me."

The carts were loaded with the normal amount of fruit and at the usual time they left Fresno with just one difference this time and that was Todd Raven sitting up next to the lead driver. At the fifty mile point they made the usual changeover of horses, and the men had a fifteen minute break before setting off again.

An hour or so later the driver warned Todd that it was around here that they were usually stopped, and money was demanded and paid. It was about five minutes later that three men suddenly rode out in front of the lead wagon and a masked rider said, "If you want to go any further friends you must pay the fare."

It was to Todd's advantage that the three mounted figures were outlined in the early morning moonlight against the white rock so as he rose to his feet and said, "No payment today boy's just drop your guns and back away then we will have a chat."

There were just a few seconds pause then a rather incredulous voice from one of the three masked men enquired, "Is that you Todd Raven?"

"Well, you have got that right." said Todd. "And who might you be?"

"Oh, someone who knows better than to try to out gun you Todd. Let us go now and you have my word there won't be any more holdups from us and the man behind this hold up business is the owner of Kingsway Market trying to get his produce on the cheap."

That satisfied Todd and he shouted, "On your way boy's and don't let our paths cross again."

Within seconds the three masked riders were away in a cloud of dust in the growing light.

They arrived at the market on time and at Todd suggestion sold their produce to everyone accept Kingsway Market. Their buyer became frantic and eventually the boss of Kingsway turned up and demanded to know what was going on. As by now all the produce from the wagons had been sold to the other market traders he started to berate his unfortunate buyer but then Todd Raven stepped in. In just a few short sentences Todd Raven told the owner of Kingsway that he was aware that he had arranged the regular hold ups of the fruit wagons and now his business would suffer as a result. The owner said he would call the marshal.

"Good." said Todd. "I have twenty witnesses who heard what the masked men said."

Two weeks later Kingsway market went out of business and a few months later under a state and government aid scheme the railroad built a spur line from San Francisco to Fresno so the fruit could now travel safely by train. Todd stayed in Fresno just long enough to see the railroad line complete then decided to visit San Francisco he found lodgings on the extreme edge of the busy city, so Tex had a decent stable and some fresh grass to eat. He did some gambling and won quite well which meant he attracted the company of an attractive youngish woman. He knew she came with the luck of winning and used her as he fancied then after a month he gave her a present and she disappeared.

He decided to visit Los Angeles almost four hundred miles to the south, so he saddled up Tex and filled the saddle bags with trail food for them both. It took Todd almost a month to complete the journey joining up with an old couple for part of the way. But after three days of listening to the old bible thumper Todd made an excuse and hurried away with Tex looking more relieved than Todd at the parting.

When they finally arrived, Todd was most impressed with the harbour and the fine views out over the Pacific Ocean. It was a busy trading port full of seaman from all over the world and of course the biggest business was brothels. With the need for women of course is the need for drink and food and the streets around the harbour were full of premises providing just that. Todd thought it ironic that a city called Los Angeles or City of the Angels should be such a sordid place.

He spent a month there after finding a place to lodge on the edge of the city with a decent stable for Tex. He got into a couple of fist fights with drunks and enjoyed knocking a few heads together. He had no reason to use his guns his appearance and general confidence persuaded any young gun slingers not to try.

Chapter Twenty Two

A sudden spate of bad weather had hit the northern half of the State of Texas and this mixture of heavy rain and strong winds had aided the final escape plans of three young army deserters from the Detention Cells at Fort Worth. Just after midnight they finally broke through their cell wall bars and escaped into the main yard. The guards were all taking shelter from the heavy rain and missed those vital minutes which allowed the three men to gain their freedom.

Ten minutes later the men were on the outskirts of Fort Worth and onto the railroad line leading to the town of Hope. Their plan now was to find an isolated farm and steal some horses and guns if possible and make their escape to the north where they had friends. The reason the three young men had deserted in the first place was because they no longer could stand the brutality of their training sergeant Frank Mitchell. To make matters worse one of Mitchell's brothers was a guard at the Detention Cells and he made sure the three were always given the worse work to do.

It was just becoming light when the three spotted the small homestead of George and Ira Olives. It was not a farm, but the small barn beside the wooden single storey house suggested horses, so they went over to investigate. George Olives who did not sleep too well was up and making some coffee when he was shocked to see three young faces staring in through the window.

Without giving it much thought and considering the weather he promptly opened the door and asked them in. He then realised by their torn uniforms that they were escapees from the cells at Fort Worth but sensibly just offered them coffee. It must be said that these young men were not violent thugs but decent young men who had been mistreated by a sergeant who was not fit to hold rank. As the four drank their coffee they were joined by Ira who after hearing their story started to cook them all breakfast.

George Olives was a retired magistrate and after they had all enjoyed breakfast and some more coffee he spoke to the three like a father. He told them that he would take up their case for them but first they must first give themselves up to the sheriff of Hope. Ira also spoke to them and convinced them that her husband would do what he promised.

"I will take you into Hope in my buggy if you are agreeable." said George. "And Jack Masters the sheriff will take matters on from there."

The three young men spent just a few minutes thinking this offer over and decided to accept and gave George and Ira their word they would not change their minds. An hour later George Olives with the help of the three young men prepared the buggy and finally they set off for Hope. Jack Masters was quite surprised to find waiting outside his office and cells George Olives and his three friends. George Olives explained to Jack about the three men's escape and the reason why they were in detention. He also told him that the Sergeants brother was one of the guards at the cells and was as unpleasant as his brother.

Jack listened to all this, and it had the ring of truth, and he made the following suggestion. He would go into Fort Worth and see the commanding officer who he knew quite well and was a decent man. But in the meantime, the three young men would stay in the Hope cells until this matter could be settled in a proper way as the conduct of this sergeant needed looking into. George Olives could go with him, and Buck Shaw would keep an eye on the three lads. They went into Fort Worth in Jack Masters two horse buggy and managed to catch the Commanding Officer just as he was coming out of the mess after lunch.

They spent an hour with him and at times he was a very angry man, at first he demanded that the three prisoners be returned to Fort Worth then on hearing the full story changed his mind. When they left he had agreed that an enquiry would commence into the conduct of the sergeant and his brother the guard immediately. On conclusion the three deserters would return to the cells for a retrial with George Olives giving evidence.

Jack Masters and George Olives started back as it was getting dark, and George was dropped off on the way with Jack arriving home about midnight. The next day when Jack arrived at the cells the three young men were repainting the inside area with some paint Buck had been given and over coffee Jack explained what had been agreed and they were delighted. The commanding officer did not waste any time within a week the sergeant had been reduced in rank and discharged from the army his brother was given twenty eight days detention in Fort Smith.

A week after that the three young men appeared at a court of enquiry and the sentence of detention was erased from their records. They were given the option of release from the army or to continue in service and they all opted to stay in the army. They all wrote letters of thanks to George and Ira Olives and the correspondence continued until the couple passed away within weeks of one another several years later.

The Italian families wine business was now doing very well and at certain times of the year employing extra local labour which was to every one's benefit. As a result, the town prospered and Hope became the envy of many of the surrounding towns in the area. State politicians like to be associated with success and one very ambitious man who aimed to be state governor built himself a very nice house on the outskirts of Hope very close to the fences of the Circle 'O' Ranch.

Very soon a dispute began between the politician and the ranch owner because the politician said the fences spoilt his view of the countryside from his house. The ranch owner made things worse by moving almost five hundred cattle into the area added to the spoilt view. One night someone cut the fences and some cattle roamed onto the politician's new house gardens and he promptly shot half a dozen and Jack Masters was called to the scene.

The cutting of ranch fences was nothing new to Jack Masters and he had developed a certain skill in assessing how this had been done. He quickly found that two sections of fence had been cut and of the most importance they had been cut from the politician's side of the property. Following this about twenty cattle had roamed through the gap created to enjoy the lush grass on the other side. Jack Masters told the politician that someone had cut the fences from his side of the property and suggested that a political rival may be out to embarrass him.

With his eye on the state governor's job the politician thought this quite likely. As a result, he paid the owner of the Circle 'O' the market price for the slaughtered beasts and donated the carcasses to the hospital in Fort Worth. The story of course was reported in the newspapers and the politician was praised for his generous act.

Jack discussed the matter with Jane his wife as he was beginning to think he had been used by this politician to gain some favourable publicity in his quest for the Governors job. He decided to go out and tell this man that he did not feel it right that the law should be used as a lever to advance a career in politics.

When he arrived at the politician's new house it was growing dark, and he was surprised to see a horse tied up outside the main door which was open. Jack dismounted and approached the main door, and he heard a woman crying. He knew that the politician wife was there plus two female servants, so he moved cautiously to the main entrance and went in. Lying on the floor with her legs bound was one of the maids the other maid lay unconscious nearby.

The maid gasped out, "A man has the master and his lady in the main room, and he has a gun."

Jack put his finger up to his lips to ensure she remained silent then he moved to the door of the main room. As he reached it he paused and listened for a moment as he heard the coarse voice of a man say, "This time I will make sure there are no mistakes and dead men cannot be elected governor, so you go first and then your poor wife."

Hearing this gave Jack no option but to smash through the main door with his gun raised and ready to fire. As he crashed into the brightly lit room the gunman spun half round and fired his first shot clipping Jack's hat. He did not fire another as two shots from Jack's gun slammed into his chest and he took his last breath in front of the open fire.

Jack quickly checked that the man was dead then he made sure that the politician and his wife were unharmed. Then he went to help the two maids in the hallway, untying one while the other slowly recovered from a blow to the head. The politician's wife showed some concern for her servants but the politician who had been the target of this thug was concerned about a bruise on his face. Jack said he would go for the doctor as the maid had a very deep cut on the back of her head where she had been knocked out.

"Please do that." said the politician. "Then he can check if a bone in my face is damaged."

Jack first dragged the body of the thug outside then rode into Hope and collected the doctor who on arriving checked the maid then the other two women before briefly looking at the politician's face which he dismissed as trivial. He stitched the maids head then told her to rest for a day which the politician's wife assured him she would do.

Jack and the doctor left with Jack making arrangements to collect the body from the garden in the morning. When he arrived home Jack stabled his horse then he had to explain all to Jane who was not impressed at all by the politician and certainly did not think him a fit person to be state governor.

After breakfast the next morning Jack briefed Buck on what had happened and then took the buggy and went out to the politician's house and collected the body brought it back to Hope and passed it over to the undertaker. He and Buck checked the 'wanted' posters to see if the man was listed but he was not and he had no identification on him.

That afternoon Jack went out to see the Politician to see if he knew who the man was the politician was having an afternoon nap, but his wife was quite helpful saying that the man had once been a member of their team. But she could not remember his name but said she was sure her husband would when he woke up.

Jack was about to leave when the politician appeared and was not best pleased that his wife had spoken to Jack.

When Jack asked what the man's name was, the politician denied ever knowing him and said his wife was obviously confused and still suffering from shock following the events of the last evening. Jack Masters was convinced the politician was lying but there was nothing he could do about it.

A month later the election for a new state governor took place and to many people's relief this man who had recently arrived in Hope did very badly in the poll. Three months later he sold up and moved south and Jane heard that he had left his wife. The house remained empty for some months then one night it caught fire in a storm and was burned to the ground. There was a feeling that someone had taken advantage of the storm to set it on fire but that was almost impossible to prove.

Chapter Twenty Three

Todd Raven had bought a semi derelict warehouse and spent some money on it and it was placed quite central to the route seaman used on their way to and from their ships. Half of the building sold drink and food and the other half catered for a seaman's need for women. It was called 'The Comfort Cradle' and it became very popular, and Todd kept his prices low and made a mint. He made sure he changed the girls around, so they were not overworked and brought fresh girls in when the need arose. There was a certain amount of resentment from other owners, but Todd could handle that and did with an eagerness that the opposition could not match.

Todd Raven had the personality that attracted a certain type of staff to him who may not have found employment elsewhere. This strange mixture of misfits were loyal to him and he could trust them and when as it always did that the urge to move on proved too great to resist he would leave the business in their hands but not just yet.

Todd enjoyed the pleasures that a woman had to offer though he did not have the appetite of his late brother Ike. What he did not realise was that some women, even those brought up in the more refined circles, might enjoy an occasional romp with a rough crude man who normally they would not pass the time of day with.

Lydia Forbes-Brown who was married to the managing director of a chain of food companies and at thirty was childless and intended to stay that way. She lived in a splendid house on the high ground just outside Los Angeles and wanted for nothing. Her husband had some odd sexual habits that she tolerated as long as she remained childless and in modern parlance she was a trophy wife. She enjoyed a morning ride on her favourite horse 'Buttercup' and it was then purely by chance that she met up with Todd Raven. She had trotted her horse for a mile or so through a woodland area when the horse suddenly pulled up clearly with a problem.

Lydia was concerned for her favourite animal and dismounted and found that the trouble was with the animal's front leg. She was now faced with a four-mile trek back to her house with a badly limping horse.

Every other day, Todd Raven took Tex for a couple of hours exercise up into the hills above Los Angeles and on this morning for the very first time came across someone else out for a ride. But they looked to be in trouble and Todd rode up to the woman and asked what was wrong. At first glance Lydia almost decided to just ignore this coarse looking brute of a man, but concern for her beloved horse made her respond.

She said in an offhand way, "See to my horse will you."

Todd Raven decided to teach this young Madam some manners his way so as he dismounted he deliberately broke wind relishing the shocked expression on the woman's face.

He then carefully examined the injured horse's front leg and did not find any tendon damage, so he checked the hoof area and found a stone had lodged between the metal shoe and the soft bone area. He easily extracted the stone with his knife and walked the horse around to make sure it had no other injuries. Lydia was fascinated by this brute of a man and found his crude behaviour somehow physically attractive.

"Perhaps I should walk him home as the foot must be bruised." said Lydia.

"Well, that is not really necessary but it's a thoughtful thing to do." said Todd, quite surprised by this rather spoilt young woman's reaction.

Then he surprised himself by saying, "In that case I will escort you home to make sure you arrive home safe."

Lydia Forbes-Brown however had other ideas about the journey home and after they had walked about a mile she suggested they take a rest for the horse's sake of course.

Lydia sat down on the grassy mound and removed her jacket and loosened her blouse then invited Todd to sit beside her. As he did so she just turned to him and said, "Now take me you animal."

So without any delay Todd did so with gusto. Some twenty minutes later and without anything more being said they resumed their journey to the Forbes–Brown residence. This time he pleasured her again, but this time they were naked in bed. From then on all the time Todd was in Los Angeles at least once a fortnight the pair would meet and enjoy each other. Lydia's husband got to know about the affair but had secrets of his own to hide so he was happy to ignore it. Despite having one of the best periods of his life there came a time when Todd felt the urge to move on. He said a brief goodbye to his friends and headed east, letting Tex set the pace for each day.

After a leisurely ten days he found himself in Flagstaff where he rested Tex up for a week got to know the sheriff after a couple of fist fights in a bar and became friendly with some old guys over a game of poker. After three months on the move Todd found himself in Kansas City and looked up some old friends.

He needed to settle down for a while and Tex certainly needed a rest, so Todd went to see the local bank manager just to introduce himself. He did not intend to start any business ventures as he had lost count of the number he had invested in, but his bank account had an accurate record and what was paid in.

The Kansas City sheriff knew him well and was amused when he heard that two newcomers to Kansas City had ear marked Todd Raven as a target for a land swindle involving plots of gold bearing ore.

One evening after Todd had enjoyed a meal and a couple of games of cards with some old friends he was about to go to his room for an early night when the two men approached him.

"You look like a man who enjoys a challenge." This was the opening line from one of the two men.

Todd immediately smelt a 'con' but he was bored and decided to see what these two clowns were on about.

So, he admitted he enjoyed a challenge and was eager to hear what they had to say. They then produced a map showing ringed in red several large plots of land and a series of surveyor's certificates stating that these areas contained gold bearing ore. Todd feigned excitement and asked how much they wanted for a plot and the men smiled at one another and said, "To you my friend just five hundred dollars in cash."

Todd decided to tease them just a mite longer so he said, "But these certificates do not have any reference numbers on them, and they would if they were really genuine as they would come out of a book held by the surveyor."

Then he looked at the two men and said, "You are just a pair of cheap con artists and poor ones at that. Get out of my sight and out of Kansas City or I will spread you both all over the sidewalk."

A deputy sheriff who had been tasked to keep an eye on the two men reported all this to the sheriff and said the men left the city an hour later heading south. The sheriff and Todd had a coffee together the next day and enjoyed a laugh at the expense of the two plot sellers.

Todd spent a month in Kansas City then felt he wanted to move again this time further east. He made the relatively short trip to St Louis where he had been before but did not intend to stay there and was determined to go on to Louisville. He spent three day in St Louis and looked up his old friends and business partners then with Tex well rested he moved on to Louisville with its growing tobacco industry. He found a place to stay on the edge of this sprawl of a growing small city a well-run stables was nearby so Tex was handy if needed. All the field work in the tobacco industry was done by the local population not yet realising how much they were being exploited by the big money from the north.

Like most men of his age Todd smoked the traditional roll ups and he enjoyed a small cigar and the first few weeks he spent in Louisville he learnt a great deal about the tobacco industry. When his local bank manger realised just how well off his client was he suggested all sorts of investments no doubt with the best of intentions. But from what Todd Raven had seen of the way the field workers and the processing workers were treated he wanted no part in the financing of the business.

He stayed another month in Louisville then decided to try somewhere else and saddled up Tex and moved on to Nashville. He booked a room at the first saloon he came to and found a nearby stable for Tex. The food at the saloon was appalling so he vented his frustration by picking a fight with two strapping young lads at the bar. The fight just about finished even and the three finished up the evening getting drunk together.

The next day he found a better place to stay at a small boarding house run by a youngish widow. The room was clean, and the food was good and plentiful and one of the men he had enjoyed the previous evenings fight with was her brother. Todd quickly found out that the young widow had been married to the deputy sheriff who sadly had been shot dead in a confrontation with two men who were attempting to rob the bank. That had been three years ago, and the sight of guns still sent a shiver down her slender frame.

When Todd Raven had asked for a room she was about to refuse him because he was armed and looked well able to use them but she had only one booking and times were hard, so she took him in.

The second evening he was there they had almost finished dinner and were enjoying some apple pie and custard when there was a thunderous knock on the door.

The young widow went to answer the door and Todd could hear angry words being exchanged then he heard a sharp crack and the young widow cry out in pain. Todd was on his feet in a flash and at the door in two strides just in time to see a man about to smack the widow again around the face.

The blow never landed as Todd pushed her aside and slammed the man up against the door and said, "Now try it with me, hero."

Needless to say, the man had no intention of taking on Todd Raven, but after being dragged into the kitchen and being told to tell all, the man, after almost wetting himself, said that the young widow had taken out a loan and had fallen behind on the repayments. Todd enquired how much of the loan was outstanding and was given a figure of several hundred dollars. Todd took out his gun and placed it under the man's chin and said, "Meet me outside the bank tomorrow at eleven and I will pay off the full amount but come here again worrying this poor woman and I will blow your head off is that understood."

The man nodded his head and almost ran from the house wetting his trousers as he ran.

Todd went back to tell the young widow and the other guest that everything was now all right, and he made some coffee for them all. Later he told the woman whose name was Rachel that she would not be bothered anymore as the loan would be settled and she would have a paper stating that from the bank.

The next morning Todd Raven went to the bank and met the man who had a colleague with him they went in to see the manager and in a few minutes the business was done. Todd had a paper stating the loan had been repaid in full which he could now give to Rachel he did tell the bank manager that he felt the bank should have compensated the deputies wife after he had been shot. The manager agreed but said the Directors just paid for the funeral because so many banks were being robbed and people shot.

Later Todd gave Rachel the paper and said, "They won't be bothering you anymore so now you can relax and just look after your guests."

Todd spent another three months in Nashville then he began to feel it was time to move on again.

Chapter Twenty Four

The Circle 'O' had been losing some of their young horses that they let roam to the north of their spread. At first they thought it might be from wolves but this was now almost unheard of so they now assumed they were being stolen. It was always a busy time on a ranch and few men could be spared to go look for some young horses that could be miles away by now. Jack and Buck were informed as a matter of routine, and they decided to take a couple of days in the hills to the north as a break from their normal routine.

By late afternoon on the first day, they found where the young horses had last been seen and quickly found some tracks heading into the far hillier country. By the time they had to camp up for the night they had found a well-established track suggesting an organised movement of horses. The nights were warm so they did not need a fire and it would have given their position away, so they settled for a cold meal.

They made an early start in the morning and both men knew moving a group of horses together can be a slow business and by mid-morning the trail of horse dung was looking quite fresh. It was at mid-day that they caught sight of the tail of the small herd and saw that only three men were trying to control them. Jack and Buck had a quick talk on tactics then Buck rode off to come round and in from slightly ahead of the group.

When Jack judged that Buck was about to be in position he rode forward and challenged the group by shouting, "I am Jack Masters the sheriff of Hope you are surrounded keep your hands away from your guns."

For a few seconds there was no reaction from the three men then one the furthest away from Jack made to gallop off but found he was staring at Buck Shaw's guns.

Within a few minutes the three men were all disarmed and then Jack and Buck realised that the three were in fact quite young. The ten young horses were all roped together so they were under control and after Buck had made some coffee for them all they started on the journey back to the

Circle 'O'. It was early evening when they handed over the horses to the delighted ranch owner then carried on into Hope with the three young rustlers and placed them in the cells. Jack had a late supper and had to tell the story of the capture of the rustlers to his two children and then they were hurried to their beds.

The next day was Friday so they could use the train to take the prisoners to Fort Worth and Jack could do some shopping as well. A few years ago, rustling cattle or horses would have been a hanging offence but now for a first offender according to his age a judge would impose a sentence of around three to five years.

For some reason when these three young men came up for trial a month later they all pleaded guilty which was sensible and were only given a very light sentence of eighteen months imprisonment. Jack and Buck were surprised but not too bothered by this obviously there was something about these three that gave them special treatment.

The three had at one time worked on the estate of a well-known state governor and this governor thought the three knew about some of the things he got up to in the bedroom with the female servants, but they did not. But he could not take that chance, so he had arranged for them to given light sentences for their silence.

A few weeks after this Jack Masters had a visit from the marshal of Fort Worth who had been given some strange information from the widow of a former crippled Civil War veteran.

Apparently just before the Civil War started her husband and two friends had robbed a train of some gold bars and hid them in a small cave in a high rocky outcrop overlooking a bend in the Snake River. They had intended to recover them when the search for the robbers quietened down but then the Civil War started and all three were conscripted into the Confederate Army.

Within two months the woman's husband had been severely wounded leaving him a cripple and his two friends had been killed. Last week as he lay dying he told his wife all about the robbery for the first time and gave her a rough drawing of the area where the gold bars were hidden. The marshal said that the widow wanted nothing to do with stolen gold bars but would like what her husband had done to be put right. He showed Jack the rough crude drawing and asked him if he would undertake a search of the area. Jack Masters knew the area of the Snake River pretty well so he agreed that he would undertake the task.

He discussed it with Buck and they both thought it would mean being away at least five days so Jack would ask Ethan Watts to go with him and Buck would look after the sheriffs duties. Jack asked Ethan straight away and the big man was very happy to oblige, and they started to make arrangements to leave the next morning with food for seven days just in case.

Later the two men studied a map of the area recently produced by the railroad and thought that the crude drawing did match up roughly with an area some ten miles northwest to the town of Hope. Both men spent the rest of the day making sure they had everything that they needed for the journey and agreed to make a start after breakfast the next morning. That evening Jack had to explain to his two children that he would be away for a few days, and they must do all they could to help mummy and not be difficult.

Jack slept well and Jane made sure he had a good breakfast Jack had his horse ready and was fully prepared when Ethan arrived. With a wave to Jane and the children they set off and for the first two hours followed the track along the bank of the Snake. It was after they had taken a break for lunch that they entered the area of interest and the first thing they did was set up a decent camp site close to the river for water.

The horses were hobbled and were quite happy with some lush vegetation to munch on. It was now beginning to get dark so they cooked their evening meal, and they now had a decent shelter should it decide to rain. They both settled down to sleep as there was no point in anyone standing guard as they could rely on their horses to warn them of any intruders. The night passed without incident and Jack woke to the sound of Ethan Watts breaking wind it was quite melodic and did not frighten the horses.

Ethan lit the fire and put some water on for coffee while Jack fried some bacon as soon as the fire was hot enough. They both enjoyed an egg and bacon breakfast and a couple of mugs of coffee. They then decided to give this area a good search but for safety reasons decided to work together. The lower rocky areas did not hold much interest but needed to be checked anyway and they spent most of the morning doing this. After a brief break for lunch, they moved further up and found several very small caves which could only be entered by sliding in on your belly they were all empty apart from evidence of animal use. By the time they had to stop they had the higher area still to search and that would take most of tomorrow.

They returned to the camp area and checked the horses and found they were fine. They just had time to cook an evening meal before darkness fell and they enjoyed their after-meal coffee in just the light of the fire. It was about an hour later when both horses moved away from the camp and over to some trees and Ethan said, "It's going to rain".

Not five minutes later it poured down and their fire was quickly extinguished, and they heard it drumming on the canvas for the next hour before it stopped.

Shortly afterwards they both settled down to sleep for the night conscious that if it rained again at least they would stay dry. When Jack woke up in the morning Ethan had already got the fire lit and was preparing breakfast. Jack played his part and made some coffee which they enjoyed with their bacon and eggs. They cleaned up then checked the horses who had wandered slightly further away then prepared to start the day's exploration.

They moved up to complete the search of the highest part of this rocky section. It was very steep in places and contained several small caves all of which they carefully searched. All the cave floors were of solid rock so there was no way anything could have been buried there. By mid-day they had completed this area and they went down and took a break before moving on to what they considered was the last section where the gold could have been hidden.

It was a slightly higher section and would take the rest of today and all tomorrow to search unless they hit the jack pot earlier. By the end of the day, they had searched the lower sections and disturbed a family of foxes who no doubt would return as soon as it became dark. They prepared their evening meal in the fading light and took one last look at the crude map the dying man had drawn. This final section and the one they had searched yesterday had the same look about them accept this last one was slightly higher. The night was dry, and the horses stayed close to where their masters slept and it was the persuasive nose of his horse that woke Jack first in the morning. The horse had become entangled with a tree branch caught in its hobble and Jack quickly freed it. Now up he set to and lit a fire and began to prepare breakfast and boil some water for coffee. Ethan woke with a blast of relieving trapped wind and soon the two were enjoying breakfast and hoping that today might see the end of their search.

After breakfast they made their way to the point where they had finished searching yesterday and began to examine these steep rocky outcrops and small caves. By mid-day all that was left was the higher part quite steep and littered with crevices and small caves. They took just a short break for lunch and a quick cup of coffee then returned to begin what was the final section.

They had completed almost half of what remained when they came across a narrow opening to a small cave just big enough for Jack to crawl through. Ethan with his bulk stood no chance of squeezing in and had to stay outside and listened as Jack told of what he could see inside. Straight away Jack heart gave a leap as against the wall of the small cave were two saddle bags caked in dust. Jack crawled over to them and felt for what was inside. His heart nearly stopped for his hands came in contact with some metal bars, they had found the gold.

He dragged one of the saddle bags to the cave mouth and passed it to Ethan and said, "Just check that we have found what we came for my friend."

As he returned with the other saddle bag he heard Ethan give a whoop of delight and then passed out the second bag to his excited friend. With both men now back out in full daylight they examined what they had found it was now without doubt the gold that had been stolen all those years ago. The saddle bags were still in a remarkable condition and still capable of carrying the gold back to Hope and then Fort Worth. The two men took their prize back down to the camp and made haste to make it back to Hope before it got dark. They did so just before the bank closed and surprised the manager by depositing to his safe keeping for the night all those gold bars. The next day under a three man escort the gold was taken to Fort Worth and handed over to the marshal there and after a judge led enquiry the gold bars were handed over to their rightful owners who made a donation to the children's school in Hope which enabled an extra classroom to be built.

Chapter Twenty Five

Todd decided to avoid any large place this time and settled for Huntsville some one hundred miles south of Nashville. He and Tex took just three days over the journey and on arriving decided it seemed just the right place to spend a quiet few weeks. He found a rather sleepy boarding house with a stable nearby with the middle-aged couple who ran the place totally disinterested in their three guests.

The small town of Huntsville had very few young people with almost everyone being over forty and any night entertainment seemed to be non-existent or appeared to be at first glance.

After dinner the first evening he was there Todd Raven asked one of the other guests who constantly read from his bible where those who had a thirst could get a drink of something other than water. The man looked quite shocked then with his eyes half closed touched Todd's hand and said, "The weak do find solace behind the stables I am told".

After finishing his meal Todd made his way out of the boarding house and round to the back of the stables. There he found a small circle of men seated around a fire passing around what appeared to be a jug of hooch. He moved up to join them and without a word being said a space was made for him in the circle. The jug reached him, and he took a sip then a swallow, and gasped it was mighty strong stuff. He stayed for almost an hour during that time two of the circle just collapsed into an unconscious state and were left where they were. When Todd left his legs felt quite weak and he had timed his exit to perfection.

The next day he visited the bank manager and the local sheriff who he recognised as being one of last night's drinking circle. During his conversation with the sheriff the matter of the 'drinking circle' came up and the sheriff assured Todd Raven that it was only an 'every other evening event'.

After some persuasion the sheriff admitted that Wednesday evening was a more popular event at the empty house at the end of the town. Todd Raven guessed this involved women but thought that they would hardly be locals and he was right. When Wednesday came round Todd made his way to this empty house to find its lower rooms dimly lit and the drinking circle members there plus some others including the bible reader. This time some local wine was being drunk and four women came into the room some discussion then took place and they slipped off into the other rooms with some of the men including the bible thumper.

After a while the women returned, and other men were accommodated, but this did not appeal to Todd Raven who had drunk almost a full bottle of the local wine and now just wanted his bed. He walked back to the boarding house with the bible thumper who was now praying for the weak souls of those overtaken by lust ignoring the fact that he had been one of those.

Todd Raven found Huntsville a fascinating place almost everyone who lived there lived two lives and he could now understand why all the young people had moved on. He managed to last there for a month and did not make any enemies and did not make any close friends either. Even Tex looked pleased when it was time to go and without giving his destination much thought Todd glanced at the map and decided on Tupelo just about a hundred miles west.

The weather was good, and they made the journey in three days and arrived in the small town just after mid-day. At first glance Tupelo seemed ordinary enough and Todd tied Tex to a railing outside of a saloon and went inside for a drink. There were about ten people inside the saloon and Todd immediately felt their combined eyes fall upon him.

"I'll have a beer." said Todd and slammed some coins on the counter and the barman, a large man with a badly scarred face, served him his drink and swept the coins into his apron pocket. Todd drank his beer then said, "Where is my change?"

The barman laughed and called out to one of the men seating nearby. "We have a troublemaker here Buck, who is complaining about the service."

The man called Buck rose from his seat and walked over to the bar and stopped about five feet short of Todd Raven.

"Well mister you have only been in this place a few minutes and you are causing trouble so you can pay a fifty-dollar fine or get the shit get beat out of you and spend the night in the lock up. What's it to be?"

Todd looked the man called Buck up and down then said, "Who is going to beat the shit out of me?"

"We are." said the barman and he and Buck launched themselves at Todd Raven from opposite directions.

Todd quickly disposed of the barman, but Buck took just a mite longer but eventually joined his colleague on the bar room floor with nobody else anxious to become involved. The town doctor, who was an interested spectator, gave both partly conscious men the once over and suggested a bucket of water and a night's bed rest. The eagerness of two spectators to throw a bucket of water over the two men suggested they were not all that popular in the town.

The doctor suggested a place where Todd could stay which had stabling for his horse was at the other end of town and led him there. He also told Todd that the town had no sheriff and that the barman together with Buck and his brother Abe who was out of town at the moment ran a fake law and order racket bullying the weak and lining their pockets as a result.

Todd found his lodgings clean, and the stables were next door and Tex would be well looked after there. The next morning after a good night's sleep Todd came down to find a good breakfast ready for him. There were three other guests and already his exploits of the previous day were known to them and the owner of the boarding house a widow just said to him, "We don't want any trouble Mr Raven."

Later that morning Todd paid a visit to the bank manager who after reading his letter of introduction from his previous manager was suddenly very pleased to see him. He went back to the boarding house and had lunch and later was having coffee with the doctor on the veranda when a man rode up and asked to speak to him. Todd invited the man to take coffee with him and the doctor and explain his business. The man sat down took some coffee then said, "My name is Abe Clancy and you met my brother Buck last night."

"Well," said Todd, "I was attacked by two men one of which was your brother and they threatened to beat the 'shit out of me' so I was only defending myself."

Abe Clancy shrugged his shoulders then said, "I can't ever remember my brother losing a fistfight especially when he had a partner to help him as well, but I have not come here seeking vengeance."

Todd looked at the doctor in surprise then said, "Then why have you come to see me then Mr Clancy?"

Abe Clancy took a final sip of coffee then said, "Buck, me and the barman have a nice little racket going on in Tupelo. Normally nobody gets hurt and we want you to join us."

Todd looked aghast then out of pure devilment he grabbed Abe Clancy by the arm and said, "I am applying for the post of sheriff of Tupelo and if I am successful you, your brother and that useless barman will have twelve hours to get out of Tupelo or face arrest is that clear."

Abe Clancy stood up a look of total surprise on his face. Then his face darkened and his anger showed and as he turned to leave he said, "You won't live to apply for the sheriff's job. My advice to you mister is get out of Tupelo fast."

He then rode off with Todd Raven's laughter ringing in his ears. As the sound of Clancy's horse faded the doctor showed concern at the situation that Todd Raven was now in. But Todd was unconcerned, confident he could out gun any of the three likely to pose a threat. A few minutes later the three men likely to threaten Todd Raven were seeking some kind of solution to their problem with the aid of a bottle of whiskey. Halfway through the bottle they decided that they would put up their own candidate as sheriff and that would be Abe Clancy. The problem was they had to get ten local people to support this nomination. Five regular drunks in the bar willingly gave their support but the other five proved to be more difficult.

The doctor, who was the chairman of the committee tasked to elect a sheriff, knew he could easily find ten people willing to nominate Todd Raven but would he take the job? By six that evening when nominations closed Abe Clancy was still two nominations light so could not stand but Todd Raven had ten nominations, so he was the only candidate and so became sheriff. He agreed to do the job for a month until a local man could undertake the roll and then made a visit to the Clancy bar. As he entered a hush fell over the normally noisy bar and the two Clancy brothers stood side by side at the far end of the bar.

"You and your brother and that clown behind the bar will be out of Tupelo by dawn tomorrow." said Todd Raven.

Then allowing for the message to sink in he added. "Is that clear enough for you?"

Abe Clancy protested. "It don't give us time to sell the place at a fair price."

"And what do you call a fair price then?" asked Todd Raven, who now had a very interested audience.

Clancy plucked a figure out of thin air and Todd laughed and said, "Only in your dreams would you get that."

Todd who had a good idea what the place was really worth said, "If you go as I suggested I will pay you this figure in cash as you leave"

He then wrote a figure on a piece of paper and handed it to Abe Clancy. Clancy looked at the figure then showed it to his brother and then they spoke quietly for a minute or so before Abe Clancy said, "We accept."

The bar-man annoyed at being left out of the consultation suddenly produced a shot gun and screamed. "The sheriff is about to be blown away."

As the shotgun swung towards Todd Raven he just as swiftly drew his right hand gun and fired. The shotgun blast just peppered the ceiling. The barman clutched his injured shoulder and lay there as the doctor came over and dressed the wound without a great deal of sympathy. Todd pointed to the injured barman and said to Abe Clancy. "Don't forget that in the morning that clown goes with you."

Todd went over to the bank and made arrangements for the money to be available in the morning then he and the doctor and his Committee talked about what to do with the bar. They decided that for the moment it would stay open as a bar but there were plenty of bars in Tupelo so to close one would not make much difference.

As he sat in his room later Todd Raven considered his position, he was now sheriff which was ridiculous for a man of his character. He resolved to rid himself of this unwanted office as soon as he could but not until the Clancy's were out of Tupelo which would be tomorrow. Thankfully the day ended without further incident and the new sheriff spent a troubled but unbroken night's sleep.

After breakfast the next morning by arrangement with the bank the sum of money was paid over to the scowling Clancy brothers. Then watched by a largely silent crowd they and their heavily bandaged former barman rode slowly out of Tupelo heading south eventually to Mexico.

By mid-day Todd Raven had handed his resignation in as sheriff to the doctor. Strangely enough now that the Clancy's had left the scene there were no shortage of people now willing to take the task on. By six that evening Tupelo had yet another sheriff, a former army sergeant who Todd thought was well able to do the job. As Todd Raven had made a present of the saloon to the people of Tupelo he was still seen as something of a local hero, and he spent another month in their pleasant company then he felt again the urge to move on. He enjoyed a farewell drink with his new friends then on a bright sunny morning saddled up Tex and headed west.

Chapter Twenty Six

It had been just over a month since the Circle 'O' and the Tall 'T' had last sent their animals to market and the money from this sale was due to be sent to the bank in Hope any day now. Three men in Fort Worth were watching the arrangements for the transfer of this money with great interest. They had a female accomplice working at the bank there who could relay to them all the details of the transfer arrangements. Their plan was to intercept the small escort on its way to Hope without bloodshed if possible, but they were not prepared to be unsuccessful in this adventure.

The bank had its own security guards, and they were reluctant to share their plans over the movement of money even with the local sheriffs involved. Even the manager of the bank in Hope did not know when the money for the two ranches was being sent from Fort Worth. The final plan was decided upon the escort of four armed men would leave Fort Worth at six in the morning with the bank manager and his cashier supervising the money being handed over to the escort.

The escort and the money would then proceed in a two-horse buggy at a sharp trot on the road parallel to the railroad line to Hope and should reach Hope just after mid-day. The three armed robbers knew from what their accomplice had told them that the escort would rest the horses at a watering point some ten miles into their journey. It was here that the robbers intended to strike hoping to take the escort by surprise if possible, but they were prepared for a shoot-out if need be.

If they took the escort by surprise they would tie them up let the horses loose and then escape with the money in their saddle bags. An unusual part of their escape plan was that once they were clear of the scene and at least five miles away they would divide the money equally among the three of them and then each one would ride off in a different direction to foil any pursuit.

On the day in question the manager and his cashier arrived at the bank early and were let in the night security guards. As arranged at 0545hrs the two-horse buggy and the four armed guards arrived, and their identities were checked. The manager and his cashier counted the money carefully as it was placed in a sturdy wooden box witnessed by two of the armed guards then the box was locked, and the key given to the senior of the guards.

The box was now taken out and secured in the back of the horse drawn buggy with a guard seated either side of it. The other two guards sat in the front one driving the horses the other at his side. With a wave to the manager, they started their journey to Hope and the two horses trotted lively away down the track. The manager gave a sigh of relief and he and the cashier went back inside the bank to enjoy some coffee the night staff had just made.

The horse drawn buggy made good progress and the four armed security men had decided that if they reached the halfway resting point for the horses early it would give them time to brew up some coffee and cook some breakfast that the early start had forced them to miss. So, the sound of the approaching horse drawn buggy earlier than expected took the waiting three robbers a little bit by surprise but they were well concealed and their horses were tied up further back.

They watched as the four guards jumped from the buggy one freed the horses and took them for a drink in the stream and to their surprise the other three started to make a fire and prepare breakfast. The three robbers waited until the four men were totally engaged in filling their stomachs and their hands had a cup of coffee in them when they struck.

The three robbers with guns drawn just suddenly appeared from out of the trees and within minutes had all four previously armed men securely bound. They took the wooden box from the buggy then tipped the buggy into the ditch. The two horses were untied from the tree they had been secured to and a slap on the rump sent them galloping away up into the hills. Without bothering to find the key they broke open the box and quickly divided the money into their three saddle bags. They then dragged the four bound men about eighty yards away from the track then they tied their money full saddle bags to their saddle pommel. They then rode off together for a couple of hundred yards before briefly conversing then riding off in three separate directions as planned.

Back at the scene of the robbery the four security guards were desperately trying to crawl back to the main track where hopefully someone would pass, and they could raise the alarm. They found they could make the best progress on their backs using their heels to propel them forward but it was a painful business but all four realised they were in deep trouble. It must have taken at least an hour before the first one made it back to the track leading to Hope and just as the second made to join him a man rode up. Within minutes although quite shocked at what he had found the man untied all four men then rode on into Hope to tell the sheriff what had happened.

The four guards however had decided to start to walk back to Fort Worth and face the music and on the way rehearse a story that was believable. Sheriff Jack Masters and his deputy Buck Shaw wasted no time in riding quickly to the scene and once they found the buggy on its side the sequence of events there became clearer.

All they knew was an armed gang had ambushed a bank escort and stolen a large sum of money but thankfully nobody had been hurt. What puzzled Jack and Buck was why had the bank escort stopped to cook breakfast halfway when normally they would drive straight on after a short water break for the horses. And for a armed bank escort to be caught off guard like this said little for their professional standard.

Jack and Buck looked around for tracks of the robbers' horses and eventually found them but were surprised to find that only three robbers were at the scene. They followed the tracks for a few hundred yards then they stopped where clearly some discussion took place. Then the three robbers left in separate directions clearly following a pre-arranged plan and giving Jack and Buck little option other than a return to Hope where it was now four in the afternoon.

It was about now that the four bank guards slowly made their way into Fort Worth dreading what was to come. They had decided on a story all four would stick to which was as they halted at the watering hole for the horses something at the side of the track caused the horses to panic causing the buggy to tip on its side throwing them off. Before they could recover they were confronted by six armed men who disarmed them and tied them hand and foot. Their two horses were freed from their harness to the buggy and ran off into the hills. One of the robbers told them they had thrown a couple of harmless snakes in their path to frighten the horses. The robbers broke open the cash box and divided the money around the six men who then dragged the tightly bound guards some distance from the track and then they rode off.

They called in at the marshal's office before going back to the bank hoping their dishevelled appearance would get them some sympathy. The marshal listened to their story it had the ring of truth but he suspected it was not the complete story, but the main fact was a robbery had taken place and he needed to deal with it. He sent off a team of four men to the scene and told the guards to report to their bank manager. More confident now the four men made their way to the bank and reported to the shocked manager what had happened.

The manager listened to their explanation then he exploded calling them useless and incompetent and when they told him about the horses being frightened by snake's he flatly accused them of lying.

Looking at all four in turn he said, "Those two horses were raised on my farm which was alive with all kinds of snakes. Their reaction would be to stamp on them, not panic as you say. So what really happened?"

The youngest of the four guards was Luke Walker recently married and desperate to keep his job and in a voice he barely recognised as his own he said, "They caught us cooking breakfast Sir."

The manager sat back in his chair. "Thank you Walker, I suspected it would be something like that, but for insurance purposes your original story will go on the records."

The manager paused then said, "This should be a lesson to you all and you will all keep your jobs but only Walker will be staying in Fort Worth you others will be moving on to other banks."

Over the next two days Jack Masters and the marshal of Fort Worth made contact and Jack passed all the information he had, and the search concentrated on three men not six but all that was found were the two buggy horses. They turned up at the trackside to Hope looking in good condition and Jack took them over to Ethan Watts for him to check them over.

On Friday Ethan put the horses on the train to Fort Worth tied securely up on the rear flat open carriage they were in fine condition and the bank manager collected them and took them out to his farm. It was two weeks later when they had a breakthrough in the case when a young man had too much to drink in Dallas and gambled recklessly at cards.

A deputy sheriff observed him lose almost a thousand dollars, but seemed almost unconcerned, so he followed him back to his hotel. The deputy allowed him to settle in his room then he paid him a visit and demanded to know where all this money came from. The man foolishly went for his gun, but the drink had slowed his reactions and the deputy easily disarmed him and placed him under arrest. A search of his room found almost fourteen thousand dollars and now he had to explain where this money had come from.

The next morning when he woke up in the cells now in the custody of the marshal of Dallas he had questions to answer with the marshal anxious to clear up a sequence of robberies and murders all involving large sums of money. The marshal and his team were a shrewd team of operators, and they knew this man had committed a crime to gain the money he had been found with there was no other explanation. A letter found on the man was from his mother and confirmed the man's name was Jacob Lee. He agreed that it was, but he sometimes used the name Lee Jacobs in some of his dealings.

"Well Jake," said the marshal. "We have several crimes around here to solve involving the theft of money but a couple involving large sums like you have were committed involving a murder and that means the rope."

The mention of the rope and a subsequent hanging had now drained the colour from Jacob Lee's face.

Over the next hour he gave the marshal all the details of the robbery that had taken place between Fort Worth and Hope including the names of his other companions. To add more credence to his story he told them that a girl working in the bank's office had given them information about the day and timing of the journey and how much money was involved and she was the sister of one of the robbers. Over the next few days contact between Dallas, Fort Worth and Hope took place and fourteen thousand dollars of the forty five thousand dollars stolen was returned to the Fort Worth bank. One of the girls who had worked in the bank's office had not been seen now for a week.

Chapter Twenty Seven

Within another week wanted posters naming the two other men in the robbery were being circulated all over Texas and the adjoining States with a reasonable artist's description. The bank manager called into his office the young Security Guard and confronted him with the evidence that there had only been three robbers not six. Luke Walker admitted he and the others had lied, but insisted he had been afraid to defy the other three men.

The manager felt some sympathy for the young man as the other three security men were much older and bigger than young Walker, so he just gave him a final warning. It was about a week later that the second of the three robbers using the name of Ben David was arrested in Kansas City after being betrayed by a girlfriend he had become tired of. The Kansas City marshal found almost ten thousand dollars in David's room and when it was suggested this could be linked to a local killing, Ben David very quickly confessed to the robbery on the Fort Worth to Hope trail.

There was some clear evidence that the third member of the gang was in Mexico and there was little chance of bringing him back into the States, so it was decided to put the two captured men on trial at Fort Worth. For those expecting a dramatic trial they were to be disappointed as the two men pleaded Guilty hoping for a more lenient sentence as no violence had been used in the robbery.

The defence counsel made much of the original statements by the four bank guards about there being six robbers and had the admitted public convulsed in laughter. The Officials from the bank were not best pleased that the bank security had been made to look inadequate and their employees liars. The judge in sentencing took into account the two men had no previous convictions known to them and in view of their guilty plea he sentenced them to five years in the state prison.

The Fort Worth bank manager was moved to the Dallas City branch, but as deputy manager and Luke Walker was considered fortunate to still be employed by the bank.

The ranch owner's of the Circle 'O' and the Tall 'T' had been paid their money a long time ago and had not had to await the outcome of the trial. But lessons had been learnt and in future the money would be transferred by train which would be quicker and safer. There had been talk for some time about a Wednesday train service to Hope giving them three opportunities a week to visit Fort Worth with most people supporting the idea it was to be considered by the Railroads Board. As the Board only met four times a year it was not a matter that would be immediately decided. The railroad never made any money over the Hope service, but the state and national government made sure they did not make a loss either by paying a subsidy.

In Dallas the sheriff had three brothers in custody Seth, Mark and Jesse Younger were all charged with the murder of two elderly sisters while robbing their home. Because of the anger in the city a trial was to be held elsewhere and the nearest suitable place was Fort Worth which had its own Prison and execution facilities. But first the sheriff had to get his prisoners safely there and he decide to move them at night in an open wagon handcuffed and their ankles secured in a gang chain.

There would be two armed guards and the driver on the wagon and the sheriff would have two other men with him so there would be a total of six guards. However, the younger brothers had friends who were reluctant to see their friends taken to Fort Worth and face almost a certain hanging. So, four of them decided that as the movement of their friends would take place at night a night ambush would be the easiest way to set them free and selected a spot on the way to Fort Worth suitable for this purpose.

Fortunately, the sheriff learned of this plot and on the night of the movement of the prisoners to Fort Worth two wagons left Dallas. The first a few hundred yards ahead of the one carrying the prisoners contained six armed men specially deputised for the occasion with the deputy sheriff in charge. It was almost two o'clock in the morning when the first wagon reached the selected ambush position, and the ambush was sprung. One thing the ambushers had to do was direct their fire at first the driver and then the guards and above all avoid hitting the men they intended to rescue. This restricted their weight of fire, but not of course that of the defenders who launched a withering response to the attack upon them. Within a few minutes the ambush had proved a total disaster and two of the ambushers lay dead and the other two were wounded and no longer a threat and were quickly taken into custody. One of the guards on the wagon had suffered a quite serious but not life threatening wound and a few minutes later the other wagon containing the prisoners came by.

Then both wagons carried on into Fort Worth first to deliver the prisoners and obtain treatment for the wounded and charge the new set of prisoners with the appropriate offences.

It was now almost seven o'clock in the morning and the doctor was roused to check his new patients and the marshal was already waiting to receive his prisoners to await their trial. It was quite a gathering at the police barracks for breakfast as the events of the night were re-run with much drama. Then they were given some beds to catch up on their sleep before they were all to make their statements. At four o'clock in the afternoon they all made their statements in the marshal's office and once this was done they were given a hot meal and then they decided to start their return journey to Dallas.

Two week later the trial in Fort Worth began of the younger brothers charged with murder and robbery. They pleaded guilty to robbery but not guilty to murder and so a jury was sworn in and the trial began in a packed court room.

The death of the two elderly sisters was explained to the court and that they had been found by their regular cleaner when she arrived one morning. The two sisters who were in their seventies were found in their night clothes with blood and bruises to their faces where clearly they had been subjected to violence. The cupboards and drawers had been crudely searched and the rest of the house ransacked. A day later Seth Younger had tried to sell some items of jewellery to a local gambler who tipped off the sheriff. The brothers were arrested, and many items identified as belonging to the sisters were identified were found in their possession.

The local doctor who had examined the two sisters at the scene of their death was called as an expert witness and asked to describe their injuries by the prosecuting counsel. The doctor stated that he had dealt with injuries of a similar nature normally caused by a fistfight in a drunken brawl, then added, "Both sisters were non-drinkers."

The defence counsel stated that the defendants denied striking the two women and was it not just possible that their injuries were caused by a fall?

"They had multiple bruises to both sides of their faces in a fall it would be just on the side of the impact with the ground." said the doctor.

That concluded the evidence and the judge briefly summed up and then sent the jury out to consider their verdict. Ten minutes later the jury returned, and the judge asked the foreman of the jury if they had reached a verdict on which they were all agreed and the foreman replied that they had.

The judge then asked the foreman of the jury to read out their verdict and the foreman stood up and said, "We the jury find all the accused Guilty as charged of the offence of Murder."

The judge asked, "Is that the verdict of you all?" One the jury replied, "It is your honour." The judge then turned to the three accused and told them to stand then said "You have been found guilty of the murder of two sisters named on the warrant and it is the sentence of this court that you be taken to a place of execution prescribed by the state and hanged by the neck until dead and may God have mercy on your souls."

There was a few seconds silence in the court then as the judge disappeared there was a great deal of rejoicing at the verdict and as the prisoners were led away to Fort Worth Prison they were spat on. It had been the ruling in Texas for some time that in cases involving a multiple execution all the defendants should be executed at the same time.

This posed an immediate problem for the executioner at the Fort Worth prison because the scaffold there was built to hang one man at a time. So work began immediately to enlarge it so that the trap door when opened would eject three bodies and the work took a week to complete. Executions now were no longer a public spectacle as in the past but a selected number of the public were invited to see justice done. The view of the execution was really quite restricted anyone invited to watch would see the person placed on the scaffold and the rope noose placed around his neck. There would be a few seconds delay as the Prison Chaplain read a final prayer then the trap door would be sprung and the accused would disappear from sight into the void below. In the past the void would have been left open so people could witness any final convulsions of the dying man but now that is closed from view.

The day came for the execution of the three brothers and about twenty members of the public had been invited to see their end some of them from Dallas. At the time appointed the three prisoners were each brought out from the main prison each had a guard on each arm and the hands were secured behind their backs. They were brought up onto the scaffold and a noose was draped over each man's neck. The executioner made some final adjustments to the rope nooses and the chaplain began his prayer.

The youngest of the three brothers was the only one to show any emotion as a large wet patch appeared between his legs. Then as the prayer finished the trap was sprung and the three bodies disappeared from view into the void below with only the tautness of the three ropes to indicate their fate. There was a collective sigh from the watching crowd and they quickly dispersed out of the prison. The executioner and his helper allowed some hanging time then went down below the scaffold with the doctor to confirm death.

A month later the trial took place of the two surviving ambushers who had been part of the gang of four trying to free the Younger brothers. Hoping to receive a lighter sentence both men pleaded guilty hoping that the fact that they had been wounded might persuade the judge that they had suffered already. However the judge was not very sympathetic and took a dim view of anyone attempting to assist someone to escape custody and gave them five years in the State Prison. So Jack Masters and Buck Shaw who had expected to give evidence had a wasted journey to Fort Worth. However, as it was the train day between Fort Worth and Hope they were able to place their horses on the flat bed truck at the train's rear and arrive home earlier than expected. The main street in Hope was much tidier now that the gravel had settled and when it rained it no longer became a sea of mud.

The grape growing had brought more business into the town and the off shoot into the separate wine making industry was beginning to take shape. New houses were being built on the edge of the town and there was no shortage of work. 'Ma's house' did good business and provided drink, food and on Friday and Saturdays nights some female entertainment for the ranch hands.

Hope was now a bustling town clearly on the up with a well behaved community and well policed by Jack Masters and Buck Shaw. Ethan Watts was chairman of the committee that ran Hopes affairs and there had been suggestions that it should have its own weekly newspaper and the publishers in Fort Worth had expressed interest in publishing the weekly Hope Gazette. It was decided to put it to the people of Hope to decide if it wanted its own weekly paper so a date was set for a ballot to decide the issue.

Chapter Twenty Eight

After a very leisurely journey west allowing Tex to make the pace Todd Raven found himself close to the Arkansas River and the bustling large town of Little Rock. He fairly quickly found a suitable place for both of them to stay in a town becoming prosperous because of the growing of cotton which was now the major industry. Having arrived quite late in the day Todd went to see the bank manager the next morning and was made very welcome. As he left the bank he met the sheriff and he realised their paths had crossed before when at that time the now sheriff was anything but law abiding. Todd Raven could tell by the expression on the sheriffs face as they met that he too had been recognised from that time ago. They had a coffee together and though not discussing old times the sheriff made it plain he would prefer if his past just remained there. Todd was quite agreeable to that everyone had a right to move on and this man had never done him any harm.

Little Rock had its fair share of bars and gambling places and the sheriff advised Todd of the ones to avoid which always seemed to be those closest to the river. He found one in the more respectable part of Little Rock during his second night called Belle's Place it was clean, well lit and the bar was far enough away from the card tables as not to distract the players. He had a meal there and played cards for about three hours and came away just a few dollars better off than when he went in.

During the time he was there not a single fist fight took place though in the distance he could hear the sound of gun shots. At the boarding house he was staying at over breakfast the next morning two of the elderly women who were almost permanent residents complained to the owner about the gunfire. The man whose wife was busy in the kitchen told the women that the sheriff had dealt with the matter and the two men would be buried later in the day.

This satisfied the two old dears and one of them turned to Todd Raven and said, "We are lucky to have such a fine man as sheriff here in Little Rock."

Her companion nodded then said, "He is also fast on the draw and a good shot."

Then both women burst into a fit of the giggles and left the breakfast table. Todd spent the morning giving Tex some exercise trotting around the outskirts of the growing town then wandered a few miles further out. He found a particular spot which he found very attractive and peaceful and let Tex lead for a couple of miles. Here he came across a small ranch where a young man was busy erecting a For Sale sign on a boundary fence. Not that far off a youngish woman probably his wife was among a group of young steers the expression on both of the youngster's faces was one of complete misery.

Todd rode up to the young man and said, "Is this your property you are selling?"

The young man looked up at Todd and he could see the young man's eyes were full of tears.

"Yes Sir. Unfortunately we have been forced to sell because we cannot repay the loan from the bank and they have already given us an extension but we still cannot pay so we have to sell to repay our debts."

"Take that sign down." said Todd. "I think you and your wife and I should have a little chat before you go any further with this selling idea."

Ten minutes later Todd and the young couple were seated in the small but beautifully kept farm house and over the next hour the young wife gave them lunch and it was explained to Todd what the nature of the debt was. Their stock would not cover the debt because they had fallen behind on the interest to be paid even though the bank had twice extended their time to pay.

To the young couple the sum involved meant only one thing everything had to be sold there was no other way. Todd Raven did the sums this was no problem to him but how could he make this young couple still believe it was their farm? It came to him in a flash he would be a sleeping partner in a three person partnership. He spent another two hours at the farm explaining what he proposed arranging for the pair who were Mark and Mary Walters to be at the bank in Little Rock at nine thirty the next morning.

On return to Little Rock Todd placed Tex in the stable and went to the boarding house and enjoyed the evening meal. Later he went again to Belle's Place and spent two hours there and bet heavily on cards and the wheel and came away a thousand dollars richer. As he walked back to the boarding house he knew he was being followed and slipped down an alley. As his pursuer walked by Todd stepped out and rammed his gun against his head then took the man's guns and tossed them in a nearby water butt.

He was about to give the man a smack in the mouth for being a nuisance when the man croaked, "I'm a deputy sheriff and the boss asked me to make sure you were OK."

Todd apologised then helped the man retrieve his guns from the rain barrel. Then together they walked the last few hundred yards to the boarding house where Todd said to the man, "Thanks for the escort and nobody will hear of the misunderstanding."

Later just before sleep finally claimed him for the day Todd reflected on the two young Walters situation and how that last act of lawlessness five years ago at the gold mine had changed his life forever. The next morning after breakfast he made his way to the bank and found Mark and Mary Walters waiting outside. Their faces lit up when he arrived and it crossed Todd's mind that perhaps they had doubted he would turn up. They went in and asked to see the manager and were soon explaining to the rather surprised official the nature of their business.

The manager was of course delighted he could get a debt off his books in such a satisfactory way and was aware even this outlay would not make Todd Raven a poor man. He did however ask if this partnership was to be put into some legal frame work and offered to put the work in train. But Todd said it was not necessary and with the managers receipt on the loan papers they left the bank and Todd was invited out to the ranch for a celebration lunch.

Afterwards Mark gave him a tour of the complete spread and Todd Raven knew then that the ranch was in good hands. Later he rode back in to Little Rock and spent some time in one other gambling joint's where it was easy to spot what games were straight and which were crooked. He won a couple of hundred dollars at cards then doubled it on the wheel then collected his winnings and went to leave the club. As he reached the door two heavies stood up and barred his way out. Then a smartly dressed man appeared and said ,"The boss would like to see you Mr Raven."

"Do I have a choice?" said Todd, "Of course" said the smartly dressed man. "But the boss would be disappointed."

"Then lead on." said Todd and followed the man up the stairs and into a well furnished office where a gray haired man rose from his chair to greet them.

The man stepped forward and extended his hand and said, "We meet again Mr Raven and this time neither of us is firing a gun at each other."

Todd suddenly snapped his fingers. "Laredo, we were in rival smuggling gangs and got involved in a shoot out. But I thought I killed you?"

The man laughed.

"For a few minutes I thought you had. But my brother got me to a doctor and I survived. But you have done well for yourself and so have I so let the past stay in the past and have a drink to the future."

Todd spent an hour with his old adversary and parted the best of friends with an invitation to visit and dine at club members rates. The next morning after breakfast he took a walk up the main street and ran into the sheriff and was invited to take coffee in his office. As they sat talking one of his deputies walked in who Todd had tangled with the other night. The sheriff introduced him as Al and said, "You may not be aware of it Todd, but he has be making sure you stay safe on the way home at night".

Todd grabbed Al's hand without comment and shook it and thanked him and in doing so made a friend for life. The sheriff then asked about Todd Raven's meeting with an old acquaintance at the 'Pink Lady' and could there be a problem there.

Todd laughed and told the sheriff that just before the Civil War he and his brother were involved in some smuggling in Laredo and they had clashed several times with the man who now owned the Pink Lady but that is now all in the past.

The sheriff grunted then said, "The owner of the Pink Lady does not have a reputation for being a forgiving man Mr Raven."

Todd laughed before saying, "Well in my case he has just given me free club membership for old time's sake."

Later that morning Todd took Tex out for a ride to the Walters ranch and had lunch there and discussed with them both some young stock they wanted to bring in to fully stock the place.

Later that afternoon he returned to his boarding house and had a rest before dinner then later in the evening he made his way to the Pink Lady where he joined the owner of the club in some fairly high stake card games. By midnight the only two players left at the table with a pile of winnings in front of them were Todd and the owner of the Pink Lady, Nathan Burke. The two looked at each other and at their winnings then they both decided that was it for the night. Though Todd insisted he did not need one Nathan Burke insisted he was escorted back to his lodgings.

The next day after breakfast Todd rode Tex out to the ranch and gave the Walters his winnings which were just over a thousand dollars. This covered the cost of the extra stock which on arrival had a fine young male calf which Todd insisted they call 'Ike'.

Most nights now Todd spent at the Pink Lady not always at the gambling tables sometimes he and Nathan Burke would just sit up in his office talking over the past.

Both of their brothers were now dead and they had lost other friends as well most of them in gun fights. Despite their less than respectable earlier careers both men were now quite successful business men and considering the time they lived in reasonably law abiding.

Over the following weeks they became good friends and that friendship was sealed one evening quite late as

Todd was about to leave the club. A man had lost quite heavily at cards on one of the other tables and had then been drinking quite heavily at the bar.

Nathan Burke was on his way across the room to his office when the man drew his gun and confronted him saying, "Die you cheating swine."

Todd just drew and fired hitting the man in the shoulder, which spun him to the ground and the gun was quickly removed from his hand. A doctor was called and the man was carried away for treatment and the sheriff was informed. A grateful Nathan Burke thanked Todd over a couple of glasses of whiskey but strangely enough this incident had spelled the end of Todd's time in Little Rock. He spent another week mostly out on the ranch where everything was going well and the new stock were settling in. But now he knew it was time to move on once again and he said his goodbyes and prepared for the journey.

Chapter Twenty Nine

A sequence of severe storms had hit the southern States of America towards the end of the year and the most recent one had left the Snake River near Hope at its highest level for years. The Railroad junction at Hope was at the moment unusable being flooded under almost three feet of water and the outlying districts of Hope were also flooded. The ranches to the north and south were on slightly higher ground and so escaped the worst of the weather. For almost a week the tracks were so muddy it was almost impossible for a horse drawn vehicle to move but Jack's store was well stocked so no one went hungry.

At last the river started to go down and the skies began to clear and in a few days things began to improve and by the end of the week the railroad line was clear of water and the line could be checked. Three days later the train service resumed and Jack's wife Jane gave him a list of goods to replenish their stock from Fort Worth. With school out for a few days Simon came with him and they had an enjoyable day in Fort Worth and came back loaded with goods.

To his surprise Jack had found parts of Fort Worth still flooded and heard that other towns not that far away the people had needed to take to the hills to survive. Gradually things began to return to normal, but the abnormal weather had caused a great deal of damage. Strangely enough the grape plantations had survived remarkably well and had not suffered any damage.

Sheriff Jack Masters and his deputy Buck Shaw were drinking a mid morning coffee when they heard a commotion outside near the doctors office. They went outside and found two ranch hands from the Circle 'O' had just been brought in they had both been badly injured in a rock fall while clearing a blocked track after the flooding. After a quick examination the doctor told Jack that they needed to be taken to Fort Worth hospital urgently. Jack got his horse and buggy ready and he and the doctor with the help of Buck Shaw got the two badly injured men aboard and secured in the back.

So Jack and the doctor made off to Fort Worth at the best speed possible leaving Buck Shaw in charge at Hope. The track side trail to Fort Worth was now in quite good condition following the floods and by resting the horses for ten minutes every hour they made Fort Worth in just less than four hours. But sadly on arrival they found one of the men had died during the journey but the doctors at the hospital felt the other man had a good chance now of recovery. Jack stabled the horses overnight and he and the doctor were found a room in the staff quarters at the hospital for the night.

After breakfast the next morning the pair after thanking the staff for their hospitality started back to Hope as they both needed to be there. They arrived back just in time for a late lunch with a queue of patients eager to see the doctor. In Jack's absence Buck Shaw had been called to arrest a man who was not local and had caused a disturbance at 'Ma's House'. The man who had been armed and was quite drunk but was now asleep in one of the cells.

Jack and Buck looked through their wanted posters, but the man now in their cells resembled none of the desperate characters depicted on the twenty odd posters they had. Jack had a look at the guns Buck had removed from him they were modern and well-kept and the type favoured by a gunfighter.

The man was now awake and was asking for some coffee and something to eat and Jack Masters told him that he could have both if he gave them his name and what he was doing in Hope. The man complied saying his name was Seth Rogers and he was looking for work, perhaps with his brother who was a ranch hand at the Circle 'O'. Jack asked him straight out if he was a gunfighter and the man gave a strange smile then said, "I have been in Mexico for the last four years as a personal guard for a rich and ruthless business man and it did require me to use my guns."

They gave him some coffee and something to eat and then Jack rode out to the Circle 'O' to see if a brother with a surname of Rogers worked there.

Jack went straight to see the foreman who had all the details of his ranch hands and the casual workers and asked if he had someone called Rogers on his payroll.

"Well I did." said the foreman. "But the poor chap got injured with another guy and you took them into Fort Worth Hospital."

Jack then told him that one of the injured men had died on the way, but he did not know who. He then went on to explain that they had a man in their cells who said he was the brother and had come to Hope looking for work hopefully with his brother at the Circle 'O'.

The foreman shrugged then said, "Well Mack Rogers is a good worker and if his brother is the same there is work here for him."

Jack left the ranch and rode back to Hope it all depended on who had died on that journey to Fort Worth and this could all end in a satisfactory manner or in a total disaster. When he arrived in Hope Jack went straight to the cells and spoke to Seth Rogers. He told him the full story of how two injured men from the Circle 'O' had been brought in to see the doctor and their injuries were so bad the doctor ordered their immediate transfer to the Hospital at Fort Worth.

"I am now told by the foreman that one of those men was your brother, Mack, but the doctor and I who took them in to Fort Worth did not know their names. But now we come to the most difficult part." said Jack. "During the journey one of the men sadly died, but the other man is in the hospital at Fort Worth and is making good progress."

Seth Rogers stood up. "So you don't know if my brother is alive or dead and I can't find out stuck in here".

Jack Masters looked the man in the eyes then said, "I'll give you a caution for being a bloody fool at 'Ma's House' then I will ride into Fort Worth with you hopefully to see your brother, but your guns stay here until the matter is resolved is that clear."

Seth Rogers was only too pleased to agree to those terms and he and Jack Masters wasted no time at all in preparing to ride into Fort Worth. But it was just past mid-day now and they would have to stay in Fort Worth overnight so Jack quickly informed his wife Jane.

They set off after a hot drink and made good progress resting the horses every hour to keep them fresh and they finally arrived in Fort Worth at four thirty in the afternoon. They stabled the horses and went on straight to the hospital where Jack Masters explained to the senior doctor there that he had brought Seth Rogers the brother of one of the two injured men from the ranch admitted the other day.

The doctor glanced at his list and smiled then said to Seth Rogers, "I am glad to tell you Mr Rogers that your brother is doing well. You may go in and see him, but please don't stay more than thirty minutes."

Forty minutes later Seth Rogers came back to where Jack was waiting in the passage with a big smile on his face.

"He is looking pretty good thanks to you and the doctor getting him here quickly and I won't forget that sheriff." said Rogers then asked, "Where do we stay for the night?"

They stayed in a nearby boarding house which Jack had used in the past it was clean and the food was good and after breakfast in the morning Jack told Seth Rogers that he could stay here for a few days if he wished. Jack knew Rogers had plenty of money so that was not a problem but Rogers said he wanted to come back to Hope to collect his guns as he felt undressed without them. Also he wanted to visit the Circle 'O' to see about work and tell them about his brother Mack.

That sounded fine to Jack Masters, so an hour later they started on back to Hope followed the same routine with the horses and arrived in time for some lunch in the sheriff's office consisting of thick soup and crusty bread and enough for three. Afterwards Jack gave Seth Rogers back his guns and he rode out to the Circle 'O' with the news of his brother and hoping to find work. The next time Jack saw Seth Rogers was when the Circle 'O' came into Hope for their weekly knees up at 'Ma's House' and he was collecting their guns at the entrance to Hope.

They had a brief chat and Jack learned that Mack was to be discharged to the care of the ranch next week and was almost fully recovered. Seth also said how much he enjoyed working on the ranch and how well he got on with rest of the hands there. Later that night as the Circle 'O' ranch hands were leaving most of them drunk Seth Rogers took charge of all their guns from Jack Masters saying, "We don't want any accidents do we sheriff."

A couple of weeks later Jack saw the foreman of the Circle 'O' in Hope and asked how Seth Rogers was doing. The foreman put his hand on Jack's shoulder and said, "You did me a favour sending him out to me Jack he's my top hand now and I could not do without him."

There was a mixture of nationalities living quite happily together in Hope after all the native American is the Indian so really that should not be surprising. But one nationality they were wary of sadly was the Mexicans and when two young Mexican riders came into Hope one evening the sheriff and his deputy were immediately informed.

They booked in for a couple of nights at 'Ma's House' and though the lady running the place was not keen to have them she needed the business and they paid up front. Jack Masters and Buck Shaw had no reason to question the two men and decided to wait until the next day and then pay them a casual visit. They had already checked through their wanted posters and there was no one of Mexican origin listed in them.

After breakfast the next morning Jack Masters went by himself to 'Ma's House' to have a chat with the two new comers to Hope. He found them quite pleasant and they said they were brothers and their names were Miguel and Jose Gomez and they were looking for work.

Jack asked them what kind of work were they interested in and both men immediately said, "Ranch work."

Jack Masters thought this strange because there are plenty of cattle ranches in Mexico. He decided to put it to them straight so he said, "Why come here looking for work when your country has plenty of ranches offering work, have you both been in trouble back home?"

The brothers looked at one another clearly uncomfortable at the question then one turned to the other and said, "Tell him."

The brother called Miguel turned to Jack Masters and said, "We both had worked for Senor Ramon Corsairs for almost five years and enjoyed our work on his large ranch. He has two beautiful daughters and recently Senor Corsairs has instructed us to teach them to ride.. But these lovely girls are not shy. In fact they are very forward and they invited my brother and me to take liberties with them and their father found out. As a result Jose and me had to flee from Mexico as the angry father would kill us and that is the truth".

Jack Masters found the story totally believable both these men were young and good looking and no doubt a rich and powerful angry father would believe anything his precious daughters told him. He told them about the two ranches not that far away one to the north of Hope and one to the south. They said they would try the one to the north first as it was the furthest away from Mexico and the vengeful father. Jack went back and told the story to Buck Shaw who agreed with Jack that it had the ring of truth. It was about a week later that Jack Masters heard that both brothers were now working at the Circle 'O' and had fitted in nicely with the rest of the hands there.

For some time Jane had been urging Jack to build an extension to the store so they could stock more clothing and he at last had found someone to do the work. It took the best part of two weeks to complete but in the end it satisfied Jane and that was what mattered.

One afternoon Jack was called to 'Ma's House' as a stranger had arrived who had booked in for two nights and was looking for two young Mexicans. Jack Masters went over and straight away he knew this was a gunman after the two young Mexican lads. There was also something familiar about this man and Jack realised he had a poster on him. As a result, he did not give the man any chance to draw and took him into custody. Then after a night in the cells he was taken on the Friday train to Fort Worth and handed over to the marshal there. Eventually, the man went for trial in Dallas charged with two killings. He was found not guilty on one charge, but guilty on the other, but for some reason was given ten years instead of the death penalty.

Chapter Thirty

Todd Raven decided to travel north for a change and settled for Springfield almost two hundred miles away. He made sure he had enough travel rations for the trip and allowed about eight days for the journey. The trip north was largely uneventful he moved through a couple of very slow moving wagons trains during the journey. On arrival he found a decent boarding house and nearby was a stables where he made sure Tex was to be well looked after.

Two sisters that had been widowed during the war ran the boarding house and their late husbands who were both sergeants would have been proud of the way they ran their immaculate establishment. Springfield was a farming area but some mining had begun but of course it was the birth place of Abraham Lincoln who had been President of the United States. There were four other guests at the boarding house all travelling on business and not Todd Raven's type at all.

After dinner that evening he went out with his guns on but had a light coat on which hid them from view. The boarding house was in the quieter part of Springfield and it was a good twenty minute walk to find the livelier area with about half a dozen bars and gambling joints fairly closely bunched together.

It now about nine thirty and the places were beginning to become busy so Todd poked his head into a couple of places to see where the most action was. The 'Black Stocking' looked promising so he went in and selected a table in the gambling section and ordered a drink. Within ten minutes three men had joined him at the table and one of the clubs dealers came over and asked if they were ready to play. They all nodded and the dealer dealt the cards and within the first few minutes Todd could see that at the moment it was a straight game. In the first five games the dealer known as the banker in this type of card game had won once. Stakes doubled in the next two games and Todd won one and the banker the other then the stakes trebled and as the cards were dealt one of the players accused the dealer of cheating.

The dealer raised his hand and two heavies hurried over to the table and the dealer pointed to the accuser and said, "This man has accused me of cheating I want him thrown out."

As the two heavies grabbed the man Todd Raven stood up and said, "Just a minute at least give the man a chance to explain his complaint."

This confused the two heavies as normally nobody argued with the dealer and the man said he had seen the dealer slip some cards from his sleeve. Todd leaned forward and felt the sleeve of the man's jacket and sure enough there were cards pushed up in the sleeve.

Todd turned to one of the two heavies, "I think you should get the owner over here to sort this out."

The man walked away to fetch the owner and Todd walked over to the bar to get a drink he had just collected it and had turned to return to the table when he heard a shot fired and he saw the man who made the complaint fall to the ground.

The man who had shot him was the dealer who stood with a gun still in his hand. As Todd moved quickly back to the table he saw a gun slide across the floor and come to rest by the body of the man who made the complaint. The dealer pointed to the dead man and said, "I had no choice he drew on me and I have witnesses." He pointed to one of the heavies.

Todd Raven knew what he was up against so he just said, "Well someone needs to get the sheriff."

Five minutes passed and the sheriff and his deputy arrived they questioned the dealer and heard his version of events and those of the heavy who backed him up. Then the sheriff turned to Todd Raven who told him he had seen the gun sliding across the floor and coming to rest by the body of the dead man. He was asked if he had seen who had propelled the gun across the floor but he had not. The sheriff was now in a difficult position the dealer insisted he had no choice as the dead man had drawn first and he had a witness to back that up, but someone else had seen a gun slid over to the dead body after the shooting.

The sheriff knew the witness was employed as was the dealer by the owner of the 'Black Stocking' and would have to back up the dealer. Nobody else in the club was able to help they were either looking elsewhere or were too drunk and confused to care. The sheriff decided to sleep on it overnight and talk it over with the local judge in the morning. He had the gun the dead man was alleged to have had it certainly had not been fired but it had been well looked after and a strange weapon for a salesman to carry.

The next morning the sheriff managed to see the other two men who had been at the card table but had left before the trouble started. They knew the dead man and said they had never known him to carry a gun in his life and in the Civil War he had been a stretcher bearer in the medical section. He then went to see the judge and told him the full story and the judge who was not a fan of clubs like the 'Black Stocking' was all for taking the case to trial and letting a jury decide the truth of the matter.

The problem for the sheriff was that his main witness was Todd Raven and if anything should happen to him the trial could not take place. The Dealer had been bailed and his movements were restricted and the trial would take place next week. The sheriff had made a rather shrewd move in holding the owner of the 'Black Stocking' responsible for the safety of Todd Raven. If anything should happen to Mr Raven all of the owners licences to operate in Springfield would be cancelled for five years.

The Dealer who had expected his boss to eliminate Raven was furious when he found out that the owners business was more important than he was. At last the day came for the trial and the court room was full and a jury had been selected and a foreman chosen. The prosecutor outlined the case stated that in a card game which had started well in the 'Black Stocking' club had suddenly stopped when the man later shot dead had accused the Dealer of cheating. One of the other players in the game found cards secreted in the dealer's sleeve and the club owner was sent for.

The prosecutor then went onto say that the other three card players left the table at this stage two not to return and the other went to the bar to collect a drink. It was as the man who went to the bar began to return to the table that the shot was fired and he saw his fellow player fall to the ground.

Then the prosecutor paused for dramatic effect and said, "But this witness will tell you that he then saw a gun slide across the floor to rest near the body."

The prosecutor then went on to say that of course the dealer will claim that the dead man drew first and he had no option than to defend himself and no doubt a fellow employee of the 'Black Stocking' will confirm his story. The prosecutor then called the two men who had been at the table with the victim and had known him for years in business and socially. Over the next thirty minutes they confirmed that the dead man had an aversion to guns as his record in the Civil War would show and both men stated that they had never seen him involved in any act of violence what so ever.

They were cross examined by the defence counsel but stuck to their evidence and then the prosecutor called Todd Raven to give evidence. Todd said his piece confirming that the gun was slid over to the body of the dead man within a second or so of him falling to the floor. He was asked if he had seen who propelled the gun across the floor but he admitted he had not. The defence counsel then asked him if he had been drinking, and Todd said, "No that is why I went to the bar for my first drink of the evening."

He was asked if he had been at the 'Black Stocking' before and Todd said he had. The defence counsel looked at his notes then said, "Could it be, Mr Raven, that you have lost money at the tables at this club and this is your way of extracting revenge?"

Todd Raven smiled then said, "No Sir, during my short time in Springfield I have been quite lucky at the tables of the 'Black Stocking' and I have checked my notes and to date I have won almost a thousand dollars."

A ripple of laughter went round the court Room and the defence counsel said, "No further questions".

That concluded the prosecution case and lunch was taken with an adjournment of one hour with the judge instructing the jury to restrict their drinking or face a heavy fine. When the court resumed it was now the turn of the defence to make their case and the accused was their first witness. He stated that he was a professional card player and did not need to cheat and the card caught in his sleeve had been an unfortunate accident which could happen when cards are dealt at speed. He had no choice but to defend himself when the man who had complained suddenly pulled a gun. He was then cross examined by the prosecutor but stuck to his story. Next to give evidence was the 'heavy' called to the table he backed up the dealer's story word for word and had obviously been coached because he was using words which certainly were not part of his limited vocabulary.

When he was cross examined by the prosecutor his very limited intelligence became obvious when clearly he did not understand the wording of even the easiest of questions. The judge decided that the man's evidence should be treated with the utmost caution and instructed the jury so. It was then left for the judge to sum up and he did so in just over thirty minutes and then sent the jury out.

They were out for just over an hour then asked for advice from the judge as they were split down the middle. He had all the jury back in court and asked them if they needed more time to consider a majority decision but they said that none of them would change their minds. So the judge ruled a hung-jury and set next week for a new trial to start. So exactly a week later another jury was sworn in and the trial started again and the same evidence was presented in the case as before. No new evidence was offered by the prosecution or the defence and by three o'clock in the afternoon the jury were sent out to consider their verdict.

They were out just over the hour when the judge was informed that they had reached a decision that they were all agreed on. With all the usual formality the court reassembled and the judge ordered the jury to return then he put the question to the jury foreman. "Do you find the prisoner guilty or not guilty of murder?"

There was a slight pause as the foreman glanced at the paper in his hand and then he said, "We the jury find the prisoner not guilty your honour."

The judge ordered the prisoner to be released from custody and with a smirk on his face the dealer hurried from the court House. He left Springfield later that evening and a week later was shot dead in Memphis during a card game.

Todd Raven spent another six months in Springfield as the younger of the two widows had decided he deserved some special attention, which he appreciated.

Chapter Thirty One

Fort Worth Prison was having some alterations carried out to improve its security and that included raising the height of the boundary wall by four feet. It was common practise to use trustees to do some of the inside heavy labouring cutting the cost of the improvement contract. Ten trustees had been selected to do this work in digging the trench to reinforce the base of the perimeter wall to allow for the extra height. Four of these that had been selected had spent months in behaving in such a way as to receive lavish praise from their jailers and achieve recommendation for the role they aimed for.

They knew that at times they would have to work just outside the wall and that would give them the opportunity to escape and a friend on the outside would on certain days be near with horses, food and clothing to make this possible.

There is a nearby park like area near the prison so a man exercising some horses was not unusual. It was on the fourth day of the reconstruction programme and things had gone well and the initial high level of security that had been evident to start with was beginning to lapse as the trustees were working well with limited supervision.

The four were working under the supervision of Mr Richards an elderly Officer approaching retirement and who had been wounded during the Civil War and needed to sit down every so often. They were on the outside corner of the wall and the view of all the other officer's there was obstructed so they decided that the time was now right so they quickly grabbed Mr Richards and gagged and tied him up. They could have knocked him out but he was a decent old stick and they did not wish to harm him.

They quickly moved over to the grassy area and spotted their friend and the horses and signalled to him and he quickly came over. Less than five minutes later the four men had changed and were riding out of Fort Worth initially along the track towards Hope but then intended to head north into the hills. Their helper returned to his home in

Fort Worth knowing that he would be well rewarded for his actions. It had been at least fifteen minutes before the unfortunate Mr Richards had been found he was badly shaken but otherwise unhurt.

It was a couple of hours later that someone reported seeing four men riding out of Fort Worth towards Hope and the marshal could arrange a posse to pursue them. The marshal and his five man posse arrived in Hope as it was getting dark and told sheriff Jack Masters all about the escape. Jack suggested that they overnight in Hope and make a fresh start in the morning and he would come with them and they accepted that idea and had some food and would sleep in the community hall.

Jack told Jane and his children of their plans and Simon wanted to come with him but his father reminded him he had to go to school. The next morning after the posse had all had breakfast Jack Masters joined up with them leaving Buck Shaw in charge. They set off across the Snake River and made their way up into the hills but it was mid-day before they caught a sight of the trail the four men had left but the horse dung was now quite dry.

Not long after that they found where the four escapees had spent the night and they began to realise how far ahead of them the four men could be. At noon they rested their horses for thirty minutes at a mountain spring then refreshed they started off again through the boulder strewn country. Suddenly their lead rider came across a rider-less horse seeking some grass in the rocky terrain it still had its saddle in place. Jack Masters dismounted and quickly examined it and the reason it had been abandoned became clear it had gone lame.

So now the four men were restricted to three horses and that would slow them up unless the unfortunate lame horse rider was abandoned like his horse. One thing did concern Jack and that was two fairly old men had a place up in these rocky hills east of where they were at the moment. He mentioned it to the marshal but he doubted if the four men knew of this.

Unfortunately, this was where the four men were now heading, as one of the four prisoners had visited the two old men just before he went to prison, with the nephew of one of the men. They hoped to obtain more food and some guns and replace the horse. One thing now was in the favour of the following posse and that was they were catching up with the prisoners and the extra weight on the horse meant it was leaving a track much easier to follow. It also became clear that now these men were heading east and Jack's warning to the marshal began to make more sense.

The marshal asked Jack if there was a quicker way of getting to the old men's place.

Jack gave the matter a moment's thought then said, "Give me one man marshal and we will quickly ride down for a mile or so then pick up the quicker trail to the old men's shack."

The marshal agreed and Jack and one man set off riding back down the rocky hills then round to the east until they found the usual track which led up to the shack where the two old men lived.

It was late in the afternoon when Jack and his companion reached the shack and saw the two old men out in their small vegetable garden. They greeted Jack Masters with a smile and they both said, "Nice to see you again sheriff."

Jack told the men the full story of what was happening while his companion took their horses into a shed at the rear. Jack asked if they had any visitors lately and one of the men said, "Oh two years ago my nephew brought a friend up here but I heard since from my nephew that the fellow is now in prison."

"Well," said Jack, "It could be that that man and his three other friends are heading here for food, guns and a horse or two."

"Well we only have old Cochise and he's not built for speed." said the old man. "And as for guns and food, yes we have them alright."

Not long after it became dark and Jack and his companion took it in turns to keep watch and were kept well provided for with coffee and something to eat. It was about two in the morning when Jack's companion gave him a shake and said, "There is someone out there coming up to the fence."

Suddenly the old man was at Jack's side, "Let me see who it is because if you go out there they could ride off, and I could lure them in."

Jack and his companion agreed and with their guns drawn they covered the old man as he went out the door and called out, "Who's there?"

Then in the dim light thrown from the lamp held aloft could be made out the shadowy figures of four men and three horses. One of the men spoke and said, "We mean you no harm old man, but we need a horse and food and a couple of guns if you have some and we can pay top dollar."

"Invite them in for a drink." whispered Jack.

"Come in for a couple of shots of my partner's hooch it will warm you up." invited the old man.

There was a muttered conversation then slowly the four men advanced towards the low building leaving their three horses tied to a rail outside. As soon as the men were inside the door the two old men moved over to the back of the room and turned up the two oil lamps. This revealed Jack and his companion with their guns drawn and a collective torrent of abuse burst from the mouths of the four prisoners.

"Shut your filthy mouths and sit on the floor or your legs will feel the weight of a bullet." said Jack.

Then he said to the old men, "Have you some strong rope we can tie these men up with until it gets light and the others arrive?"

Within minutes some old but still strong rope was produced and the four men were tied hand and foot and propped a couple of feet apart against the wall of the shack. The old man then gave them each a drink of the hooch and then it was just a question of waiting until it was daylight.

The two old men went to their bunks for a couple of hours leaving Jack and his companion to sample the hooch if they wished. It became light just before seven and the old men made some coffee for them all. Then one of the old men told Jack about their old horse called Cochise he had been called that because they had bought him from an Indian from one of the Reservations and he was rather unique because he had been "Indian Broke."

That meant he had been broken in as a colt by Indians and their tribe defied the European tradition of mounting from the left and they mounted from the right. For them it was the sensible way to mount because the wild horses they caught and broke had manes that fell mainly down the right hand side of the neck and as they rode bareback grasping the mane to hoist them onto the horses back was the best way to mount. As any rider knows trying to mount a horse in the unaccepted way is upsetting to the horse with unpredictable consequences.

Jack thought about this and realised that if these men had taken Cochise who ever tried to ride him would have been in for a nasty shock when he tried to get into the saddle. It was almost mid morning when they heard the sound of horses approaching and a few minutes later the marshal and the rest of the posse arrived. Of course the marshal was delighted that they had the four men in custody thanks very much to the help of the two old men and they all had a sip of the hooch before making a start back to Fort Worth.

The lame horse had now recovered well enough to carry its rider back to Fort Worth at no faster pace than a trot. The four prisoners rode with their hand tied and their horses secured to another member of the posse. They took the easier route back mostly alongside the railroad line and arrived in Fort Worth just as the light was failing. The prisoners were delivered straight back to the prison and would face charges under the Prison Rules which would mean an extension to their sentences.

Jack was a guest for the night at the police headquarters and enjoyed a good meal, pleasant company and a comfortable bed for the night. After breakfast the next morning he started off back to Hope and arrived in time for lunch after checking with Buck Shaw that all was well. After lunch he had to tell Jane all about the pursuit of the four prisoners and the capture at the old men's cottage.

When his two children came home from school he had to tell the story again this time he added the piece about Cochise the 'Indian Broke' horse this fascinated Simon who wanted to know if there were many still around. His father gave it some thought and imagined that there must be quite a few. He knew what the next question his son was going to ask and it quickly came when he said, "Do you think I could have such a horse for my birthday Dad, then Sue Ellen could have mine."

Jack said he would think about it, but could not imagine why anyone would want to mount a horse from the right it was so un-natural.

The next morning Ethan Watts came to see him and said someone was sleeping in the community hall and entering and leaving by the rear window. Jack went to have a look and sure enough it was clear someone was sleeping there and using some old curtains as bedding and there were traces of bread crumbs on the floor. He had a word with Buck Shaw who said he would spend the night in the community hall in case the night intruder returned and Ethan Watts was informed.

So before it became dark Buck Shaw found a comfortable chair in the hall and waited for the arrival of the night intruder. It was quite early at around nine at night when he heard a noise at the back of the hall and he realised it was a window being raised. He drew his gun as a precaution and waited for the intruder to appear in the main hall. He did and to Buck's surprise it was a small boy and Buck quickly holstered his gun and said quietly, "What are you doing here at this time of night my young lad."

The startled boy burst into tears and Buck took him by the hand and after closing the rear window went over to Ethan Watt's house with his captive. Here the boy was given some supper and some hot milk and asked to explain what he was up to. He was from a large Italian family and he had to sleep with two elder brothers who had been bullying him so he had run away. Ethan Watts gave him a bed for the night and the next day took him home and the worried mother and father promised to sort the matter out. Two days later the boy saw Ethan Watts again and told him he now had a small bed of his own in his big sister's room and they got on really well.

Chapter Thirty Two

Todd Raven having enjoyed Springfield for sometime decided to head east and decided on Nashville in Tennessee some three hundred miles away. He took plenty of track rations and allowed Tex to make the pace and the journey was pretty uneventful and lasted sixteen days. Nashville was on the Cumberland River and there was a fair amount of river trade and a growing tobacco growing industry.

Todd's first priority was to find decent accommodation for himself and his horse and he spent most of first morning there doing just that. He settled for an establishment ran by a widow and her daughter who was engaged to the local deputy sheriff. There were stables nearby ran by two black brothers but owed by the widow and clearly very well run. So Todd Raven had found decent lodgings and so had Tex and their arrival in Nashville had started well. The widow had asked Todd not wear his guns during meals and he was quite happy to conform but always wore them when he went out.

All the night life in Nashville was located down near the river and the majority of the gambling houses were down there as well as most of the bars. Todd did not venture out the first night but stayed in and listened to what his fellow guests had to say. There were only two both tobacco buyers and were attending for a crop auction in the next day or so. One who had just a little too much after dinner wine tried it on with the very attractive daughter of the widow and Todd Raven put a stop to that with a quick rebuke which carried menace. Todd Raven had not noticed but his actions had earned a nod of approval from the widow.

The next morning after breakfast he paid a visit to the bank manager and introduced himself. After a quick glance at his files the manager greeted him warmly and offered him coffee and asked if his visit was business or pleasure? Todd explained that he was not sure yet but he was going to have a good look around and then asked where the real action was. The manager smiled then said, "They tell me that the

'Fallen Angel' is the best gambling club and pretty straight apart from the dice games and the 'Wheel of Fortune'."

So that night after dinner Todd made his way down to the river area and quickly found the brightly lit 'Fallen Angel'.

The club was quite crowded and the bar was busy and on the far side were some tables where some card games were in progress. Todd could see there was an upper floor where he could hear the sound of the 'Wheel of Fortune' in action. He moved over to the card tables and waited for an opportunity to join in.

He did not have to wait long as a very disgruntled man rose to his feet and said, "You boys are raising the stakes too high for me."

Todd quickly took his place and brief introductions were made and it was explained that a limit had been agreed that nobody raised more than fifty dollars during a game and Todd nodded his agreement. He spent four hours at the table with his three new friends and they collectively drank a full bottle of whiskey. Todd paid for the whiskey because he had won about thirty dollars and they all agreed to meet the next evening with slightly higher stakes on offer.

Todd arrived at his lodgings just as the daughter's boy friend was leaving and they gave each other a brief greeting. As soon as Todd was in the door the mother locked up for the night and Todd had the feeling that she made sure her daughter's liaisons did not become too amorous. Todd slept well in the comfortable bed and the next morning after breakfast decided to take Tex out for a ride around the outskirts of Nashville.

The stable lads quickly readied Tex for his outing and soon they were enjoying the air from the higher ground with a fine view over the river and the tobacco plantations. Todd spent a couple of hours in the saddle then brought Tex back to the stables where the stable boys washed Tex down and gave him some fresh hay. Todd went in to his lodgings and had a quick wash and then enjoyed some lunch with two new lodgers who had replaced the tobacco buyers who had moved on.

Strangely enough the two new lodgers were reluctant to discuss their business, which to Todd meant they were not the usual buyers or salesman. So what were they?

Todd had a rest on his bed in the afternoon and when he came down for dinner the two men were anxious to know where the best gambling clubs were. He told them that they were down by the river, but some were a bit dodgy, so take care.

Both men laughed and one said, "Oh we can take care of ourselves and we are a little too smart for these Southern Jarheads."

Todd realised then that these two men were professional gamblers from up north hoping to make some easy money down in the southern states, well they could be in for a surprise. They had dinner which Todd enjoyed but the two men just picked at their meal and left quite a lot on their plate. This did not go unnoticed by their landlady who gave both men a far from friendly look when serving coffee.

Later Todd left for the 'Fallen Angel' and was pleased when he saw the two men heading down towards the river. He joined up with his friends of the previous evening and it was agreed that fifty dollars was the maximum that anyone could raise during a game.

The evening came to an earlier than planned end when a shooting took place upstairs over a dispute in the wheel of fortune clubs. The sheriff was called and the 'Fallen Angel' was closed early, so Todd went to his lodgings just forty dollars better off.

He was enjoying a drink with the land lady and her daughter when the two other lodgers came in both had been in a fight and had got the worst of it. The land lady and her daughter rushed off to get water and towels to clean up the men's faces and Todd could not resist saying, "So much for the southern jarheads."

Later they got the men's side of the story, which was that they saw some obvious cheating going on and complained, but were chucked out by the club's heavies and beaten up outside.

The daughter said she would tell her boyfriend who was deputy sheriff in the morning and he would sort this out, and she asked what the name of the club was. The two men were reluctant to say, but after some persuasion finally admitted it was the 'Red Garter Club'.

The landlady reacted in horror before saying, "But that is mainly a seaman's brothel."

But the two men insisted it had gambling tables where the cheating had taken place.

The next morning after breakfast the daughter kept her word and went and informed her boy friend that two of their lodgers had been assaulted at the Red Garter Club. The sheriff was standing nearby when she passed this information on and she was not best pleased when both men burst out laughing.

Seeing she was annoyed, the deputy sheriff said, "Anyone who uses the Red Garter is asking for trouble. It would be closed down but it provides a service for the drunken river crowd who, if they could not go there, would cause trouble in the better parts of town."

The daughter Sally came back with the advice from the sheriff for the two lodgers try somewhere else for your enjoyment. Todd Raven found the whole episode most amusing but he knew the two men did not. That evening after dinner when on his way to the Fallen Angel to meet up with his new found friends he realised that his two fellow lodgers were following him. He stopped just outside the Fallen Angel and told them he was meeting up with friends for a card game.

The two lodgers explained that they would try that luck on some of the other tables and made their way inside. Todd followed on and joined his friends at their usual table and after a couple of drinks table stakes were agreed with a maximum call of a hundred dollars.

The evening passed pleasantly enough with Todd winning a couple of hands and losing the odd one. But just before midnight trouble flared in the far corner of the smoke filled room and not to Todd's complete surprise the gunfight that followed involved his two fellow lodgers.

The players on all the tables grabbed their stake money in the race to get out of the club to avoid being involved. Todd his pockets bulging with his winnings backed up against the bar waiting to see how things developed.

The sheriff and his deputy came through the door and advanced on the group of men who had all drawn their guns in a face off. Todd with his guns clearly in view walked over to the sheriffs party and said ,"May I join you?"

The sheriff nodded and now the three of them advanced towards where the trouble had flared with one man laying flat out and another nursing a wound in his shoulder.

"Put your guns down boys and back up against the wall." Called out the sheriff, his voice firm and strong.

There were a few seconds of hesitation before one by one the guns fell to the floor and the men backed up as ordered except for one. He grabbed one of the other men and with a gun to the other man's head made for the door. A shot rang out and he dropped the gun and clutched his shoulder dropping to his knees in agony.

Todd Raven holstered his gun and turned to the sheriff and said, "There is always one who has to spoil things, isn't there sheriff?"

An hour later six men would spend the night in the cells including the man Todd had wounded. One man had been shot dead in the quarrel over cards and one wounded. The dead man was one of the lodgers and the wounded man was his companion, so there was only Todd to serve at breakfast but he received some admiring glances from the widow.

She had been given the full story from her daughter who had heard of Todd's part from her boyfriend. It turned out the two lodgers were professional gamblers from St Louis who were looking for a place to buy into. No charges would be brought over the incident because guns had been drawn on both sides of the argument. The wounded lodger recovered quite quickly and went elsewhere to try his luck.

Todd Raven stayed in Nashville for a few months more and enjoyed the generous hospitality that the widow was now supplying. She was a handsome woman who had looked after herself but this closer relationship did not please her daughter. Todd Raven found out why one evening when he heard the two women having words in the kitchen.

He heard the mother say, "Why do you object to my relationship with Mr Raven. You will be off to live with your deputy sheriff when you are married."

Then the Daughter replied, "No mother, when we are married he will give up his job and run this place and you can take it easy."

Hearing this Todd decided it was time to move on and he left the next morning heading north for Louisville about one hundred and fifty miles away.

Chapter Thirty Three

Todd Raven found Tex eager to be on the move again and they did the journey easily in five days and quickly found a boarding house with good stables nearby. The Ohio River was close by and was an important part of the local tobacco trade and a major influence on the growing economy. Louisville was well run and had a sheriff Todd Raven had met before though they were not exactly friends.

The next morning after breakfast Todd introduced himself to his local bank manager and as he was leaving the bank he bumped into the sheriff. They exchanged nods but did not speak though no doubt the sheriff did speak to the bank manager about his departing client. After a bread and cheese lunch at his boarding house he was enjoying a coffee on the porch with the man who ran and owned the place with his wife when a horse and trap pulled up outside.

"It's my wife's sister Dolly." said Todd's companion. "She and her husband run a small ranch about five miles outside of town".

The woman was quite distressed and ran into the boarding house almost in tears and the man put down his coffee and went in to see what all the fuss was about. He came back out a few minutes later and said, "It's their neighbour. He has given her husband Jack a good hiding over a dispute involving their access to a stream that crosses both their properties. The sheriff can't do anything because Jack went onto his land to complain and was in the eyes of the law trespassing."

Todd Raven gave the matter a few moments thought then said, "I could go out to the ranch and lodge there for a few days and perhaps help sought the matter out."

At that moment the two sisters came out onto the porch and the man put Todd's offer to the one called Dolly. She looked at Todd and said, "Well you are big enough Mr Raven, but our neighbour is a nasty piece of work. But you would be very welcome."

Twenty minutes later Tex and Todd Raven were following the pony and trap out towards the ranch some five miles away.

When they arrived Todd was immediately impressed with the small ranch. it was well-kept, all the buildings were in good condition and brightly painted. They had a variety of livestock. Cows, kept mostly for milk, some pigs, sheep and lots of chicken. But in a separate pen they had half a dozen fine young horses.

He was invited inside and met Dolly's husband Jack who was resting in a chair his face badly bruised from the encounter with his neighbour. Dolly showed Todd where he would sleep in a small bedroom at the rear of the single storey house. Dolly then went to prepare dinner and Jack explained to Todd the main reason for the dispute.

"Mark Warren wants to buy our place and Dolly and I do not want to sell and that it what this is all about. This nonsense about this stream not having enough water in summer for the two ranches is rubbish, even in the driest of summers it has never dried up".

Jack then told Todd of why he went over to Warren's ranch to speak to him and what led to the assault.

"I know one of Warren's ranch hands and he is a decent guy and he warned me that Warren was planning to use explosives to divert the stream away from my land that is why I went over to his ranch to confront him. When I confronted him about him trying to divert the stream he went berserk and he knocked me out cold and one of his men brought me home stretched out over my horse."

Todd wandered around the neatly arranged room and admired the large framed map of the area hung on the wall. It showed Jack and Dolly's ranch outlined in red and nearby was the Warren ranch clearly shown in green. The stream in question was clearly visible and could be traced back into the hills almost to source of its spring.

Todd looked at the map for a couple of minutes then said to Jack, "Who owns this land?" then pointed to the area where the stream flowed down from.

Jack laughed, "Well nobody with any sense it's just all high ground made up of rocks and small gullies and there is nothing for an animal to graze on accept rabbits."

An idea was beginning to form in Todd Raven's brain, but he needed to discuss it with his bank manager and that would have to be in the morning. They enjoyed a fine meal that evening and Jack was feeling much better just before ten o'clock as they were enjoying a final drink there was a knock on the door and Todd went and answered it with his guns drawn. It was a ranch hand from the Warren ranch with a letter for Jack and having delivered it he quickly departed.

The letter contained an offer for the ranch, quite a reasonable one, but with suggestion that failing to accept within forty eight hours would be foolish on their part.

Dolly was clearly upset, but Todd told her not to worry and advised them to go to bed and leave things now for him to sort out as he had a plan.

After breakfast the next morning Todd saddled up Tex and rode into Louisville and tied up Tex outside the bank. He had to wait twenty minutes as the manager was with a client but as soon as he was free Todd was ushered in and the manager immediately ordered coffee. As they sipped the excellent brew Todd asked about the price of land in the area and the manager rang for a clerk to bring the latest State Surveyors land list. The bank manager then showed Todd some prime farming areas and the price per acre. Then Todd pointed to a map on the bank managers wall which was a replica of the one Jack and Dolly had.

Todd pointed to the area he was interested in and asked, "What is the price the government want for that per acre then."

The bank manager laughed, "Are you serious Sir? The only thing you can grow there is poor."

Todd insisted he was serious and would later tell why and again asked the price.

The manager consulted the latest list then said with a smile. "It's a dollar an acre and I think that's over priced."

It took Todd Raven a further twenty minutes to explain to the manager why he was serious then he purchased five hundred acres which encompassed the spring source and the stream down to its fork to the two ranches.

The bank manager now aware of how this would settle the feud immediately sent a messenger with the signed documents to the state offices only a couple of miles away. He then assured Todd that they would have conformation of the purchase by this time tomorrow and the two men shook hands. Todd then rode back to the ranch and gave Tex a rub down and some fresh hay then went into the house to find Jack and Dolly had received another warning from Mark Warren that they now had only twenty four hours left before he would take action.

Despite this threat Dolly was laying out the lunch table and soon they were enjoying a pleasant light meal. Afterwards as they were enjoying their coffee Todd told them he had enjoyed a busy morning with his bank manager. Then he stood up and walked over to the large map that was framed on the wall and pointed to the area where the stream began its journey down to the two ranches. Then he said, "Guess who owns that land now?"

Jack and Dolly looked at one another dreading to think it was Frank Warren.

Todd laughed and said, "We do."

It took a few seconds for the full implication of what Todd Raven had said to sink in then both Dolly and Jack gave a cry and grabbed Todd in a close embrace then danced across the floor.

It took a few minutes for the initial emotion to subside and then the two of them wanted chapter and verse on the whole business. Over now, something stronger than coffee Todd told them about the morning's events the price and the land purchase being registered in the state office with written acknowledgement of the sale being assured by tomorrow.

Todd then turned to the couple and said, "You realise that as soon as that paper of ownership is in your hands you control the water that flows onto the Warren land and if you wished you could be as unpleasant as he has been and with the law of ownership on your side."

Dolly looked at her husband and shook her head, "No Todd, we are not like that and after all it's the animals that would suffer."

Then the pair looked at Todd and said, "But we can't pay you the five hundred dollars for some time but we will."

Todd laughed. "You owe me nothing. The Deeds are in your names just call me a sleeping partner who may turn up now and again for a bed some decent food and pleasant company. For the next hour they almost finished the bottle then Dolly fell asleep and Jack carried her to the bedroom. Later he joined Todd on the porch then they heard Dolly busy in the kitchen preparing dinner and they crept in and finished off what was left in the bottle.

Later that evening after dinner they sat out on the porch with their coffee and just talked until almost midnight then it was a rush to get to bed. Then next morning after breakfast Todd and Jack rode into Louisville and collected the signed deeds from the bank manger who told both men that if there were any problems with Frank Warren the bank's solicitors would handle it. He also suggested that once Jack's wife had seen the documents the best place for their safe keeping would be in the bank and as Jack had an account there would be no charge for this service.

They rode back to Jack's ranch and showed Dolly the deeds which proved now beyond doubt that they owned the land that which encompassed the stream and the spring as its source. They were enjoying a coffee in celebration when three men rode up led by Frank Warren. Warren strode up to the door and Todd Raven opened it before he could demand entry and said "What do you want?"

Warren seemed surprised by the appearance of Todd Raven but he then said, "My business is with the owner, not his lackey."

Jack appeared at Todd's side and said, "Come in Mr Warren. Mr Raven is a dear friend and colleague and now a business partner."

This completely put Warren out of step as it were and he entered the house struggling to gain control. He was invited to sit down which confused him further, but he did manage to blurt out in sheer desperation. "Your forty eight hours are up."

To his complete and utter amazement Jack and Dolly burst out laughing and Warren got to his feet and angrily said, "You won't find it so funny when my men come and throw you and your belongings out into the cow shit."

Todd Raven looked at Warren and said, "Just sit down and listen to what Jack has to say and stop making a damn fool of yourself with your stupid threats."

Jack then stood up and waved the deeds in the air and said, "Recently Mr Raven on behalf of Dolly and myself offered to try and solve the problem that existed between your ranch Mr Warren and mine. This problem was over the water that flowed equally between the two ranches and your ranch not having enough during a dry summer."

Jack looked at Frank Warren and smiled then said, "Well now the problem has been solved, because Dolly and I and our partner Todd Raven own all the land the stream crosses before it reaches your ranch Mr Warren including the spring where it all begins."

They spread the Deeds out on the table so that Warren could see them he closely read through them and as he finished gave a strange cry. He quickly recovered and said "Name your price for the deeds and you will have my word you will never be short of water, what say you?"

Jack and Dolly just laughed, then Jack said "Let's forget the past Frank we will never see you short of water we can make a fresh start as from now if you are agreeable?"

Warrens face now was quite pale and he got to his feet.

"Let me think about it and I'll see you both tomorrow." and he walked slowly out of the house.

Todd watched him mount his horse ignoring the questions his curious ranch hands were asking and they quickly rode away.

The very practical Dolly was preparing lunch and as Jack and Todd waited on the porch for the summons to eat they both wondered what Frank Warren would decide to do.

After a pleasant light meal they enjoyed some coffee and then they all decided to take a rest. Jack and Dolly on their bed, but Todd stayed in a comfortable chair on the porch.

Chapter Thirty Four

Frank Warren was halfway through a bottle of whiskey and he still was not drunk he summoned the young Mexican girl from the kitchen to bring him something to eat. She was fearful of Frank Warren when he was drunk and her mother had warned her to keep him at arm's length but this time he made no move to molest her.

Later he walked outside and spoke to a couple of his men and one was dispatched to try and find someone Warren wanted to see. The man arrived about an hour later and Warren spent some time with him and together they finished off the whiskey.

"What's the name of this guy who has called all this trouble then?" At last the man from the deep comforts of the armchair enquired.

"Oh, it's Todd Raven some saddle tramp they befriended." said Frank Warren.

Despite the large amounts of whiskey consumed, the man sprang to his feet and made for the door. "Thanks for the drink Mr Warren, but I don't intend to cross swords with Todd Raven, even for double the money."

As he heard the sound of his hired-gun ride away Warren smashed his glass on the wall in anger in anger and screamed to Maria to bring more whiskey. But the Mexican girl had sensibly left for the quarters she shared with her mother and Warren was forced to collect his own whiskey and later fall into a drunken sleep.

In the morning he woke in a foul mood and found Maria's mother in the kitchen. She ignored his abuse and cooked him breakfast and made him coffee. He then rode into Louisville and saw the bank manager and asked if he could challenge the purchase of the deeds.

The bank manager smiled then said, "I am not a legal expert Mr Warren, but from what my solicitor has told me you would be wasting your time and your money in pursuing such a course of action."

Frank Warren just stood up and walked out without another word and made his way to the nearest bar. His mood now was poisonous and after a few drinks several elderly men having a drink on one of the tables laughed loudly at something one of them said. Warren thought they were laughing at him and stormed over to them and knocked their drinks off the table.

The bar keeper walked over to stop things getting out of hand, but Warren was now in no mood to back down. As one of the old men struggled to grab his glasses from his waist pocket Warren assumed he was reaching for a gun and promptly shot him. All hell broke loose and the sheriff was called while Warren, who had been overpowered by the angry bar customers, faced a lynching had not the sheriff intervened. Sadly, the elderly man died that evening so the charge was now murder. As the man was a retired teacher , he had never carried a gun in his life, so Warren's prospects did not look good.

The trial was set to take place in the Louisville court in two weeks time and as Frank Warren had friends and money he had retained a top Legal counsel to defend him. His legal counsel quickly decided that their defence would rest on the God given right of all american citizen's to bear arms to defend themselves.

The judge appointed to try this case quickly realised that choosing a jury who would be impartial in this case would be difficult as the principals in this case had many friends. So a requirement in the jury selection was that each person selected for jury service was required to swear on the Bible that he had not been or was a friend of either the deceased or the accused.

The large court house was packed for the opening day of the trial and the judge in his opening remarks made it quite clear that he would not permit any disturbance to take place during the trial despite the emotions that were running high at the time.

The prosecuting counsel began by outlining the events of the case how on this particular day four elderly friends were having their usual morning drink together discussing old times. They were completely unaware of the accused a man called Frank Warren who none of them had ever met before was drinking at the bar. They of course did not know that the accused was having a very bad day in his business dealings and was in a rather foul mood.

At this point the defence counsel was about to object then thought better of it and remained quiet for the moment. The prosecuting counsel went on saying the accused had several drinks at the bar then became annoyed at the laughter coming from the table where the four elderly men were seated. He went on to say, "Witnesses will state that the accused stormed over to the elderly men's table and swept all their drinks off the table into their laps. Then as one of the old men fumbled at his waist for something the accused drew his gun and shot him in the chest, a wound from which he later died."

The prosecutor paused then said, "The old man was not carrying a gun and had never done so in his life so there was no reason for this dreadful act a clear case of murder."

A succession of prosecution witnesses followed first the barman then the three companions of the old man all gave their evidence clearly. This took most of the first day and the first day ended with a doctor giving the cause of death which was a gun-shot wound to the chest causing a great loss of blood and shock.

The second day of the trial started with the Defence counsel pointing out to the jury that every American citizen has the right to bear arms and defend themselves. He then walked over to the jury and slowly looked all of them in the face and said, "If I came to your house at night drunk and carrying a gun and banged on the door and threatened your wife and when challenged by you dropped my hand down towards my waist you would be justified in shooting me is that not so?"

At this most of the jury nodded and the defence counsel smiled and said, "But I was only reaching for a letter I was asked to deliver."

The defence then questioned the barman and asked how many drinks Frank Warren had been given. The barman said he could not remember but it was more than three.

The defence counsel then asked, "Do you feel responsible that a man who you allowed to drink more than was good for him shot someone?"

"No Sir." replied the barman. "I am paid to sell drinks the more I sell the more I get paid."

Next to be called in turn were the three companions of the dead man and they were all asked who were they laughing at and could the accused have thought they were laughing at him. Each of them gave a similar answer that they were laughing about their exploits of the past years. When asked if it might have been that Warren thought they were laughing at him, they replied, "He was so drunk who knows, but we had never met him before."

The defence was about to call the accused to the stand but the judge decided to adjourn for lunch.

After lunch Frank Warren was called to the witness box and asked by his defence counsel to explain his actions in the bar that led to the shooting. Warren in a clear voice stated that he had some bad business news and after seeing his bank manager he went to the bar to forget his business troubles with a few glasses of alcohol.

"Did this improve your mood?" asked his defence counsel.

"No Sir, it made it much worse and I was convinced that a group of men sitting at a table nearby were aware of my business failure and were finding it highly amusing."

"Then what happened?" asked his defence counsel.

Frank Warren looked at the jury and said, "To my great regret I foolishly went over to ask them what they found so funny and to show my annoyance I swept their drinks from the table."

He paused and then went on, "One of the men dropped his hand to his waist and I thought he was going for his gun and my instinct for survival took over. Without thinking I drew and fired my weapon, mortally wounding him."

The defence counsel turned to the judge and said, "No further questions Your Honour."

The prosecuting counsel now took the opportunity to question the defendant. He began by asking Warren if he normally drank himself into a state where he did not know the difference between right and wrong. Warren replied that in normal circumstances he was a moderate drinker, wine with his dinner and a whiskey before bed.

He was then asked about his business dealings as it was said he was a ruthless competitor and he admitted that he did have a reputation for going hard for his target. The prosecutor satisfied he had got enough from the defendant said, "No further questions Your Honour." and Warren returned to the dock.

The summing up then began with the prosecution leading the way with a complete outline of the events of that day leading to the fatal shooting in the bar. The defence counsel then followed and gave a view from the defendant's side of that same day's events and when he finished the jury were instructed not to discuss the case with anyone outside the jury room and he adjourned the case for the day.

The next morning the judge began his summing up and ran through the evidence in careful detail. He then said to the jury, "In our country it has become an accepted practice that if two men confront each other with guns and one of the two men dies as a result there is no charge of murder."

He paused to allow these words to register with the jury then went on, "But here you have a case where in a confrontation only one man is armed but is convinced by the other man's hand action that he is reaching for his weapon when in truth he is fumbling for his spectacles."

The judge allowed these words to sink before going on. "A totally sober man may well have still had the wit to realise the old man posed no threat, but as one has heard before when the drink goes in the sense goes out. The problem you have to solve today is whether or not it is a reasonable action for a man beset by business problems, which are of his own making, to over indulge in drink and in doing so allows himself to confuse the fumbling of an old man searching for his spectacles as a threat to his life." The judge then sends the jury out to consider their verdict.

The jury were out two hours then came in for advice as they were clearly unsure of what they should do. The foreman asked if an alternative charge to murder was available the judge smiled and with some sympathy said no and the jury went back to think again. They came back with a verdict of not guilty, but Warren had a charge of drunk and disorderly and discharging a firearm recklessly to face and got two years imprisonment. Todd Raven thought the jury got it about right and stayed on in Louisville for another six months then felt the urge to move on.

Dolly and Jack tried to persuade him to stay, but he felt the time was right to move on and he liked to go while still friends with everyone. He was unsure where to go but a toss of a coin decided his future for the next few months and with a well stocked saddle bag of trail provisions he and Tex headed west early on an autumn morning.

After a week on the road Todd decided to take advantage of the train and treble the speed of their travel and in doing so it was not long before they reached fresh ground at a place called San Angelo about a hundred miles from the Mexican border.

Chapter Thirty Five

The people of Hope were enjoying a prosperous ending to the growing season with the grape plantations producing their best harvest. Various parties had been held all over the town but very little trouble had occurred that required the intervention of either the sheriff or his deputy. That is until the following Monday morning when a man's body was found behind the community hall with a kitchen knife thrust into his chest. One of Ethan Watt's dogs found him and the body was cold and it was clear he had lain there all night.

He was fairly quickly identified as the husband of one of the Italian women and the poor woman thought he was on the night guard duty at the winery. When Jack Masters checked at the winery they said he had not reported for duty that night and they had to get someone else to cover his duties. Jack and Buck began to think that the night guard had arranged to see someone before starting his duties and that was probably a woman. Did she kill him or was it her jealous husband or other lover they had to start their investigation before the trail went cold.

Jack went to see the wife who was not as upset as he expected her to be and he felt able to ask her did she think her husband was seeing another woman. The woman shrugged then said, "Pedro was a passionate man and I was unable to satisfy him so he tended to wander and he found plenty of women willing to give him what he wanted."

Jack now felt he was getting somewhere so he asked, "Do you know who his latest fancy woman was then?"

The woman thought for a moment then said, "I think he was seeing two. One was the wife of a railroad worker and the other was married to the man who has recently opened the timber yard."

Jack knew there was only one railroad worker living in Hope and he looked after the station there and his wife was rather a pretty little thing. But the man who had opened the timber yard had a tall fair haired wife not unattractive, but hardly the sort to stray.

Jack discussed what he had found out with Buck who was off to Fort Worth to keep the marshal there informed of how the investigation was going. Jack decided to go and see the railroad worker first as he considered him the prime suspect. He lived in a small single storey wooden house neatly kept and freshly painted. As Jack arrived he could hear the sound of two people talking and some laughter in the conversation. He knocked on the door and the woman answered it quite quickly and invited him in and offered him coffee. Jack declined the offer and said he was investigating the death of Pedro Calvert whose body was found behind the community hall in Hope this morning.

"We had heard of his death." said the railroad worker, "But we did not know him, although I might have seen him use the train."

His wife nodded at what her husband was saying and Jack had a feeling that both were speaking the truth. As Jack left the house the wife followed him out and said, "Don't tell my husband, but a month ago that horrible man asked me to meet him secretly, but I told him to go away."

Jack made his way home the timber yard couple would have to wait until tomorrow as he could not keep Jane and her dinner waiting. Later that evening once their dinner had settled and the children were at last in bed Jane asked him about the murder and who were his main suspects and Jack had to confess he was probably left with just one. Of course Jane wanted to know who that was and Jack said he thought that the timber yard owner's wife was one of Pedro's conquests so it could be him.

It was just as they were going to bed that night that Jane suddenly said, "Of course these Italians are passionate people, so it could be that Pedro's wife had suffered enough and decided to rid herself of a worthless husband."

This gave Jack much to think about and it was sometime before he could get to sleep. The next morning after breakfast he went over to his office and discussed the case with Buck Shaw and they looked again at the murder weapon. It was a kitchen knife with a razor sharp blade of a type found in most kitchens. As a weapon of choice it would suit a women rather than a man who would more likely have a heavier hunting knife.

Jack and Buck went to where the body had been found hoping to find some extra clues to the killer's identity but they found nothing. Jack decided to pay Pedro's wife a visit and found the couples small wooden house with a small garden quite well looked after. He found Pedro's wife packing her belongings as she was moving into Fort Worth with her sister as the small house was only rented to them by the winery whilst her husband was employed.

Jack decided to ask the woman a straight question and said, "Did you kill your husband, Mrs Calvert?"

The woman did not answer but sat down and poured out two glasses of wine. She took two or three sips then said, "Can you prove I killed my husband sheriff?"

Jack stood up. "Not at the moment but I am getting closer to the truth and you have knives in your kitchen similar to the murder weapon."

Mrs Calvert pointed to the door ."Please go and leave me to grieve in peace, but here is my sister's address in Fort Worth."

Jack Masters went back to the sheriff's office and told Buck all that had occurred and they both had to admit Mrs Calvert was either innocent or a good actress.

Jack took the weekly train into Fort Worth and discussed the case with the marshal who felt, as Jack did, that the widow was the chief suspect. Her sister's address had been checked and the two were now living together in rather a nice house which the other sister's late husband had owned.

On the marshal's advice Jack went to see the timber yard owner's wife when her husband was at the yard. The woman was quite open about her previous relationship providing it was kept from her husband and Jack agreed to this. The woman stated that they often met behind the community hall, but Pedro was terrified that his wife would find out as she could be quite vicious when roused. Jack asked if she was prepared to say this in court on oath. The woman said certainly not and asked him to leave.

Jack passed all this onto the marshal in Fort Worth who took legal advice and were told they could not force the woman to appear and in any case she would say nothing.

Pedro Calvert was buried in Fort Worth Cemetery with a grieving widow and a supportive sister at her side some members of the winery were there as were Jack and Buck.

It was almost three months later that Lisa Calvert's sister with a badly bruised face came into the marshal's office in Fort Worth one morning saying, "Now the bitch has tried to kill me."

The marshal sat her down and gave her something to drink and gradually managed to find out from her what had caused the upset between the two sisters. Gradually the full story came out that after dinner the previous evening the two sisters had polished off a full bottle of wine.

It was then that her sister confessed to killing her husband because of his numerous affairs and said that she had a nice sum of money he had been stealing from the winery at night. She tried to persuade her sister to sell up and start a new life together down south. They argued about it and more wine was drunk and her sister grew violent and punched her in the face so she went to her room. Then during the early hours her sister attacked her with a knife, but her sister was so drunk she easily fought her off.

The marshal asked, "Where is your sister now?"

The woman replied, "I think she was in her room when I left the house probably packing to clear out."

The marshal, a deputy and the woman made their way over to the house with the intention of arresting the woman. When they arrived all was very quiet and the marshal feared the woman had fled.

They went inside and were guided to the sister's bedroom and thrust the door open to find the woman lying flat out on the bed with a gaping wound to her throat and a blood stained knife still grasped in her hand. The body was still warm and a bag lay beside the body with over a thousand dollars stuffed inside.

As far as he could tell the woman was dead but the marshal sent his deputy to fetch the doctor to confirm death. The doctor arrived and confirmed death and the body was removed leaving the sister very upset at the outcome to their quarrel. She then was required to make a statement while the facts of this incident were still fresh in her mind.

Jack Masters was informed the next morning and asked to enquire at the winery if they had been losing money. The man and his wife who owned the business kept very accurate accounts and they showed that money had gone missing on a regular occasion in small amounts and in total added to just over a thousand dollars.

This information was passed onto the marshal who a week later returned the money to the winery owners. So the case was closed with the records showing that Pedro Calvert was killed by his jealous wife who then escaped justice by killing herself.

The sister found she could not live in her small house any more after her sister had committed suicide in one of the bedrooms, so she had moved east.

A telegraph office had now been established in Hope giving them an emergency line to Fort Worth instead of an almost thirty mile horse ride. It was used mostly by the bank and the sheriff's office, but occasionally by the doctor seeking a second opinion.

The Friday night and Saturday night's frolic at 'Ma's House' by the cowhands from the two ranches normally never created any problems for Jack and Buck but one weekend their girl friends in Hope staged a 'blockade' on 'Ma's House'. The girls did not mind their boyfriends enjoying a drink there it was what followed on from there that they were going to put a stop to. This of course raised the hackles of the ladies brought in from Fort Worth to provide the bedroom entertainment and was their living. The ridiculous thing was, of course, that of the sixty or so men using the facilities over the two nights only about five had girlfriends in Hope.

Fortunately the standoff only lasted an hour on the Friday night when Jack Masters on the advice of his wife persuaded the small number of ranch hands in the first group to stay loyal to their girls. The word quickly spread to the ranch hands due on the Saturday night and only those without local girls turned up. Jack realised that a difficult situation had been resolved and thanked his wife who reminded him she needed a new dress.

Slightly further west as the train service had developed and had been further extended to carry more passengers and freight it also carried money. And in the past whereas stage coaches carried the money in strong boxes between banks now trains were providing a faster and more secure system of transfer. It came as no surprise to Jack and Buck that soon they began to receive wanted posters with details of train robberies involving quite large sums of money.

These outlaw gangs chose their spot usually at the top of a steep gradient where the train was forced to slow right down to walking pace. They would jump onto the selected coach as it passed through a cutting force their way in by gun point and then escape with the loot as the train picked up speed having tied up the guards. The rest of the gang would have their horses nearby so they could make a clean getaway and the robbery would not be detected until the train reached the next station.

The railroad companies responded to these robberies by enlisting the help of the newly formed Pinkerton detective agency. This agency had started off in New York and some of its methods had come in for some criticism. It frequently used former jail birds to infiltrate gangs and provide them with information about their future plans. It was also said that in an effort to achieve convictions some of the evidence provided was quite dubious but despite this they did manage to slow down the wave of robberies. Much to Jack Master's amusement he had a letter asking him to join the Pinkerton Agency, but he declined the offer as he was very happy where he was as sheriff.

Chapter Thirty Six

San Angelo is a cattle town on the Concho River rough and ready with the six gun still the main way of keeping the peace and Todd Raven felt immediately at home. Within an hour he had found a decent enough stables for Tex and nearby a small boarding house run by two Chinese that would do. It was now mid afternoon and the place was reasonably quiet before the ranch hands from the outlying ranches came in to let off steam. Some had been on the trail for weeks and had lived on a diet consisting of just beans so for the next few days every step they took would be followed by the breaking of wind.

After a decent meal that evening Todd ventured into San Angelo and was lured into the Golden Star bar by the music and the lights. He almost turned round and came back out because as he entered he received the benefit of about twelve ranch hands breaking wind freely at the bar. He walked quickly over to the far side of the room and sat down at a vacant table and waited for some service.

A young Mexican came over and said, "Beer or whiskey mister?"

Todd replied, "I'll have a beer please."

The 'please' caught the young Mexican by surprise, but when he returned with the beer he said with a smile, "Enjoy your drink Sir."

Todd Raven spent a couple of hours at the same bar watching with a keen interest the antics of the ranch hands enjoying their first night back from bringing a herd back from Mexico. As one point the local sheriff and his two deputies walked in. They looked capable men and sensibly let the moderate behaviour of the cowhands continue.

Just after eleven o'clock Todd made his way back to his lodgings and as soon as he was inside the door one of the Chinese locked up for the night. He found the bed clean and comfortable but he found sleep slow to lure him, but eventually it did and he spent a peaceful night.

A tap on his door woke him instantly and his hand reached for his gun, but it was only the older of the Chinese men with a morning coffee. A short time later he went down for breakfast and enjoyed eggs and bacon and some more of the strong coffee. He then sat out on the porch and was given a morning news paper which had on its front page headline *Pinkerton Agency fail to stop Train Robbery.*

Todd read through the article which told of a large sum of money guarded by a team of Pinkerton agents had failed to prevent the money being stolen in a daring raid as the train passed slowly through a steep cutting and the robbers sprang aboard.

The Pinkerton Agents were overpowered by the robbers after a hornet's nest had been thrown into the compartment holding the money. The robbers were all wearing protective clothing against the stings of the angry insects, but the agents were so badly stung they jumped from the moving train in a panic. The robbers got away with fifty thousand dollars and some gold coins.

Todd found the newspaper story amusing as he had no time for the Pinkerton agency and had heard several stories about some of the people they employed. Strangely enough the same news paper was in front of the sheriff that morning and with some delight he drew the attention of it to his two deputies. Only a week ago a Pinkerton agent had tried to lure his two men away with talk of more money and a chance to travel all over America.

The sheriff noticed that the train that had been robbed was on its way north from Houston so it had taken place not that far away. The same thought had occupied Todd Raven's mind, but it depended just how disciplined the gang were. Some men would find it hard to resist the women and the attractions of the south coast gambling dens and it would take a strong leader to keep them under control. But that is exactly what this particular gang had, Matt Kelly was as fast with his fists as he was with his guns and not one of the other three gang members would challenge him.

It took them three days to reach San Angelo and their four horses were on their last legs and would take days to recover. But they booked them into the best stables in town and then the best hotel for themselves and all four spent an hour in separate hot tubs to wash off the travel grime.

The first night they were there they had their meals served in just one of their rooms and it was two days before they ventured out in public. On the leader's instruction they now were all in worn but clean clothes and moved about in pairs and not together as a four. The intention of their leader was to stay in San Angelo for about five days to rest the horses then make a more leisurely journey further west to El Paso a distance of about five hundred miles. Matt Kelly made the rules of their stay in this town quite clear.

No. 1: Don't get drunk
No. 2: If you have a bet, your limit is ten dollars as you are a cowhand
No. 3: If you want a woman use her, pay her and don't get involved.

Without realising it Todd Raven passed the time of day with Matt Kelly on the evening of the gang's third night in San Angelo. Todd had taken quite a fancy to the Golden Star and had a few games of cards with some of the older clients including the local doctor. They always played for just a few dollars, with the winner of each game buying a round of drinks. They had a vacant chair this particular evening and Kelly asked if he might join them.

They agreed and he had a friend with him who was quite younger and he sat just a few tables away. The newcomer only played four hands and won once and paid for a round and then took his leave. Todd noticed the way the man wore his guns and decided that he and his companion certainly were not cowhands resting after a cattle drive. Later that evening the doctor commented on Todd's dry cough which had become worse recently and advised him to cut down on his smoking.

Todd whose cure for most of his ailments was a glass of whiskey asked the doctor if he always noticed the ailments of his opponents at cards.

The doctor laughed then said, "Yes I do and that chap who joined us briefly for cards must keep bees because I noticed his hands had the result of several bee stings on them."

That night as Todd lay on his very comfortable bed he gave what he had learned tonight a great deal of thought. The sheriff of course would be very interested and if one man's hands had evidence of insect stings so might the others and a search of their rooms might be interesting. But this did not appeal to Todd Raven he was not an informer but if he had now become suspicious how long would it take the sheriff and his deputies to take a closer look at the four new comers. He was still turning the options over in his mind when he fell asleep and he was woken by a tap on the door by the older of the two Chinese men with his morning coffee.

An hour later after enjoying a very satisfying breakfast he decided to go and see how Tex was doing in the very comfortable stables he was housed in. He found him being led round a small exercise yard with four other horses and realised they were the mounts of the four new comers. He decided to take Tex for a short ride and had him saddled up and rode briskly out to the north for a couple of miles then more slowly back into town again.

As he arrived at the stables his card playing partner was checking over the condition of the four horses and Todd saw this as an opportunity to have a chat. As Todd Raven dismounted from Tex the man called Matt Kelly said, "Enjoy your morning ride?"

"Yes." said Todd. "Your horses in good shape?"

"Yes." said Kelly. "They needed a good rest and they have had one."

Todd decided to take the bull by the horns and said, "Have the hands improved this morning or are those stings still bothering you?"

Kelly looked up in surprise then quickly said, "Ok big mouth how much to keep your mouth shut?"

Todd Raven laughed. "I don't want your money, but the Doc who you played cards with last night said to me this morning that he thinks you keep bees because you had some stings on the back of your hands."

Todd let that sink in then went on. "Now if he should mention that to the sheriff he might link that to the train robbery and the use of hornets so perhaps it might be a good time to quietly get out of town."

Matt Kelly nodded his thanks and quickly slipped away and Todd went back to his boarding house and had a coffee and read the papers until it was time for lunch. After lunch his cough was bothering him so he had a couple of glasses of whiskey and then went for a lie down. He slept for an hour and felt better and sat on the porch until dinner which was roast chicken and quite delicious.

He decided to go out about eight o'clock and made his way to the Golden Star and joined up with the doctor and two of his friends for a game of cards. They had been playing for about an hour when the sheriff came in who came straight over to the doctor and said, "He's left town you should have told me earlier."

The sheriff then turned to Todd Raven. "I'm told you were seen talking to him late this morning."

Todd Raven asked, "Who?"

"Matt Kelly." said the sheriff. "By the stables."

"Oh yes." said Todd. "I had just taken my horse out for some exercise for about an hour and this man you say was Kelly was walking four horses around the yard."

"Do you know him?" asked the sheriff.

"Not really." said Todd. "I played cards with him briefly last night here with the Doc. He seemed OK."

"Well." said the sheriff. "He and his three friends have left town in rather a hurry and we suspect they were involved in that train robbery. They certainly fit the description."

Todd played cards for a couple of hours and then left about even and as soon as he was in the door the Chinaman locked up for the night.

Two days later Todd received a letter and when he opened it there was just a short message which said. 'Check your saddle bags and Thanks'.

He went down to the stables after breakfast and took Tex out for a ride and checked his saddle bags and found a thousand dollars inside.

Todd did not need the money and he did not want the money, so wondered what should he do. If he handed it to the sheriff it would be like trying to buy his way out of trouble with a display of false honesty while hiding the larger sum with his gang somewhere else. If he told the truth he would be guilty of aiding and abetting a wanted criminal gang and that would mean ten years at least. He could not leave San Angelo yet as that would raise even more suspicion from the sheriff. So he decided to leave the money in his saddle bags and destroy the letter he had received. Nobody with any sense would keep their money in a saddle bag in a stable so it should be safe enough.

He had given some thought about leaving San Angelo, but he decided to stay for a while longer. He was also being kept awake at night by this cough so he decided to have a word with his card partner, the doc, for a remedy.

That evening during a drink break when they had playing for an hour he mentioned his problem cough to the doc. He did not show any great sympathy but said, "Come and see me at ten o'clock tomorrow morning."

That night Todd Raven was woken several times by bouts of coughing and in the morning he found some spots of blood on his pillow. The next morning after breakfast he went to see the Doc as arranged and submitted to an examination and admitted that he had coughed up very small spots of blood.

"Can you give up smoking?" asked the Doc. Todd Raven shook his head.

"In that case," said the Doc, "in six months it will kill you".

Chapter Thirty Seven

Todd Raven returned to the boarding house with a couple of bottles of medicine the Doc had given him. One contained something to help him sleep at nights and the other contained honey to ease the soreness in his throat caused by the coughing. He was also told quite bluntly that there was no cure for his condition but if he stopped smoking he would extend his life by perhaps another year.

He managed not to smoke until after lunch when he was enjoying his coffee on the boarding house porch it triggered a bout of coughing and he quickly threw the offending weed into the street. Later he went to his room and had a spoon full of honey which eased his throat and he had a short sleep. When he woke up he sat on his bed and thought about how he should now conduct his life and resolved to try and reduce his smoking or quit it all together. It was now time for dinner and at least his appetite was still good.

After dinner he made his way to the Golden Star and joined the Doc and his friends at their usual table and took some pleasure in breathing in the nicotine filled air. He ordered a bottle of sweet wine to everyone's surprise except the Doc's who nodded his head in approval. The sweet wine would not burn his throat as the whiskey would and was a sensible choice. They played cards and chatted for about two hours then they made their separate ways to their homes.

On the Doc's suggestion Todd asked for a cup of warm milk when he went to his bed that night and this did not surprise the Chinaman one bit. He drank the milk and had a measure of the medicine and went to sleep quite quickly dreaming quite a lot but not suffering from any bouts of coughing. He woke with a start as the Chinese man tapped on the door and brought in his morning coffee. Todd lay there for a few minutes desperate for a smoke but resisted the urge and sat up and sipped the hot drink.

After a good breakfast he decided to go for a ride and walked over to the stables and had Tex saddled up. They then rode up into the high ground for a couple of hours never more than walking pace because Todd had a lot to think about. He realised that if he was to extend his life he must give up two of the things that in the past had always given him pleasure and that was smoking and whiskey. One of the other things he always enjoyed was having a woman but that desire was always triggered by several glasses of whiskey. He had to face the facts that life without these vices was worth living and it needed to be seriously considered.

He rode Tex back into San Angelo and saw him looked after in the stables with a special treat of some fresh sweet hay. He walked over to the boarding houses and had a wash and then enjoyed some lunch. Afterwards he took his coffee on the porch and sat there for most of the afternoon and only had one slight fit of coughing.

He sat there until it was time for dinner and he really enjoyed the beef meal and the sweet wine that was served with it. Later he made his way to the Golden Star and joined up with the usual group on the far table from the bar. Todd had his now usual bottle of sweet wine while all the others were on whiskey.

They had been playing cards for almost two hours when a silence fell over the Golden Star. Two men had entered the bar with guns drawn and one was collecting the money lying on the tables while the other was standing guard. Todd waited for his chance that for a second the collector was between him and the man standing guard.

The moment came and he sprang to his feet his chair crashing back and he fired twice and the man standing guard crashed to the floor. The man collecting the money dropped his hat full of cash and was about to reach for his guns when he saw the look in Todd's eyes and the smoking guns in his hands. His hands dropped to his sides and quickly a crowd removed his guns and the sheriff and his deputy arrived.

Todd of course was the centre of attention with everyone telling the sheriff how this man had taken on the two armed robbers. The sheriff still remembered the train robbers and how Todd Raven had been seen talking to one of them and now he had shown he was good with a gun. The Undertaker had arrived to take the dead robber away and the sheriff asked Todd if he would come over to his office in the morning and make a statement and Todd agreed. Todd then left for the boarding house and as the sheriff was about to leave the Doc took his arm and said, "A word in confidence sheriff if you please." They spoke for a couple of minutes then they both left.

Arriving at the boarding house Todd asked for a cup of warm milk then went up to his bed. He drank the milk and had a tot of the medicine then slipped into his bed and despite the excitement of the evening when fairly quickly off to sleep.

His night was full of dreams few of which he could remember in the morning and he woke to the sound of the knock on his bedroom door and the smiling Chinese man and his morning coffee. He longed for the taste of tobacco smoke to join that of the coffee but he resisted the urge and finished his coffee then had a wash and a shave and got dressed. He made his way down for breakfast and enjoyed his eggs and bacon and the strong coffee.

Just after nine o'clock he walked over to the sheriff's office to make his statement as requested. The sheriff was there with just one of his deputies and asked him to run through what happened last night with him before writing it down. Todd did just that and told him in great detail the events as they had taken place right up to when the sheriff had arrived on the scene.

The sheriff nodded his head and said, "Please write that down for us now, if you please Mr Raven." Todd did as he was asked.

Though Todd was not aware of it the sheriff had now got it firmly fixed in his head that Todd Raven was a Pinkerton agent. The problem was the Pinkerton detective agency did not always cooperate with the local sheriffs because of local corruption and the agency was frequently retained by insurance companies to investigate local claims. The sheriff's suspicion had been first been alerted when

Todd Raven had been seen with the suspected train robber and now he had been shown to be very skilled in the use of the gun. The sheriff also knew it was pointless him telegraphing Houston and asking the Pinkerton agency if Todd Raven was one of their agents because the agency never discloses its agent's names. Todd walked away from the sheriff's office and back to the boarding house and spent the rest of the morning on the porch with a coffee desperate for a smoke.

At last it was time for lunch and he found there were two other guests in the boarding house now a married couple though they did not look particularly devoted.

Todd enjoyed his lunch then decided to have a rest on his bed and took his coffee up with him. He had just settled down when he heard the newly arrived couple come into the room next door and as he dozed off to sleep their voices suggested that all was not well. He spent probably an hour in fitful short spells of partial sleep broken by an irritation in his throat and a desperate urge for a smoke. He sat up on his bed and lit up a small cigar took two puffs which triggered a bout of coughing only suppressed by a spoonful of honey.

He was now wide awake and tidied himself up and went down stairs and sat out on the porch where one of the Chinamen brought him a cup of coffee. He stayed there until it was time for dinner and then went inside to enjoy what had been prepared for them this evening.

He enjoyed a fine steak dinner, but the married couple on a nearby table did not seem too happy with their meal or rather the man didn't who complained that his steak was uncooked. It was taken away and given more cooking time, but still this did not satisfy the man who stood up and walked out. His wife just carried on with her dinner and later when they were served coffee she joined Todd Raven on the porch. She sat down next to him and apologised for her husband's behaviour.

Todd told her to forget about it and perhaps her husband was worried about something. At this the woman gave a dismissive shrug then said, "The only thing that he's worried about is that I will catch him with his latest tart that he's picked up at one of those bars he goes to."

As she said this she burst into tears and Todd took her hand to console her. In between her sobs she said, "Please help me to my room."

Todd had little choice than to escort her up the stairs.

He opened her room door and as he helped her inside he was now very conscious of her scent and how attractive she was.

"I would offer you a drink but there is none in this room." she said.

"Well," said Todd, "If you would like a drink I have a bottle in my room next door"

"Lead the way." said the woman. "And my name is Alice."

Two minutes later they were enjoying some sweet wine in Todd Raven's room. After two glasses Alice rose to her feet and turned the lamp down to just a glimmer of light and said, "Make love to me Todd. It's been so long I've forgotten what it feels like."

It was just after eleven o'clock when Todd heard Alice's husband come in. Thankfully, Alice had returned to her room about fifteen minutes before, after a memorable evening in Todd's room.

The couple stayed another week and while Alice's husband carried out his nightly foray to satisfy his need for coarse sex, Todd had found something to take his mind off smoking.

When the married couple left they both seemed to be in a better humour than when they arrived and that evening Todd Raven made a return to the Golden Star. He made his way to his usual table and joined the Doc and the usual small group. The Doc looked at him and said, "We thought you might have been unwell old chap."

Todd laughed. "No, I met up with an old friend and we had a lot to talk about but she has gone back now."

Todd had a bottle of sweet white wine during the course of the evening and sniffed the nicotine soaked air appreciatively and won slightly more than he lost.

Towards the end of the evening just before they left the club the Doc whispered in his ear, "The sheriff thinks you are a Pinkerton man."

Todd smiled then said, "Well why destroy the illusion then Doc and you can be the President."

They laughed then left the Golden Star and made their ways to their separate places of rest.

Todd now disciplined himself into a regular routine conscious of his slowly declining physical condition. The yearning for tobacco was still there but he satisfied it by his nightly visits to the nicotine charged air of the Golden Star. He was determined not to end his days gasping for breath in some home or other and already had a plan for a more dramatic end to what had been a quite exciting life. But for the time being he would stay in San Angelo. He liked the place and the people there.

Most days he took Tex out for an hour or so and sometimes longer and on this particular day he spent a couple of hours talking to some trappers up in the hills. He came back in time for lunch then spent most of the afternoon out on the porch in the shade as it was a very warm day. His exit plan was now finally worked out and was extendable to keep pace with his physical condition. As he sat on the porch he ran through the plan. It was perfect and it gave him a feeling of amused satisfaction.

He sat there until it was time for dinner which was as usual very filling and satisfying and he enjoyed the company of some new guests, two elderly gentlemen here for a funeral. After dinner he made his way to the Golden Star for his nightly dose of nicotine and to see his regular friends for some card games. A bottle of sweet wine was brought to him as soon as he was seated while the others had their usual beer or whiskey. They played cards and talked of many things then just after eleven decided that was it for the night. Nobody had lost or won much it was that kind of gambling and that way you all stayed friends.

Halfway back to his boarding house Todd felt he was being followed and stood back in the shadows to see if that was so. He eased his guns in their holsters ready for use just in case, then waited if a pursuer should appear. It was one of the deputies who was startled when Todd moved out to face him then said rather shame faced, "The sheriff is concerned for your safety Mr Raven."

Todd said, "Thank the sheriff, but there's no need and goodnight."

With that he walked back to the boarding house.

Chapter Thirty Eight

Sheriff Jack Masters made his way to his office after taking his two children to their school. Buck was already there, giving some breakfast to their one prisoner who was awaiting collection by the Fort Worth marshal. About six items of mail had been brought up by the Monday train from Fort Worth. Five were the usual wanted posters, but one was personal and addressed to sheriff Jack Masters.

Jack could not remember the last time he had received a letter and he sat down and opened this one with some curiosity, but first checked the post mark. That gave him no clue as to the sender as it was quite indistinct, so he opened it anyway and scanned the brief message. It read quite simply, 'Your time is nearly up Jack and I am coming to get you. A good place for this final showdown will be on the banks of the Snake. Until then keep your guns ready.'

There was no signature and it was a complete mystery to Jack Masters who may have sent it and for just a moment he thought it might have been a joke then thought better of it.

He showed it to Buck who dismissed it as from some saddle tramp Jack had arrested and sent down trying to extract some revenge. But at the back of Jack's mind he felt that there was more to it than that but was determined that Jane would not find out. Life in Hope was pretty good the winery was doing good business and this provided work and income for the small town.

The two ranches to the north and south were doing well and Ma's House had built another extension. They now had trains three days a week on Monday, Wednesday and Friday. The Wednesday service collected livestock from the ranches for the Fort Worth market so there were cattle trunks coupled to the passenger carriage of the train. The marshal came from Fort Worth and collected the prisoner Jack and Buck were holding and at Buck's suggestion Jack showed the marshal the letter he had received. The marshal read it then said, "I would not worry too much. If someone was serious about getting you he would hardly give you warning of his intention, it would be a sudden shot out of darkness."

Jack could see the logic of that and tried to put the matter to the back of his mind as there were plenty of other things to concern him.

On Saturday morning Jack took Simon fishing at a rock pool on the Snake they had been there a couple of hours and had had a couple of bites but most of the fish became wary of the slightest movement. Jack noticed someone on the other bank and the contents of the recent letter sprang to mind then he realised that that person was also fishing and he relaxed and began to enjoy his morning.

After four hours they packed up and went home with three good sized trout for dinner that evening. It was Buck's turn for duty that night as Jack had covered the night before and 'Ma's House' did another good nights business. One of the ranch hands who had only been working there a few weeks got a little too drunk and Buck had to lock him up for the night as he wanted to fight everyone.

The first letter that Jack had received had now almost faded from his mind until about a month later he received another again with an almost obscure post mark. The message was almost the same but this time Jack made no mention of the letter to Buck. An outbreak of violence in Fort Worth prison led to three deaths and six prisoners accused of being involved in their killings. It was thought that three should be lodged in the Hope cells and three in the police cells in Fort Worth. They would be held for almost two weeks until the trial started so it kept Jack and Buck busy.

The three prisoners were quite young and aware that if found guilty they would hang, but strangely enough none of the three appeared to be the violent type. Jack discovered that the other three men held in Fort Worth Police cells were the instigators of the violent assault and these three now in Hope cells just became involved.

The trial when it began did not get off to the best of starts the jury were sworn in and the trial began but at the end of the second day the judge was taken ill and had to be replaced so it all had to start all over again. The judge then adjourned the case early on the second day of the restart because he considered two of the jury appeared to be drunk.

The next day when they adjourned for lunch he forbade any hard liquor to be consumed by the jury under punishment of a heavy fine.

As the trial proceeded it became clear who the real culprits were and the three younger men were in fact guilty by association by being in a nine man cell where three died. Two prison guards who witnessed some of the violence were unable to say who was chiefly responsible for the blows that killed the other three inmates. That is why all the remaining six inmates were charged with their death.

The prison medical officer was called and after he had given evidence regarding the three dead prisoners he was asked if he examined the remaining six prisoners for injuries. He admitted that he had and he had found slight injuries to three prisoners and confirmed they were the ones lodged in Fort Worth police cells. The counsel representing the defendants was now in a quandary with half of the men he represented more deeply involved than the other half who could be totally innocent.

The judge sensing his dilemma agreed to an adjournment for the day and met both counsels in his chambers to try and seek a solution to this turn of events. An ideal solution would be for the three to have separate representation but that would mean a retrial and there was no legal precedent for this. It was decided by the judge to let the trial carry on with the prisoners who had all pleaded not guilty to be cross examined by both counsels. This took the best part of two days and the first to face this were the three men who were considered the ones who had been the most involved.

The judge was about to begin his summing up when the jury foreman stood up and asked the judge if at this stage the jury could ask for the judge's advice. The judge gave this some thought then cleared the court room of the public then asked the foreman what was causing the jury their concern. The foreman cleared his throat and said "Your Honour we are being asked to give a verdict on the actions of a group of men who have violently killed three others but it is clear that only three men took part in the killings but we are being asked to try them as a group." He paused and then went on "If we find them guilty we will convict three guilty men and three innocent men so you see our dilemma your Honour."

The judge thanked the foreman for his opinion and then adjourned the case for the day as he wished to give the case some consideration before recommencing the next day. After he had his dinner that evening the judge spent several hours reading through his law books to confirm the powers he held under the state legislation.

The next morning the judge called the prosecuting counsel and the defence counsel to his chambers to inform them of his decision on how the rest of the trial was to proceed. As soon as the court was assembled the three prisoners that were considered not involved in the violent crime were brought into court. The judge formally discharged them from the case and they were sent back to prison to continue their sentences.

The case then continued with the other three prisoners being brought back into the dock for the judge to begin his summing up of the case. This took until lunch time and the jury would not be formally sent out to consider their verdict until the court resumed after lunch. The action of the judge in discharging the three other defendants was already exciting the reporters as being a very unusual course of events.

When the court resumed after lunch the jury were sent out and it was anticipated they would not take long to reach a verdict. In fact it took two hours and then they returned and the court refilled and waited as the judge gravely asked the foreman if they had reached a verdict they had all agreed on.

The foreman said. "We have your honour"

"And what is your verdict?" enquired the judge.

"Guilty as charged your honour." said the foreman.

A sigh of satisfaction ran around the court and they waited for the sentence to be pronounced and it came almost straight away. The judge looked at the three men standing in the dock and said, "You have been found quite rightly in my view guilty of murder not once but three times and the penalty for this is quite clear, you will suffer death by hanging and may God have mercy on your souls."

He then indicated with a wave of his hand that they should be taking away, which was of course back to Fort Worth prison.

The state and national newspapers all covered this trial and commented on the judge's action most were in favour, but one or two were critical.

The hangings were due to take place in one week's time and of course they all would take place together as was the law. An appeal was heard and dismissed two days after sentencing. Relatives of those that had been murdered were invited to attend the hanging, but it was no longer open to the public just a few selected officials.

The scaffolds had been erected in the stable yard and during the execution the Prison was locked down. There were about thirty spectators present when the three prisoners were led out to the scaffold with their hands bound behind their backs. Once on the scaffold their ankles were secured and a hood was placed over their heads and the rope noose put in place around their necks.

The prison chaplain started to read a prayer and as he reached its end he gave a nod and the executioner sprung the trap and the three bodies plunged through to their death. The spectators began to move away, but one or two stayed for coffee with the prison governor in the prison board room.

After the yard had cleared the prison medical officer went beneath the scaffold to confirm that all three prisoners were dead then their bodies were removed and taken away for instant burial in the prison grounds. Jack Masters had been invited over by the marshal, but decided not to attend as he had plenty to do in Hope and he had seen enough death in the Civil War.

The next day the papers were full of the story of the hangings in Fort Worth Prison and when Buck collected the letters from the train station there was one for sheriff Jack Masters. Buck knew straight away it was another letter full of threats and for a moment or so he considered burning it at the side of the track. But he knew that was quite wrong so he brought it to the sheriff's office and gave it to Jack. He opened it straight away, but it was brief and just said, "Time's nearly up for the showdown."

Chapter Thirty Nine

The last couple of weeks had been slightly cooler at nights in San Angelo and Todd Raven had been sleeping better though he was aware that he had lost some weight. He had developed a good friendship with the Doc who was well aware that Todd did not intend to tolerate a slow lingering death from this enemy in his chest. They played cards most nights with a select group of friends never for very high stakes and drank a fair bit though for Todd it was now just sweet wine.

They were always kept amused by the antics of others in the Golden Star which in the past would have resulted in gun play but now it was usually a drink thrown in some ones face and a brief brawl.

Most days Todd would take Tex for a couple of hours of a gentle ride in the hills because it was important to keep them both fit for the final adventure he had planned. One evening quite late as they were about to leave the Golden Star they heard the sound of gun fire from further up the street in the direction of a rather rough area dominated by the Diamond Lil brothel.

They watched with interest as four men from the sheriff's office hurried past to investigate the disturbance. The deputy with them called out as they went past, "Can you come with us Doc we may need your help."

The Doc could hardly refuse so he followed on behind and was pleased to find Todd Raven had joined him. They took about ten minutes to reach the scene and found there were two bodies lying in the street outside the brothel and were told two more were lying injured inside. The Doc examined the two men outside first and they were obviously dead so he went to go inside but the deputy sheriff stopped him.

"You can't go in Doc because there are three half drunk gun toting fools ready to blast anyone stupid enough to try and go through the door."

"But those two wounded men could bleed to death" argued the Doc.

The deputy looked very unhappy.

"I'm sorry Doc, but I don't want to see anymore lives wasted tonight."

Todd walked over and had a few words with the deputy. Then the deputy spoke to his men and they moved to the windows of the brothel. Todd walked over to the door and picked up a chair that was lying on the porch outside glanced over to the deputy and then threw it through the door towards the bar. The three drunks inside fired a volley of shots at nothing in particular, but in doing so had betrayed their positions and a return volley of accurate fire came from the deputy's men with devastating results.

The siege was now over and the Doc was able to treat the one surviving wounded man as the other had now passed away. None of the three gunmen had survived the deputies men's volley of shots which at least saved San Angelo the expense of a trial. The deputy sheriff thanked Todd Raven for his help and said, "You Pinkerton men are certainly well trained."

Todd looked at the Doc with a quiet smile, but said nothing. The story would be worth a couple of bottles of free wine and that was reward enough.

He and the Doc walked back down the street then went their separate ways to their places of abode. Todd had his warm milk and the Chinaman then locked up for the night and they all went to bed. Todd had a good night's sleep with barely any dreams thanks to Doc's strong medicine and woke in the morning to the sound of a tap on the door and the smell of fresh coffee as it was placed on his bedside table.

It was a fine morning and after he had enjoyed a good breakfast he collected Tex from the stables and rode out into the hills. After a while he then dismounted and let Tex nibble the grass while he ran through his plans and decided it was time to write another short note. He rode back into San Angelo saw Tex well looked after at the stables then went to his boarding house for lunch.

In the afternoon he wrote the short note sealed it in an envelope then as usual he paid the conductor on the train leaving San Angelo five dollars to post it elsewhere. The conductor had heard that this man was a Pinkerton agent and was quite flattered that he had been asked to post these secret messages as this was the fourth time he had been entrusted to do so.

After dinner that evening Todd as usual made his way to the Golden Star and met up with the usual crowd and for the first hour they had to retell the events of the previous late evening. Then they got down to their usual game of cards but found plenty of free drinks came their way all evening. Just before they normally left for their for their homes for the evening the deputy sheriff paid the Golden Star a visit but it was Todd Raven he had come to see.

He waited until they finished playing they last game then very politely asked Todd if he would come and see the sheriff in the morning about ten o'clock. Todd equally politely agreed and they all began to make their way to their various homes.

On arriving at the boarding house the smiling Chinaman handed Todd his glass of warm milk then quickly locked up for the night. Todd once in his room drank his milk then downed his nightly dose of Doc's medicine, stripped off his clothes and climbed into bed. He gave some thought to what the sheriff wanted then the Doc's medicine took over and he slipped into a deep sleep.

He woke with a start to the sound of a tap on the door and realised it was morning and it was the Chinaman with his coffee. He sat on the side of the bed and sipped the strong brew he could not believe how quickly the night had passed without a single dream. He finished drinking the coffee and went to stand up but had to sit back down on the bed as a wave of dizziness swept over him. The Doc had warned him he should expect this as his problem progressed but the effect was short lived. He washed and dressed then went down for breakfast.

His appetite was still good and he enjoyed a full breakfast and a couple of cups of coffee. He then sat on the porch for twenty minutes before starting to walk over to the sheriff's office for the ten o'clock appointment. He arrived just as the clock chimed the hour and was immediately offered coffee and the sheriff thanked him for his help at the Golden Star the other night.

Todd waved his thanks away saying he had only done what any citizen would do in the circumstances. The sheriff however was not having any of this and leaned forward and said, "Come now Mr Raven you are a Pinkerton agent. It's not a secret anymore, everyone in San Angelo is aware of your identity."

Todd stood up. "Sheriff I am not a Pinkerton man, but I like San Angelo and will be here a couple of weeks more then I will be on my way."

Then with a wave he walked out of the sheriff's office and as Todd walked away the sheriff turned to his deputy and said, "That bastard is definitely a Pinkerton man and in code he was telling us in a couple of weeks his job here is done."

The deputy looked at the sheriff in admiration realising how much he had to learn before he could hope to be a sheriff. Todd walked over to the stables and checked on Tex who was being walked around the yard with two other horses then satisfied he was being well cared for he went back to the boarding house.

He sat on the porch until it was time for lunch then went inside to find there were two guests who had arrived apparently hoping to buy into a tobacco business that was requiring some investment. At lunch they ignored Todd's friendly greeting so he sat with his back to them and pretended they were not there.

After lunch Todd went up to his room and lay on his bed and ran through the plan he had made. He knew that the Doc had got his condition about right, but he needed to be well enough to complete the journey to the chosen spot and with just enough life left in him to complete the task.

At dinner the two new guests were more affable and Todd guessed the business had gone well. As usual he made his way up to the Golden Star to spend the evening with his friends and the evening passed without incident with the only loss to their pockets being the cost of the drinks.

The two new guests were leaving in the morning after breakfast and were settling up with the Chinaman now and were quite amused when Todd was brought his hot milk. They all went to their rooms and the Chinaman locked up for the night and once in his room Todd sat on his bed and sipped his milk. He had felt pretty well all day apart from a couple of dizzy spells one when he got up quickly in the porch after lunch and one just before he left for the Golden Star that evening.

He barely coughed at all now and the craving for tobacco had gone, but so had his energy level and he needed to watch that. He took his nightly dose of Doc's medicine and settled down in his bed and turned the small oil lamp down to a faint glimmer. It was not long before sleep claimed him and the small amount of morphine in his nightly medicine ensured a deep sleep with hardly a dream included.

It took two taps on the door to waken him and then the smiling face of the Chinaman and his morning coffee to start the day. When eventually he went down to breakfast he found the other guests had already left to catch the train to Houston. He enjoyed his breakfast and had his second cup of coffee on the porch in the early morning sunshine.

He spent almost an hour out there then as he rose to come in he felt dizzy so he sat down and within a few minutes felt fine. He handed in his coffee cup and told the Chinaman he was taking his horse for a ride until lunch then walked slowly to the stables and collected Tex. They went for a gentle trot up into the higher ground around San Angelo then Todd found a flatter stretch and he enjoyed a brisk short gallop.

Just before mid-day they came back down into the town and Todd saw Tex given a good wash down and some fresh hay at the stables then he went to enjoy his lunch.

Two new guests were at the lunch tables they were elderly sisters here for the funeral of their brother. Over lunch they insisted in explaining to Todd that they had not seen him for years as they had supported different sides in the Civil War.

Todd was glad when the sisters had to leave for the funeral service and he could go to his room and rest. He laid on his bed for a couple of hours his mind running through the final details of his plan.

At dinner that evening the two sisters had returned from the funeral but were in deep conversation on their table and Todd was allowed to eat his dinner in peace. He took his coffee on the porch and then made his way up to the Golden Star for the evening's entertainment. All his usual friends were there and there were more than the usual gang of drinkers at the two bars. Doc explained that there was a new singer in the usual group of women who sang a couple of songs and danced on the bar top to amuse the drunks.

Todd had his usual bottle of sweet wine and they played a few hands of cards then there was a big cheer from the bar area and the female group of girls including the new one jumped up on the bar top and began to dance and sing. Todd did not think they were anything special they were the usual bar fodder brought in to lure the drunks to buy a few more beers. They did the usual routine and finished with them turning round and waggling their backsides in the air to great applause.

During the evening they did this several times more but Todd and his friends had seen this all before and took little interest and at the usual time they all decided they had had enough for the night and settled up. Todd walked part of the way home with the Doc then said goodnight and walked slowly back to the boarding house. The Chinaman brought him his hot milk then locked up for the night and Todd went up to his room.

Chapter Forty

He undressed and then sat on his bed and drank his milk then he measured out his dose of medicine and swallowed it. He slipped into the comfortable bed and turned down the small oil lamp then lay there thinking that shortly his bed would be harder than this and his nearest companion would be Tex his faithful horse. Sleep came fairly quickly but this time it was not completely dream free and he was almost glad when he woke to the sound of a knock on his door.

His mouth was very dry and he enjoyed the strong sweet coffee even more this morning. He took his time dressing then went down for breakfast thankful that he still had a good appetite. He ate a full breakfast and as usual took his second cup of coffee out onto the porch. Thirty minutes later he made his way to the stables and had Tex saddled for his morning ride then at a gentle trot they made their way out to the north of San Angelo.

They had almost reached a wooded area where he allowed Tex to browse when he became quite dizzy and he had to hold onto the saddle pummel to avoid falling off. The feeling passed and he then carried on with the usual routine he had established on these morning rides. With about thirty minutes to go before lunch he began the ride back into San Angelo and saw Tex well looked after at the stables.

At the boarding house he had a quick wash then went down to lunch and enjoyed some locally caught fish and some salad. Later he took his coffee out on the porch for a while then spent an hour on his bed. He had a detailed map of the area between San Angelo and Hope and had marked off his route and the proposed overnight stopping points during the journey. He had decided to restrict himself to twenty five miles a day so as not to overtire himself though of course Tex would consider that a stroll.

It was soon time for dinner and he tidied himself up and made his way downstairs to see what there was to eat. He was now the only guest in the boarding house and tonight there was steak for dinner and very tasty it was too with a full range of grilled potatoes and vegetables. Todd Raven also managed a small portion of apple pie before the usual coffee then sat back and wondered if he had the energy to go out tonight. A thirty minute rest on the porch and the persuasive voice of the Doc eventually drew him once more to the Golden Star and his usual circle of friends.

The place was crowded as usual and they took their place at their normal table and the young bar tender brought over the normal selection of drinks including Todd's bottle of sweet wine. The new young lady had excited the attention of some of the older drunks and a couple of brawls broke out during the dance performance and the sheriff was called. His threat to close the place for a week was enough to calm things down and there was no further trouble.

Todd and his friends left at their usual time and he and the Doc walked part of the way home together. Just before they said goodnight Doc said, "Fancy a smoke?"

Todd looked at him in horror and said, "That's a disgusting habit." They both laughed and went their separate ways.

When Todd arrived at the boarding house the Chinaman was waiting with his hot milk and wished him a smiling goodnight. He went up to his room and sat on his bed and sipped the milk until it was finished then undressed took his medicine and climbed into bed.

He lay there thinking about his day then gradually the medicine did its work and he slipped into a deep and almost dreamless sleep until two sharp raps on the door brought him back into the land of the living. The smell of fresh strong coffee was a good way of being greeted into the new day and Todd sat up in bed to sip the reviving brew.

As he finished his morning coffee he had already decided that he would start his journey to Hope in four days time so on the day he left he would send the final letter. It would take eight days to make the journey to the final rendezvous point so everything should be ready.

He washed, dressed and went down for breakfast and as was now his normal routine took his second cup of coffee onto the porch. He had already arranged with the Chinaman for him to supply some food for a week's travelling and Doc was going to give him some extra medicine for the journey. He went round to the stables and took Tex out for his usual exercise up in the hills but this time he found a quiet spot and spend twenty minutes or so practising his draw. He had a growing weakness on the left side of his body which meant his normal practice of drawing and firing both his guns in any encounter was now out of the question.

But his right side was as yet unaffected and his hand speed in the draw was still second to none. Pleased with his performance he remounted Tex and they trotted back down into San Angelo both looking forward to their different types of lunches.

Todd had his lunch then spent an hour on the porch then went to his room until it was time for dinner. When he went down for his evening meal he found two guests had arrived both were Chinese and were in a lively conversation with his Chinese host.

Todd enjoyed the meal and took his coffee on the porch as the after dinner conversation with the new guests was very loud. Later he made his way to the Golden Star to join his friends. The Doc was a little late as he had been helping to bring a baby into the world. Of course they all stopped playing cards and drank the baby's health wishing her a long and happy life. Todd drank his usual bottle of sweet wine and around eleven thirty they decided to go to their beds and paid what they owed.

Doc walked part of the way back with Todd and he told him that he would be off in a few days and would like a large bottle of his medicine for the journey. Doc offered to give him the prescription should he need more, but Todd said one more bottle would be enough. The Doc understood and they just said goodnight as they parted.

The Chinaman had Todd's milk ready and he wished Todd goodnight and rushed back to his Chinese guests. Todd got to the top of the stairs and entered his room and placed the milk on the small table by the bed as he turned to take off his outer clothing his world tipped sideways and he fell back on the bed.

The dizzy spell lasted less than a minute then he was able to sit on the bed and drink his cooling milk. After drinking the warm milk he completely undressed for bed and took his nightly dose of medicine. Then he slipped into bed and settled down feeling now completely relaxed and comfortable. In a few days it would be the hard ground as a mattress and just Tex as a companion but he was used to that and the nights were warm.

He drifted off to sleep quite quickly with barely a dream that he could remember in the morning which arrived with two knocks on the door. It was the Chinaman with his morning coffee which filled the room with its fragrance. Todd sat on the bed and drank his coffee tomorrow would be his last day in San Angelo so he would write the last letter today and have it ready to post tomorrow.

The Chinaman had all his travel rations ready it was all neatly packed and would slide into his saddle bags. He went down to breakfast and was given a friendly wave by the other Chinese guests then enjoyed a full breakfast. He took his coffee on the porch then later on he had some final business with the bank manager which took almost the rest of the morning. It was almost lunch time when he returned and he sat out on the porch until lunch was ready and when he went in to enjoy his food he found the other guests had gone.

The rest of the day and evening passed as all the others had and on his return from the Golden Star of course his hot milk was ready. As he sat on his bed and finished the milk before taking his medicine he thought, "I shall do this one more time then it's the final journey."

The next morning began with the Chinaman's knock and the hot fragrant coffee later he went down to breakfast as usual he took his second cup of coffee on the porch then an hour later collected Tex and went for a ride in the hills. He returned just before lunch and told the stable boss tomorrow he would be leaving San Angelo with Tex after breakfast. He then went for lunch and afterwards stayed on the porch for an hour then went to his room until dinner.

Later he went down and enjoyed his dinner and then made his way to the Golden Star for the last time.

He enjoyed his last evening at the Golden Star he paid for all the drinks and as the evening ended he said his farewell to his friends with a firm handshake and then left with the Doc. As they parted for the last time the Doc gave Todd a final bottle of medicine and wished him well on his journey, then a brief handshake and they went they separate ways.

At the boarding house the Chinaman had his hot milk ready and with a goodnight Todd went to his room. He drank his milk undressed and took his medicine and then climbed into bed. Sleep came fairly quickly and was almost dream free but for the first time he was awake when the Chinaman tapped on his door with his morning coffee.

He washed and then went down for breakfast and sat at the table to finish his second cup of coffee. He then collected his kit from his room and came down and settled his account with the Chinaman giving him a generous tip.

Then he collected Tex from the stables and settled his bill there. He made sure all his kit was secure on the saddle and the rations were in the saddle bags and now he was ready to go. The final letter was sent in the usual way and then Todd began his journey in warm bright sunshine with Tex setting off at a leisurely trot.

The journey to the western bank of the Snake River was completely uneventful and took the eight days as planned giving Todd Raven a complete day of rest before the final confrontation was to take place.

In Hope Jack Masters had received the final letter and had only shared the contents with Buck Shaw in the strictest confidence. The short message in the letter could not be clearer it was a challenge for a shootout at the wooden bridge at the bend in the Snake at noon on the 10[th,] which was tomorrow. Both Jack and Buck knew of the spot it was even shown on the map so he told Buck he would be there.

On the morning of the 10th Todd had a wash in the Snake River and then had breakfast and some hot coffee kept hot on a small fire. Tex was content finding plenty to eat grazing freely well out of the line of fire. Todd prepared himself as the time drew near then he saw his adversary arrive on the other side of the Snake. He moved into position and waited for Jack Masters to do the same and a few moments later Jack moved onto the end of the wooden bridge.

They were now eight yards apart and Todd Raven said, "I'll count to three and fire, so get ready ... One - Two - Three."

Both men's right hands moved as in a blur and two shots rang out as one. Both shots struck the target aimed for. Todd Raven slumped forward. Jack's bullet had lodged near Todd's heart, but Todd's bullet had struck the soft wood of the bridge just in front of Jack Masters. Jack raced over to Todd just in time to hear his last words.

"Take care of old Tex Jack. He's been a good friend."

The next day Todd was buried in Hope's cemetery and Tex enjoyed the final years of his life as Sue Ellen's horse.

The End

BV - #0104 - 100223 - C0 - 197/132/14 - PB - 9781804672402 - Gloss Lamination